APR   2021

THORNLIGHT

CLAIRE LEGRAND

THORNLIGHT

ILLUSTRATIONS BY
JAIME ZOLLARS

Thornlight
Text copyright © 2021 by Claire Legrand
Illustrations copyright © 2021 by Jaime Zollars

The text of this book is set in Adobe Garamond .
Book design by Sylvie Le Floc'h

Library of Congress Control Number: 2021933801

ISBN 978-0-06-269666-3 (hardcover)

First Edition

21 22 23 24 25 PC/LSCH 10 9 8 7 6 5 4 3 2 1

Greenwillow Books

For lionhearted Finley,

who has been patiently waiting for this one

Storm Witch
Ruins

Harvester
Shelters

Harvester
Trails

The River of the Clouds

The Royal
Storm Halls

The City
of Aeria

The Fall
Gate

Flower
House

The
Cliffs
of
Westlin

THORNLIGHT

Once, in a land of seven kingdoms called the Star Lands—

Oh, wait.

That's a different story.

That story is about a witch named Quicksilver, who embarked upon a perilous adventure to save all of witchkind from a villainous figure called the Wolf King—who was indeed villainous, but not in the way you might think.

This story is about another brave girl, though she would be the first to tell you that she's not very brave at all.

And she would be wrong.

.1.

THE SUN AND SHADOW TWINS

Once, in a troubled realm known as the Vale, in the province of Westlin, in the capital city of Aeria, on the broad road called First Street, in the rooftop garden owned by the florist Nash Orendown, perched on the garden's stone wall amid a soft green carpet of morning glories, a girl named Thorn searched the sky for signs of lightning.

And found none.

"Great storms," Thorn cursed quietly, gripping her broom. "Brier will be in a terrible mood when she gets home. The skies are far too quiet."

"Give them a minute," said Mazby, wiggling his rump in the air before pouncing into a clump of morning glories. A dew-sprinkled dragonfly zipped away. Mazby's beaked head poked out of the morning glories, his dark crown feathers gone askew. "Why don't the dragonflies just let me eat them?"

"Would you just let yourself be eaten, if a thing twenty times your size were hunting you?"

"Only twenty times bigger?" He puffed out his chest and thrust his yellow beak into the air. "I'd say at least thirty."

Thorn held out her palm. Never one to miss an opportunity for petting, Mazby jumped onto it. Thorn scratched his soft white chin, and Mazby's eyes fell closed in blissful surrender. Purring, he gently kneaded his claws—eagle talons on the front feet, cat's claws on the back—against her palm.

"On second thought," Thorn conceded, with a small smile, "perhaps you're *twenty-five* times bigger than a dragonfly."

"Quite right," said the grifflet, and turned around three times in Thorn's palm—just as an angry voice exploded from the street below.

"Thorn! I don't pay you to dawdle and dream, do I? Get your sorry behind down here at once!"

Thorn jumped off the wall. "Coming, Master Tuwain!" she

shouted back, grabbing her cap. With Mazby clinging to her shoulder, she ran for the iron stairs that stretched from the roof to the road.

"That man always seems to know when I'm about to settle down for a nap," the grifflet grumbled as Thorn hurried down, her broom's handle clanking on each step. When she tumbled out through the creaking, vine-covered gate and onto First Street, she crashed to a stop at the feet of a tall brown-skinned man wearing a fine black coat and a bright red cravat.

Master Tuwain glared down at her, his bushy black eyebrows quivering with outrage.

Thorn peeked out from underneath the brim of her cap and offered an apologetic smile. "I was only taking a short break—"

"Tell me, Thorn Skystone," Master Tuwain began, his voice smooth and gentle, "are sweeps meant to wander around rooftops and gaze at the sky? Or are they meant to stay in the gutters and clean our streets?"

Mazby, who hated when Master Tuwain used that unctuous tone of voice, poked his head out from under Thorn's long, tangled brown hair. Thorn clamped his beak shut with her fingers. Mazby let out a muffled trill of indignation.

"They're meant to stay in the gutters, sir," Thorn answered.

"It's just that Mr. Orendown, he's my father's friend, you see, and he lets me take my breaks in his garden—"

Master Tuwain waved his hand. "At what age do I typically prefer to hire my sweeps?"

Thorn swallowed hard. "Fifteen years old, sir."

"And how old are you?"

In that moment, with Master Tuwain looming over her, and people all up and down rain-soaked First Street looking over to see what the trouble was, Thorn felt like an errant dog being punished for doing its business on the rug instead of outside.

"Twelve years old, sir," Thorn said meekly, her cheeks burning.

"And why did I agree to hire you?"

Thorn answered, but it came out so soft that only Mazby could hear it. She held her broom close to her chest—a shield between her and the world.

"What was that?" Master Tuwain cupped a hand around his ear. "Are you a mouse or a girl? Tell me. Why did I hire you?"

A small crowd had gathered around Number Thirty-Four First Street. Thorn wished she could sink into the muddy cracks between the wet cobblestones and live forever in the cool, dark underground. In such a place, no one could find her and yell at her.

No one could mistake her for her sister, and then feel disappointed when they realized she wasn't.

"You hired me, sir," Thorn said, her voice a mere thread of sound, "because my sister is a harvester."

"And not only a harvester," Master Tuwain carried on, "but the best one we've got." Then, realizing how many people were watching and whispering, he said, rather louder than he needed to, "Rest assured, Thorn, that were it not for your sister, you would—"

But then the most famous girl in Aeria turned the corner onto First Street, and everyone flocked to her instead.

"Brier!" they called, waving their hats, offering up gifts—frosted cookies wrapped in sparkling paper, bundles of silver coins, chunky knitted scarves. "How are the storms looking?"

"Brier, tell us! How much lightning did you gather today?"

"Is it true, what people are saying?"

"Are the storms fading?"

Brier Skystone of the Vale, riding down First Street on the back of her unicorn, Norojedzia, waved at her many admirers. Everyone she laid eyes upon seemed to stand taller and straighter.

"Storms go through cycles," said Brier, addressing the crowd with a smile. "Sometimes they are loud and energetic. Sometimes they retreat to rest."

Thorn stepped back into the pink rhododendron bushes flanking Number Thirty-Four's front door and, with a pang in her chest, wished that she was already out of sight, back at home.

The people of Aeria followed Brier down the road with shining eyes. A bold few even rushed forward to drape garlands of paper flowers around Norojedzia's neck.

Brier looked exactly like Thorn in every respect—same pale skin, same large brown eyes, same long, wavy brown hair. But if you stood the two girls side by side, you would immediately see past the physical similarities and notice the differences.

One girl had shining eyes and an easy smile. One girl wore her hair in a tidy, practical bun rather than letting it fly about loose and tangled. One girl knew exactly what to say and how to say it. One girl was a blazing bright sun.

The other girl was nothing but a shadow.

Brier looked around the street and found Thorn hiding in the flowers. Then she glanced at Master Tuwain, who was still scowling. Brier's mouth tightened. She turned Noro toward Number Thirty-Four.

Thorn shrank back into the bushes. Maybe if she wished it hard enough, she would truly disappear.

"Please, don't worry," Brier was saying to the crowd. "And please don't listen to rumors. Noro and I work in the mountains every day. We see the storms up close. If there was reason to worry, we'd be the first ones to tell you. Isn't that right, Noro?"

Noro, who Thorn knew would be bristling at the indignity of wearing flowers around his neck like a child's pony, said in his rich, smooth tenor, "Quite right, Brier."

Then he pawed one white hoof against the cobblestones and let loose residual lightning from his long spiraled horn. The sour, hot smell in the air cut through the damp fog of Aeria's streets, and when tiny white sparks snapped about Noro's horn like firecrackers, the crowd cheered.

Brier reached down into the bushes, found Thorn's hand, and pulled. Thorn dug her heels into the mud for only a moment before giving up and scrambling onto Noro's back. The slight heat of Noro's magic prickled Thorn's legs, but with Brier there, she wouldn't be truly hurt.

"My sister, Thorn!" Brier twisted on Noro's back so she could throw an arm around Thorn's shoulders. "The best street sweep in Aeria!"

Master Tuwain let out an incredulous guffaw, but the rest of the crowd drowned him out. They pumped their fists into the air and cheered as Noro carried Brier and Thorn down First Street toward home.

Thorn forced a smile and waved back at the crowd, but it seemed silly to be called the best sweep in Aeria, for it wasn't true. She was too distractible, too caught up in her art and her daydreams. And anyway, who cared about being a sweep? Her wages were nothing compared to Brier's. She might as well go hunting around the gutters for spare change.

Besides, none of those people were cheering for her. They had eyes only for Brier. Thorn wished her sister would stop trying to make anyone care about her, the shadow twin. She knew Brier meant well, but it was humiliating to sit on Noro's gleaming white back in her stained, stinking sweep uniform as the crowd chanted her sister's name.

But still, Thorn waved. She smiled until her cheeks hurt. She didn't blink, for then her embarrassed tears would fall. In general, she was terrible at holding back tears, but that didn't mean she would stop trying.

They turned onto the tiny grassy path that led to their home on the edge of Aeria. Rain clung to the willow trees lining the path; mist lined every patch of yellow-flowered clover.

"I love you," Mazby whispered, hidden inside Thorn's coat. He was the only one Thorn talked to about how little she thought of herself. "I think you're wonderful. I like the way you smell. You're the best friend a grifflet could ask for." He butted his head beneath her ear. "You excel at finding the truly quality trash. You're also good at making Master Tuwain angry, which is fun to watch."

That, finally, made Thorn laugh, just as Noro brought them to the red front door of the Skystone family's tiny yellow cottage. It was called Flower House, so named for the profusion of flowers that surrounded it—foxgloves and hydrangeas, heliotropes and blue-speckled violets.

The flowers were Thorn's; the name was Brier's.

Noro's cold blue-purple eyes narrowed as Thorn dismounted. "Every day I hope that you'll come to your senses and send that vermin up north, where he belongs."

"The word is 'grifflet,'" Mazby corrected, scrambling atop Thorn's cap so he could glare up at Noro. "Or does your *brilliant* unicorn brain have trouble with words?"

"Grifflet. Vermin." Noro tilted his slim white head. "Doesn't seem to be much difference to me."

Every feather on Mazby's kitten-sized body poofed in

righteous fury. "Careful, horsey. I'd hate to have to claw up that pretty coat."

"Just as I'd hate to have to put my horn through your tiny rat's heart," Noro said smoothly.

Brier dismounted and whirled on them. "Enough!"

Everyone fell silent. Thorn realized that Brier, who only a little while ago had been beaming, now looked ashen and exhausted, her eyes watery and red.

All the blood in Thorn's body at once ran slower and hotter.

"Brier, what's wrong?" she asked.

Brier shook her head fiercely, entered the cottage, and hurried through the kitchen to the sunroom at the back of the house. The sunroom was built of green-tinted glass, and though it never got very sunny—nowhere in Westlin ever got very sunny—it was the warmest spot in the house. Thorn liked to work there, in the midst of her curling ivy plants and fuzzy slenderleaf ferns. The room was full of her art—pieces of colored glass and metal hanging on wire; sculptures of unicorns and lightning and Brier herself, fashioned out of scrap metal and painted tin.

Thorn joined Brier on the stone balcony outside the sunroom and looked down on the land below.

Flower House sat on the easternmost border of Westlin.

From its balcony, Thorn and Brier could peer over the stone wall and look down the high cliffs. The sheer black rock was ribboned with dozens of thin waterfalls that flowed from the sparkling mountain rivers of Westlin to the murky bogs of Estar far below.

And between the mountains and the bogs was the Break—a dark chasm, hundreds of miles long, that divided the province of Westlin from the province of Estar, cutting the realm of the Vale in two. Quakes shook the Break day and night. Sometimes they opened the chasm a tiny bit wider.

Even from such a great height, Thorn could see the darkness seeping out from the Break onto the surrounding land, like murky scum flooding out from a swollen river. She could see the flashes of white lightning as the soldiers of the Vale fought the monster that lived inside the Break—the monster that, according to their parents' brief letters, was closer than ever to emerging.

No, not the monster, Thorn told herself. The Gulgot.

You know its name is the Gulgot, their parents' first letter from the war front had read. *Say it aloud. Say it often. Do not simply call it "the monster." A monster is frightening and mysterious. But a thing with a name—the Gulgot, this creature, whatever it looks like, whatever rage or hunger burns in its blood—is something we can defeat.*

The Gulgot climbs nearer every day. Darkness floods out of the Break ahead of him, faster and faster. You can't trust anything in Estar now. Not the trees. Not the bridges. Not the ground. Nothing that the Gulgot's wickedness and anger have touched.

We must face the darkness and light it up until it can no longer hurt us. We will *do this, my loves. You can be afraid, yes, of course you can, but do not let that fear rule your hearts.*

Then, at the end of that first letter: *P.S. Thorn, don't leave your art all over the house. Keep it to the sunroom, please.*

P.P.S. We love you both. Our love for you is fiercer than the combined might of all the storms in the Vale.

P.P.P.S. Try to keep Noro and Mazby from killing each other.

Sometimes, if Thorn squinted very hard and held her breath until she felt dizzy, she thought she could pick out the ant-size shapes of her parents, somewhere below in the chaos.

It had been far too long since their last letter.

"Brier, what is it?" Thorn asked. She hesitated, then placed her sweaty, filthy hand on Brier's cold, tingling one. Brier always hummed with lightning after a day in the mountains, and Thorn never felt quite worthy enough to touch her.

Brier—older by five minutes—leaned hard against the railing, her ferocious glare fixed on the war far below.

"Nothing," she said at last. "It was a long day, that's all."

But Brier was not as good at lying as she was at everything else. Thorn saw the truth plain on her face.

"The storms are fading, aren't they?" whispered Thorn.

"No, they're not," Brier replied flatly.

"I heard one of the other harvesters yesterday, when I was doing my evening sweep, near the square. He said the latest harvest could power only ten eldisks, if we're lucky."

Brier pushed herself away from the railing. "Thundering skies! Don't believe every single thing you hear on the streets. And you shouldn't eavesdrop, you know."

"But Brier—"

At the door to the sunroom, Brier whirled. "You're not stupid, Thorn, no matter what everyone says. So stop acting like it."

Then, her dark eyes flashing as if they held lightning inside them, Brier stalked into the cottage, leaving Thorn alone.

Thorn crossed her arms over her chest, wishing she could disappear into the fine, tangled mess of her hair. Each time she tried to inhale, her breath caught.

No matter what everyone says?

She closed her eyes and pressed her lips tight until the tears tingling behind her nose faded. She would not let such thoughts sink their familiar claws into her heart—that she was stupid, and dirty, and small. A mere sweep. The shadow sister.

Not today. Not again.

Brier hadn't meant to sound so hateful. Brier loved her; she said so every day before kissing Thorn's cheek and leaving with Noro for the mountains.

And if Brier hadn't really meant such cruelty—and she hadn't, she *wouldn't*—then maybe Brier was just tired. She'd had a long day in the mountains. She missed their parents, just like Thorn did.

Or maybe, Thorn thought, her stomach flip-flopping, Brier knew a secret, and she didn't want Thorn to find out.

.2.

THE REBEL BOLT

The next morning, after a sleepless night, Brier threw on her long harvester coat and sneaked out of the house when dawn was but a hint in the sky.

Not even the sweeps had awakened for their morning rounds. Not even Thorn, who often left the house in near-darkness. As she'd once told Brier, it was easier to avoid talking to people before the sun came up.

Brier paused at the archway that led to the overgrown garden behind their cottage. Wisteria vines hugged the wrought-iron frame, their heavy blossoms an eerie soft purple in the misty almost-light.

Brier lightly dragged her fingers across the petals and waited.

Noro swore to her that unicorns possessed exceptional hearing and could hear even the flowers when they laughed. It was, he had instructed her, the easiest way to call for him without anyone else knowing.

Brier wasn't sure she believed him. She always felt like such a fool, tickling the flowers like a child who still believed in stories of immortal stars and witches with magic in their blood.

But it wasn't smart to doubt a unicorn.

"You called?" Noro said dryly, appearing to Brier's right.

She flinched. "Great storms, Noro! Do you have to be so quiet all the time?"

"I cannot help my incredible natural grace." Noro shook a long lock of wavy white hair out of his eyes. "Surely you should be used to it by now?"

"Yes, yes," Brier grumbled. "Unicorns are graceful and magnificent and perfect and always land on their feet."

"Precisely. Take that, cats."

Brier climbed nimbly onto his back, and Noro glided through the damp, sleepy streets of Aeria toward the mountains. His hooves, just as hard and unbreakable as his horn, hit the cobblestones without a sound.

"It's quiet this morning," Brier remarked after a few moments, unable to bear the silence any longer. "Too quiet."

It wasn't the city itself that bothered her—streets slick with rain, flowering vines framing every dark doorway, Queen Celestyna's castle towering silent and white overhead. Word was that more people had fled earlier in the week—two whole families, gone from their houses just like *that*. Probably they were heading for the forested southern lands, which were so far away you could walk for weeks in the wild before finding one of their cities. Brier thought they were cowards, those people—abandoning the Vale right when it needed them most. But even *that* didn't bother her at the moment.

What *did* bother her was the sky.

It was gray and still as stone. No thunder rumbled; no distant lightning flashed.

Noro didn't speak until they stepped onto one of the winding dirt paths that led up into the mountains. Soon, these paths gave way to narrow, pebbled trails; tall pines became stubby ones. The wind grew unfriendly—though not as unfriendly as Brier would have liked.

Friendly winds meant stormless skies.

"You should have told her," said Noro. Even the morning birdsong seemed muted.

Brier wondered: Did the birds know? Could they read the storms?

Did they know what was to come?

She imagined it happening, on some quiet gray morning: every bird in the Vale fleeing in a cloud of black feathers—just before the Break opened and the Gulgot clawed its way out at last.

"Ow," Noro remarked mildly.

Brier was twisting her fists in Noro's silken mane, as if ready to throw a punch.

She released him. "Sorry."

"Angry about something, are we?"

"The skies. The world."

Noro let out a puff of laughter. "Ah. That again."

"Noro, what if—?"

"You should have told her."

Brier ducked beneath a low-hanging pine branch. The soaked needles drew wet fingers down her spine. "Told who what?"

"You were cruel to her."

Brier looked away, her throat tightening. "Thorn doesn't need to know. No one needs to know."

"I agree that the general population doesn't need to know that the end is near," Noro continued, his voice maddeningly calm, "but your sister is a fine keeper of secrets. You wouldn't need to worry."

"She couldn't handle it," Brier said at once. "She'd go completely wonkers. She's so . . . weepy and wibbly."

"In some ways, yes, she's not as strong as you," Noro replied. "In other ways, I'd say she's in fact far stronger."

"Hah!"

"I'm not joking, Brier."

Brier fumed silently on Noro's back. Low-lying gray clouds drifted around them like an army of gathering ghosts.

Then, up ahead, past a few rocky rises covered in patchy clover, a crackling light flared, brilliant and quick. A soft rumble followed; Brier felt it in her ribs.

Lightning.

Brier's spirits lifted. She urged Noro into an easy trot. When she was eight years old, she'd spent a few weeks practicing this gait on one of the queen's shaggy work ponies. The royal horse masters had used the beast to teach Brier how to ride before she was matched with Noro.

Never again would she sit on a horse's back, jostled around

like a sack of feed. Noro's trot—the least graceful of his gaits—was so smooth it felt like skimming across the top of rippling water.

"And what good would telling Thorn do?" Brier asked as they made for the crackling air where the lightning bolt had flashed. "She'd sit around and worry about it until she made herself sick, and for no reason. The storms will come back."

"And if they don't?" Noro sailed over a shallow ravine and landed quietly on the other side. "You'll be at the thick of this, Brier, whatever happens next. And I don't care to see you bearing the weight of it alone."

Brier pulled heavy plated gloves from her pocket. "You're worried for me, Noro?"

"Constantly," he replied. "Gloves on?"

Torn between pride and delight—Noro didn't *need* to worry about her, she was perfectly capable of taking care of herself; but, oh, to be worried about by a unicorn was a precious thing few people enjoyed—Brier said shortly, "On and ready."

Noro let out a low hum. "We're close. I can smell it."

They flew over a ridge of rock and emerged onto a grassy plateau bordered by sheer black cliffs. Above loomed the mountains, draped in cloaks of cloud.

And in the middle of the plateau, a single bolt of lightning waited.

Noro stopped short. One of his long white ears pricked forward; the other swiveled backward.

Brier's heart pounded as she watched the bolt hovering a few inches above the ground, threads of energy spinning around it. The bolt shivered, as if it was ready to fly apart into a thousand pieces.

No one knew lightning better than a harvester, but this was like no bolt Brier had seen before.

Lightning ran and raced, jumping from cliff to cliff like a snow lion. Only unicorns were fast and nimble enough to chase it. Lightning was wild and untamed, and did everything it could to avoid capture.

It certainly didn't stand around *waiting*.

"What the thunder is this?" Noro whispered. One hoof pawed at the rocky ground.

"You're acting horsey, Noro," Brier said automatically.

Noro's leg stilled. He cleared his throat. "Thank you."

"Why is it just standing there waiting for us?"

"I have no idea."

The bolt of lightning shimmered and twisted. Brier had the

oddest, most distinct feeling that it was *staring* at them.

"Perhaps we should leave it be," Noro said slowly.

"And lose a harvest?" Brier scoffed. "Not on my watch." She clapped her hands. The thin plates of bindrock lining her gloves crashed together with a tinny clang. "Let's go, now!"

Noro could have disobeyed, if he'd been free to. He was certainly strong enough to fling Brier off his back. He could have run away through the mountains and left all trace of humans behind.

But Noro wasn't free. Since the moment they'd met four years ago, when he'd been so charmed by Brier that he'd momentarily lost his senses and allowed her to ride him, they had been bound. Brier's will was his will. Once, long ago, when witches still lived in the Vale, the Old Wild would have been strong enough for Noro to resist the call of any human.

But the Old Wild—the oldest, wildest power in the world, the power that stretched from horizon to horizon and lived inside every tree and human and beast—was not what it had once been. It was quieter, weaker, harder to find. This was what Noro told Brier and Thorn when they dared to beg him for a story about the Vale of years long past.

Nevertheless, Brier felt a tingle of the Old Wild rush through Noro as she ordered him forward—a moment of quiet rebellion. Not because he didn't love her, but because he was a creature meant to live free.

His body shuddered; his horn sparked. Then he rushed at the lightning bolt, faster than a snow lion, deadlier than a diving hawk.

Brier's eyes watered. She threw up her gloves, sifted her fingers through the air. The bindrock plates soldered to the fabric sizzled and thrummed. But it was Brier's fingers, Brier's blood, that did the real work.

Some girls were born with a talent for singing or sword fighting, or for art, like Thorn.

Other girls were born with a nose for lightning.

Brier rubbed her metallic palms together, clapped once more. Her gloves flared to life. The fine hairs on her body stood straight up. Her nose and mouth stung from the lightning's heat.

And still the bolt waited.

And waited.

And *waited*—

Noro dodged the bolt at the last moment, veering away

so Brier could gather it up. He arched his neck, aiming his horn.

Brier reached for the bolt, fingers spread wide, blood connected to bone connected to muscle connected to skin and glove.

Her fingers met the light's edge.

The bolt shot up off the ground, and instead of zipping and zagging away as she expected—

CRA-ZACK!

The bolt twisted around in midair, whipping out one crackling white tendril of light. It hit Brier in the chest and sent her flying.

She did not land well.

She hit the ground at an odd angle, heard a few sickening snaps.

White-hot pain flared up and down her body—her arm, her leg, her skull.

But none of that was worse than the burning sensation in her chest, where the lightning had struck her. Her heart was on fire, climbing up her throat. She couldn't cough, couldn't breathe.

"Brier?" came Noro's terrified voice.

Something wet and scorchingly cold fell onto her skin.

Unicorn tears?

It was the last thing Brier thought before the world turned black.

.3.

THE GREAT GLASS HALL

Celestyna Hightower the Twelfth, Queen of the Vale, Master of the Realm, Daughter of Westlin, and Mender of the Break, sixteen years old and small for her age—a fact of life that she despised—sat on her throne, watching her harvesters squirm.

Eleven harvesters. Not twelve.

Someone was tardy.

Queen Celestyna loathed tardiness.

"You come before me incomplete," she said. "Why?"

A few tacky seconds crawled past before one of the

harvesters spoke. It was the eldest, a pale, pointy-nosed man with a scraggly gray beard. What was his name?

"Begging your pardon, Your Majesty," said the man slowly, "but there was an incident this morning, you see . . ."

Queen Celestyna sighed, lifting her eyes to the ceiling. Among the vaulted white rafters, slender-necked mistbirds called back and forth from their nests. Others flitted through the air, their periwinkle tail feathers fluttering and iridescent crown feathers shimmering.

One sent a gob of white dung flying to the floor. It landed with a plop right at the feet of handsome young Lord Wycklin, son of the governor of Estar, who had the gall to shriek and flap his hands. He shot a nasty glare up at Celestyna, his mouth twisting.

As if it was some sort of hardship, to be nearly soiled by one of his queen's exquisite mistbirds, which filled Castle Stratiara with soothing song, day and night.

As if it wasn't Celestyna's generosity that had given him a home in her own castle, his people a home in her city—while his province, Estar, far below the capital, fell to ruin at last, after years of growing darkness. Once Estar had been a thriving province of greenery and life, just as Westlin was. Now it was a wasteland.

Westlin would be next, Celestyna knew. The darkness flooding out from the Break would coat everything in ruin.

Celestyna set her jaw and glared until Lord Wycklin dropped his gaze to his boots. And to think, Celestyna thought angrily, that *this* was the kind of person her advisers wished she would marry.

A bird boy hurried over from his perch at the back of the room, his long gray coattails flapping. He mopped up the soiled floor, then scurried back to his seat.

"An incident," Celestyna repeated.

"Yes, Your Majesty," continued the old harvester. "There was a strange bolt of lightning. Very strange, indeed. It . . . Your Majesty, it struck our young Brier."

"Lightning," Celestyna pointed out, "is known to strike."

The harvesters shook their heads.

"This was different," insisted the old man.

Farver. His name was Farver Pickery. Celestyna's mind retrieved the information for her.

Sometimes she imagined her mind as a tired, stooped scholar. The poor thing had reached the end of her life but was doomed to forever roam the libraries of the world, searching for a book that did not exist. Alone, and lonely.

Quietly Celestyna dragged the fingernails of her right hand across the stone arm of her throne.

Better to be alone forever than to trap anyone else in the horrible web her family had woven.

"The lightning was waiting for Brier on the Black Ridge Flat," continued Farver Pickery. "That's what Norojedzia told us. And he and Brier are the fastest pair we've got—"

"I know," interrupted Celestyna, because now she remembered the name.

Brier Skystone—the girl with lightning in her blood. So said Celestyna's harvesters, and her forgers, and the simpering, silk-robed flatterers among her court.

They believed Brier was the girl who would save the Vale.

Celestyna's fingers longed to claw something.

Most days she figured the Vale could not be saved. But if anyone was going to do this impossible thing, it would be Celestyna herself. It *had* to be. After all, her parents had named her the Mender of the Break, right before they—

Before *she* had—

Celestyna swallowed hard. She did not blink, and soon her eyes dried.

"Is Brier dead?" she asked.

Farver Pickery bowed his head. "No, Your Majesty, but she's badly hurt."

"Because the lightning struck her."

"Yes, Your Majesty. It jumped back and, well . . ." The man fell silent, his mouth twisting.

Celestyna lost her patience. She couldn't stand the sight of the old man's tear-bright eyes. It pierced her heart, and heartache was something she could not afford.

"Speak," she said, "or I'll send you to Estar for three straight rotations."

Farver's wrinkled, sallow face went sallower and wrinklier. The air in the throne room stilled.

To Estar.

To the Break, and the monster.

To war.

This was a worse threat than the vast dungeons, worse than being taken to the far northern mountains and left shoeless in the high snowy peaks.

For the war at the Break was a war they would lose.

Celestyna knew it.

Farver Pickery knew it.

Probably even lightning-girl Brier Skystone knew it.

But still they fought, because what else was Celestyna, Queen of the Vale, supposed to do? Let the Gulgot climb out of the Break and devour them all at last?

Not that she hadn't thought about that more than once— sitting back in her throne, putting on her most comfortable slippers and her most beautiful gown, and drinking a steaming mug of tea as the world crumbled around her.

At least, from her throne room, she would have a good view. And it would be such a relief to stop fighting.

She listened to Farver Pickery speak, watching her reflections in the glass lining her throne room.

It was a hall of windows and glass doors and mirrors. Sitting on her throne, Celestyna was surrounded by images of herself: a too-small, too-young queen with hazel eyes and fair skin dusted with shimmering cerulean powder to match the mistbirds. Her hair was a long fall of soft waves and smooth ringlets—silver streaked with lavender, sky blue, and stormy gray, just as her parents' hair had been. And against her cheek fell two alarmingly crimson curls that called to mind her father's bright red blood.

Celestyna stared at her reflections and suddenly felt too tired and hopeless to even clench her fists. The eyes of her entire court were fixed on her. She wondered bleakly what they were thinking, and wished that she could go to one of them, so they could hold her and stroke her hair, and tell her that she could rest for a while, and that someone else would worry about the Gulgot, the Break, the realm.

But there was no such person left for Queen Celestyna the Twelfth. Besides Lord Dellier, her family's oldest adviser and friend, she was alone. The eyes in her throne room did nothing but stare in silence. Some of them, wondering how they could bribe her to bring their loved ones home from the war. Others, hoping she might marry them.

"We're worried the lightning is changing." Farver nervously took off his cap, smoothed down his wild gray hair, then put the cap right back on his head. "It went at young Brier with ill intent, Your Majesty. It was waiting for her like a hunter stalking its prey."

"What was today's harvest?" Celestyna interrupted once more.

She ignored the lords and ladies and advisers gathered in her throne room. They were growing restless; they were starting to whisper behind their satin gloves and beaded fans. A few merchants in tasseled coats, sitting at a table in the corner, scowled and glared. They'd been so desperate for trade that they'd traveled to the Vale from their distant southern forests and far northern mountains—and now here was the Vale's queen before them, overwhelmed and useless.

Celestyna tried not to look around at anyone, but her mind buzzed with nervous questions.

Did they think she sounded afraid?

Did she sound too young, too weak?

Would the merchants soon flee the dying Vale, as had so many others before them?

Would they take what remained of her people with them, leaving her truly alone at last?

Farver shook his head. "I'm sorry, Your Majesty, but we harvested enough lightning for only seven eldisks today. What with young Brier hurt—"

"Seven?" In her shock, Celestyna forgot about being too young or too weak. She shot to her feet, her silver-and-violet skirts swirling about her ankles. "You dare to come before me with so little?"

The courtiers milling about the room stopped their murmurings. Bright eyes latched onto her from beneath lace veils and feathered hats.

Vicious, the eyes were, and amused.

And afraid.

Celestyna stood trembling before her throne. "You insult me." Her voice came out just as shivery and red-hot as her tired insides. "I provide you with unicorns, I pay you wages. I entrust the safety of our people to you, and this is what you grant me in return? A good day's harvest should yield us two hundred eldisks."

She paused, swallowing with difficulty. "And you bring me seven. Only seven weapons with which to fight the end of our world."

Farver Pickery raised his hands. "Your Majesty, it's the storms, they're changing!"

"Enough." Celestyna's cheeks were on fire. Her heart kicked and fumed. She was gratified to see Farver Pickery flinch.

Lord Dellier cleared his throat and stepped forward. He had fair, wrinkled skin and grave brown eyes. In recent months, his neat cropped hair had turned gray. Celestyna tried not to think about that too much.

"Perhaps," said Lord Dellier, "it is time to send word east, to the Star Lands." He paused. "You'll recall, Your Majesty, the stories our scouts have told us about the two young witches who fought—"

"I said *enough*." Celestyna glared at Lord Dellier until he looked away. Her head pulsed with panic. *She* would be the one to save the Vale, not some upstart pair of eastern witches nobody had ever met.

"Witches made the Break," Celestyna said, raising her voice until every piece of glass in the throne room rang with it. "We don't need any more witches here, especially not outsiders who don't understand the Vale and everything we have endured."

She lifted her chin and glared at her court. "Bring Brier Skystone to me at the dawn bells, or I'll banish all of you to the bogs of Estar and hunt the lightning we need myself."

Her harsh voice startled the mistbirds into a flurry. A few feathers of lilac and dew silver drifted to the floor. The courtiers ran for them; there was no better hair ornament than a genuine mistbird tail feather.

Celestyna stormed down from her throne, her armored guards clanking at her heels. The ladies nearest her hurried away, laughing nervously.

She pointed to the doors at the far end of the throne room, hoping she looked taller and more frightening than she felt. "Get out. All of you, get out. *Now.*"

Celestyna stood with her arms rigid at her sides and her

head held high, watching her court flood out the doors. They stared at her over their shoulders. They whispered and laughed and cursed and shook their heads. Lord Dellier hesitated, but Celestyna stared him down until he too turned and left. A pang seized her heart as she watched him walk away, his dear gray head looking grayer than ever. He was the only person in this castle who seemed as tired as she was. He didn't deserve her glares.

But Celestyna couldn't bear for even Lord Dellier to see her in that moment. Once the room was empty of everyone but her two armored guards, she returned to her throne. There she sat, breathing tightly—head high, eyes hot, mouth wobbling, jaw tight.

If she opened her mouth, she might cry, or scream until her voice ran out. Her guards waited at her sides, patient and silent. She wished they would let her cry upon their shoulders, and nearly commanded them to do so. She wished they would leave her alone but then quickly banished the thought. It was a fear that often kept her from sleep—that she would awaken someday to find her castle empty, everyone fled north or south to other lands. The Break would open wide to swallow her city, and she would be the only one left when her country fell at last into darkness.

She stared at her reflections until her tears were gone. Dusk had fallen, and at this time of day, her imagination always got the best of her. In the nearest window, her reflection changed. She no longer saw her own image, but instead that of an old witch, huddled at the mouth of a cave. Wrapped in chains. Dusted with snow.

A single word came to Celestyna's mind, one of the last her mother had whispered:

Fetterwitch.

Some people's nightmares were full of monsters and murderers.

Celestyna's worst dreams were of the cave witch who lived in the mountains behind her castle.

Shivering, she rose in the shadows, turned away from the darkening windows, and left the throne room, her guards in step behind her.

In the west wing of the castle, in the private parlor where not even her flustered clutch of huffing, puffing ladies-in-waiting dared follow, Celestyna sat down to supper. Beside her, arched windows overlooked the Westlin mountains. Above them stretched a thick gray sky. She stared at it, too tired to eat.

"So many clouds," she whispered to herself. "So little lightning."

The next instant, the parlor door flew open and her sister hurried inside—Princess Orelia, twelve years old, wide-eyed and determined, with silver ribbons fluttering in her long golden hair.

Orelia's tutor bustled behind, waving a fistful of papers. "Your Highness, we are not quite finished yet!"

Orelia whirled around and shut the door in the old woman's face with an impertinent little curtsy. Then she went at once to Celestyna and held her hands.

"What was that all about?" Orelia said quietly, looking hard at Celestyna's stony face. "I was there, you know, in the throne room. I saw what happened, before Madame Berrie fetched me. I got free of her as soon as I could." She blew out a tiny sharp breath. "I saw your face, Tyna. You almost cried in front of everyone."

Celestyna did not answer. She held herself very still.

Orelia pressed on, gently. "Oh, Tyna. You look so sad. What is it? Say something, won't you?" She paused, then sat on the velvet-cushioned bench beside Celestyna. "Mama said never to cry, not when you're queen. Remember? But here, with us two, we can do whatever we want."

Celestyna laughed only once. She pulled Orelia close, so her sister would not see her face. She could never be too sure what it would show—especially when Orelia brought up their parents.

"Mama said many things about being queen," Celestyna murmured.

"She said, 'Don't ever yell,'" Orelia began, doing a fair impression of their mother's voice.

Celestyna shut her eyes against memories so horrible she could never look directly at them. "And she said, 'Don't ever cry,'" she added.

"Don't laugh too hard."

"Don't be too nice."

"But don't be too mean!"

"Don't wear too much lace on your gowns or paint on your lips."

Orelia's stomach growled. She laughed, snorting a little. "Don't be scared where people can see."

"Don't love too much."

"I don't like that one." Orelia hugged Celestyna's arm. "It's cruel."

"I like it." Celestyna stroked Orelia's hair. It was still lovely and fair, as it had been on the day she was born. With each stroke, Celestyna imagined her heart calming until it was just as smooth and unsullied as her sister's long, loose curls.

Soon her mind was clear, and her parents were dead and gone, as they had been for two years. She thought the words until they stopped hurting: *dead and gone*.

"Don't love too much," Celestyna said quietly, staring out the window. "Do you know, I think that's my favorite rule of all."

.4.

THE CHARRED WEB

Thorn dragged her weary feet through the front door of Flower House as the evening bells at Castle Stratiara began to ring.

She hung up her broom and cap and kicked off her boots. She took off her coat and dropped it onto the bench by the door. Mazby promptly collapsed onto the coat, yawning, and Thorn shifted the fabric into a nest around him. She crept sock-footed into the kitchen to the sound of his purrs.

There, at the threshold, she stopped dead.

Past the kitchen and its hanging copper pots, past the sunroom cluttered with Thorn's art, sat Brier.

She was huddled on the balcony, tears streaking her face. Noro lay behind her, propping up her shaking body with his own.

Thorn's heart dropped to her toes. She ran to the balcony and skidded to a halt.

Brier's harvester coat was singed black. Beneath it, her favorite gray tunic hung in limp shreds.

And on her exposed chest and throat, shimmering from silver to black to silver again, stretched a web of darkness. It was as though someone—or some*thing*—had painted a storm cloud across her skin.

"Oh, Brier," Thorn murmured, reaching for her.

"Don't touch it!" Brier snapped, fresh tears spilling down her cheeks. She twisted away from Thorn and cried out in pain. Noro bent his long white head over her shoulder and blinked; a single crystalline tear dropped from his great eye and slid down Brier's neck.

When it touched the charred web, the tear sizzled, gave a small cry as if it had been burned, and vanished. A tiny column of smoke rose from the spot, stinging Thorn's nose.

She sat back on her heels. "I don't understand."

"My tears should heal anything." Noro's voice sounded

charred and brittle, like Brier's skin. "I healed her broken bones, the break in her skull, but this . . . Thorn, it won't budge. It's a burn, I think, but nothing I do affects it."

"It's fine," Brier muttered, pushing away from Noro. "It just needs time to heal on its own."

But the moment Brier stood up, she let out another little scream of pain and crumpled back to the mossy gray floor.

Thorn caught her, expecting Brier to push her away. Brier wasn't the touchy-feely sort.

But Brier hid her face against Thorn's neck and wept.

Mazby crept onto the balcony, his yellow eyes wide, one of his front legs raised in confusion.

"I've got you," Thorn whispered to her sister. Her chest clenched in fear. What had scared the unscare-able Brier so awfully? What had hurt her?

And if whatever it was had managed to hurt *Brier*, who had survived years of harvesting without even a scratch . . . what then?

But Thorn did not allow her terror to pull tears from her eyes. Not this time. Instead she stroked Brier's tangled hair, which had fallen loose from her bun. "I'm here now, and you're safe."

What a funny, obvious lie that was.

Brier was the protector of this household—the rider, the fighter, the lightning girl.

How could a shadow protect the sun?

"But that doesn't make any sense," Mazby insisted. "You saw wrong."

Noro's gaze dripped with scorn. "Oh, yes? I, a unicorn with perfect vision, somehow *saw wrong* when a lightning bolt struck Brier in the chest and knocked her flat?"

The three of them had gathered in the sunroom while Brier slept in her bed upstairs, the burn covered with a thick bandage and a cooling salve. Night breezes slipped through the open windows; Thorn's strands of metal and colored glass chimed softly. Noro lay curled up in a corner—his muzzle more slender than usual, his legs daintier, his tail mere silver wisps. It was a funny trick of unicorns, to be able to fit into small rooms despite their size. Noro had told Thorn and Brier that this was a sort of magic that only worked when the unicorn was at home—a comment that had made Thorn cry and Brier beam with pleasure. A unicorn thought of Flower House as *home*.

The feathers on Mazby's head were an indignant crown as he

glared up at Noro. "I'm only saying that lightning doesn't attack people."

"It does now."

Thorn hugged her favorite pillow to her chest. If she pressed her nose to just the right spot on the embroidered fabric, she could smell her mother's perfume.

"I wish Mama was here," she said quietly. "And Papa too."

"We should write to them," Noro said. Fireflies attracted by his horn bobbed throughout the room. "They should know what's happened."

"*We* don't know what's happened," Mazby argued.

"We know Brier's hurt. That's enough."

"And what'll they do?" Mazby's voice grew shrill. "Come rushing home from war before their rotation's complete? Risk being exiled?"

Noro stared coolly at him. "Calm yourself. You're starting to sound like a squirrel."

The force of Mazby's gasp knocked him off his cushion and into a basket of fabric scraps. When he clawed his way free, a rose-colored tassel clung to his feathers.

"How dare you," he sputtered. "Thorn, will you let him get away with such comments?"

"Ah, of course," murmured Noro. "Grifflets never fight their own battles. They must hire bigger creatures to do the fighting for them."

Mazby screeched a battle cry and launched himself at Noro with claws extended.

Thorn caught him gently between her hands and brought him to her lap.

"Unhand me at once!" he cried.

She caught his beak between two fingers. "You'll wake Brier. And hasn't she been through enough today?"

Mazby's feathers flattened. He swallowed and nodded meekly.

"And this is the first time you've seen lightning act in such a way?" Thorn asked, releasing Mazby's beak.

Noro nodded once. "It has always tried to escape capture, but it has never turned on a harvester like that."

Thorn stared at the floor, trying to quash the rising swell of fear in her chest.

"That harvester I heard, and the rumors going through the city. About the storms fading, and the harvests getting smaller." Thorn looked up at Noro. "It's true, isn't it?"

Noro's expression gave away nothing. "What does that

have to do with the lightning attacking Brier?"

"Because if the storms are fading, if the harvests are growing smaller, if lightning can *attack* us, then maybe . . ."

Thorn fell silent. It was such a stupid thought.

You're not stupid, Thorn, no matter what everyone says. So stop acting like it. So Brier had said. But what if Thorn *was* stupid? It would make sense, wouldn't it? Their parents had explained to them long ago: twins start out life as one tiny little baby inside the mother's womb, until eventually it splits apart and becomes two.

When Thorn had first learned this, the world had suddenly become clear to her. When she and Brier had split apart, Brier had taken all the good with her—the strength, the smile, the grace, the confidence. Her veins carried away the talent for lightning, leaving Thorn's with a talent for . . . what? Sweeping?

It wasn't fair, but it was how the world had worked out for Thorn:

A strong twin, and a weak twin.

A good twin, and a . . . well, not a *bad* twin, but certainly not an impressive one.

A sure and sunny twin, and a twin who preferred to sit alone and make art out of trash.

"Go on," Noro said gently.

Thorn swallowed hard. She scratched her left arm. Another shadow-twin thing: when Thorn got nervous or scared or felt bad about herself, she felt itchy, and first rubbed and then scratched and then clawed at her skin until Mazby or Noro or Brier stopped her.

"Maybe," Thorn said, "the lightning has tapped into the Old Wild. And is using it to turn against us."

An unbearable stretch of silence followed.

A firefly bumped against a window.

Noro stood. His voice was strange and rough. He sounded less like Noro and more like the crash of storms. "I'll thank you not to speak of the Old Wild again, not until Brier is well. Even a unicorn's heart can only bear so much at one time."

Then Noro left. In his wake trailed a pulsing, frigid sensation. A vein of magic, maybe? Had Noro's sadness made it stir? The shadows in the room deepened. Or was it simply the fading lantern light?

Thorn sat very still, breathing thin and slow, cradling Mazby in her palms, until the feeling passed.

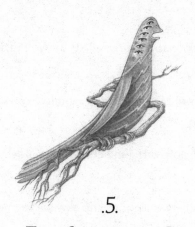

.5.

THE SHIVERING CUB

Once, when the world was young and savage, shadows had souls.

The light of the two moons cascaded to the ground in tiny crystalline flurries. Trees sang to one another in rumbling voices about the patterns of sunlight in their leaves.

Before humans and witches, before dogs and horses and mistbirds—even before the unicorns—there lived mammoth beasts with earth and wind in their veins instead of blood.

They breathed through lungs spilling over with yellow-flowered clover, and saw the world with limpid eyes that glimmered of dark seawater.

They inhaled rain and exhaled snow, inhaled fire and exhaled ashes.

They tore down mountains and rebuilt them with the hides of their own dead.

They moved slowly, trailing cliffs and valleys and forests in their wake.

The horizon between ocean and sky, between meadow and stars, was a shifting, blurry divide.

It moved—often.

Sometimes the beasts would awaken to a ground frosted with stars and a sky churning with waves.

Sometimes there would be no stars at all. Long days of darkness stretched out for an age until, without warning, the skies would burst awake again, spilling shimmering falls of lily-colored light to announce a new dawn.

And the beasts would blink sleepily in wonder—eyes stinging, frozen-over snouts puffing out clouds of steaming air—and roar.

It was a celebration, those roars, and a declaration:

We are awake, too.

The cub, shivering in the dark, was very old, and yet too young to remember those times.

His mothers had explained it to him, though, long ago.

On his darkest days, he recited their stories to remind himself that while he was now alone, he had not always been.

If he had once had a name, he could no longer remember it.

He knew he was a cub. His mothers had called him that, before the end.

"Cub," he said to himself every few hours, or every few days, or after months had passed and he had tired of silence. His old voice tore like brittle paper. Sometimes the sound terrified him because he had forgotten his voice existed.

"Sleep wildly, my little cub, and dream of the stars." That's what his mothers had often told him.

But he never slept, not anymore.

He crawled.

And he craved.

.6.

THE PAINTED LIE

The next morning, Thorn woke up groggy-eyed from a night of worried sleep. She stumbled into the kitchen and was cooking Brier's favorite breakfast—eggs scrambled with onions and diced tomatoes from their garden, served with thick buttered toast—when someone pounded on their front door three times.

BAM!

BAM!

BAM!

Thorn jumped. The spatula flew out of her hands.

Mazby, foraging for beetles in the flower box outside the

kitchen window, thrust his head through the curtain. One twitching black leg hung askew from his beak.

"Manners, Mazby." Thorn dumped the eggs onto a plate.

Mazby swallowed. "Who do you think that could be?"

BAM!

BAM!

BAM!

No one ever came all the way out to Flower House for a visit, not since their parents had gone down to the Break for their war rotation, and not since their friend Bartos had grown up and been recruited. Brier saw her friends while out in town or up on the mountain. And Thorn's only friends were Bartos and Brier.

Thorn undid the latches with shaking fingers. She couldn't help thinking that if Brier were the one answering the door, her knees wouldn't be so wobbly.

Be Brier, she told herself. *Be Brier. Be Brier.*

She opened the door and tried to smile the way Brier would.

"Good morning," she blurted as the door swung open and hit the wall. "How can you help me? I mean . . ." She shook her head; her fake smile hurt. "How can I help you?"

Five members of the royal guard were towering over her

on snorting, beribboned warhorses. The guards wore sky-blue cloaks and felt caps topped with mistbird feathers. There were two female guards and two male, including the stout, stern captain on the lead horse—and bringing up the rear was a bony, gangly, huge-eared seventeen-year-old boy with curly brown hair and a few pimples on his pale cheeks.

Thorn was so relieved to see him that she felt lightheaded. "Bartos? What's going on?"

Bartos's face was stern, but his eyes were kind. He had been a friend of their family for years, ever since Thorn's father hired him to help tend the gardens. Bartos had eaten suppers with them, and given both Thorn and Brier piggyback rides before they grew too big for such things.

But then Bartos became a member of the royal guard. Many people were dying in the war. More darkness flooded out from the Break every day. The queen needed more soldiers.

And Bartos had always been the sort of boy to go where he was needed most.

"We have come to bring Brier Skystone to the queen," said the captain. His silver sash glinted impressively in the pale morning light. His tawny brown skin shone with old battle scars.

Perched on the coat rack, Mazby bleated in alarm.

"It's all right, Thorn," said Bartos, a little nervously. He scratched behind one big ear. "The queen only wants to talk to her."

"But why?" Thorn asked.

The captain of the guard raised a single black eyebrow. "It doesn't matter why. The queen orders it." He peered more closely at Thorn. "Are you Brier?"

"Brier? No! No." Thorn resisted the urge to wipe her palms on her trousers. "I'm her sister, Thorn. I can fetch her for you, though. She's sleeping. I'll wake her up. I'll get her. If you don't mind waiting? You can just wait right here, I'll only be a moment."

Desperate to cut off her own blabbering, Thorn glanced frantically at Bartos before slamming the door shut.

She waited, catching her breath. She counted to ten.

Then she ran upstairs to the attic room she and Brier shared, stubbed her toe on the iron frame of Brier's bed, and shook her sister awake while hopping around on one foot.

Brier moaned and turned over, blinking awake.

Thorn gasped and stopped hopping. *"Brier."*

"Is it bad?" Brier coughed.

Gingerly, Thorn pushed aside the collar of Brier's flannel

sleep-shirt. Mazby fluttered down to Brier's pillow and chirped sadly. Tears sprang to Thorn's eyes at the sight of Brier's burn. It looked as if it had gotten worse overnight—larger, shinier, shiftier.

Brier yanked her shirt closed and sat up. "I'm the one who's burned, and you don't see *me* getting all snivelly."

"I'm sorry, it's just . . ." Thorn wiped her eyes with the back of her hand, her chest aching. Why couldn't she be dry-eyed and square-jawed and strong, like Brier? "You look awful. Your skin's so pale, and you have big shadows under your eyes."

"Well, I feel awful too, so that makes sense. What was all that noise downstairs?"

"The royal guard is here. The queen has summoned you."

Brier's dark eyes widened. "Why?"

"Maybe she knows about the . . ." Thorn gestured at Brier's chest. "Maybe she wants you to tell her what happened."

"Or maybe she wants to shut me up so I can't talk about it," Brier said grimly. "Lightning fighting back? People will panic. Better to get rid of me and not risk it."

Brier flung back her covers, swung her legs out of bed, marched toward the door—and stopped. Swayed on her feet. Clutched her chest and moaned.

Thorn hurried over, and Brier leaned against her.

"It's like there's this giant icy fist, clutching my lungs," Brier wheezed.

"You have to stay home," said Thorn.

"I can't ignore a summons from the queen."

"You can hardly walk!"

"Oh, so I should tell the guards, 'I'm sorry, I'm not feeling well, so I'll just stay home, if it's all the same to you'?"

"No." Thorn stood, and if her heart had been pounding before, it was now ready to fly out of her chest. "I'll go instead."

"That's the stupidest thing I've ever heard," Brier spat. "You don't have a burn on your chest, you don't talk like me, and the minute the queen sees you going all trembly and weepy, she'll know you can't possibly be me."

Thorn's eyes stung. "I thought I wasn't as stupid as everyone says."

Brier's face softened a little. "You're not. But you're also not *me*."

"Believe me, I know that very well."

"Let her do it," said Noro, his voice floating up through the window from the balcony below, which joined with their father's gardens by way of a stone path. "I'll help her."

Brier narrowed her eyes at the floor. "You won't be able to ride him. The Old Wild only permits one rider per unicorn. You know that."

"I can bear the pain," Thorn said. "And maybe it won't be so bad for me. We are twins, after all. We share more than most."

"And the burn?"

"Wait right here." Thorn hurried downstairs to the sunroom and gathered the supplies she needed. She ignored the front door and the shifting shadows outside the windows as the queen's guards no doubt grew impatient. Hopefully Bartos could keep them distracted for a few moments longer.

Back in the attic, Thorn sat on the floor across from Brier and thrust a small mirror into her sister's hands.

"Hold this," she instructed, and then, before she could talk herself out of it, Thorn got to work. She examined Brier's burn closely, then unbuttoned her own shirt, dipped her fingers into a jar of lumpy, charcoal-based paint, and smeared it onto her chest. Her fingers were deft and sure—first black paint, then silver.

She cleaned off her hands and hurried to the closet door. She grabbed Brier's harvester coat and the singed tunic beneath that. Gingerly she changed, careful not to smudge her paint job, and then gathered her long hair into a tidy knot on the top of her head with a cord of blue-dyed leather, as Brier liked to do when she went up to the mountains.

Thorn took a deep breath.

Be Brier. Be Brier. Be Brier.

She turned around, straightening her shoulders.

Mazby trilled with pleasure. "Oh, that'll do nicely!"

Thorn tugged on the end of Brier's coat sleeves. They were a little too long for her.

"Well?" she managed. *Be Brier.* She tried on Brier's smile. No matter how many times she'd practiced that easy grin in the mirror, it still felt strange, like too many teeth were trying to fit into one face. "What do you think?"

"Stop fiddling with your sleeves," Brier said at once. "I don't do that. And can your smile be a little less—"

"Thorn," came Noro's calm voice, from below. "The queen's guards are getting quite restless."

For a few seconds, Thorn and Brier stared at each other— one in a singed harvester's coat, the other in a faded sleep-shirt. Brier moved first, opened her arms. Thorn's breath caught. Brier wasn't a hugger.

But then Brier hesitated and stepped away. "I suppose I shouldn't. I don't want to muss the paint."

Thorn's disappointment left her speechless.

"Go on, then." Brier limped back to bed. "Don't lose my job. And don't be too . . . *you*."

Too soft, in other words. Too scared. Too trembly and weepy.

Thorn bit her lip and nodded, tugging her coat straight. "Mazby, stay here."

The grifflet's feathers went rigid. "But—!"

"You're my friend, not Brier's. You'd give us away."

Thorn looked away before she could see Mazby's feathers droop.

Downstairs, she took a deep breath and opened the door. She nodded primly at the guards and made straight for the entrance to their father's garden. She ignored Bartos's wide eyes. He would know at once, of course, that she wasn't Brier. She held her breath, waiting for him to tell the others.

But he stayed silent.

Noro emerged from the gardens, his midnight-blue gaze steady and cautious, and Thorn had to concentrate on climbing onto his back without showing the truth—that she wasn't used to riding a unicorn, and it *hurt*.

I am not yours, Noro's entire body seemed to say. This wasn't like riding Noro alongside Brier; this was different. This was *trespassing*.

As Noro had told them, on days when he could bear to speak of it, there were still some faint traces of the Old Wild floating through the world. Once a unicorn had been bound to its rider, there could be no other without consequence. Petting was one thing; riding was quite another. Someday, maybe, as the Old Wild continued to fade, anyone would be able to ride any unicorn they pleased. Noro would be as tame and gentle as a farmer's old horse.

But that had not yet happened, so Thorn gritted her teeth, settling as carefully as she could onto Noro's back without letting her discomfort show. Her legs, her fingers, her feet—every part of her that touched Noro felt scorched, as if she'd brushed against a hot oven and couldn't move away from it. Instead she had to keep her hands to the flame.

And keep Brier's smile on her face.

Be. Brier.

"All right, then." She ducked underneath the wisteria blossoms as she and Noro left the garden. "To the queen?"

Bartos, standing behind the other guards, shook his head, his eyes wide.

What are you doing? his expression seemed to say. *This is madness!*

But Thorn ignored him.

The captain of the guard once again raised his eyebrow. "To the queen," he agreed.

Thorn was not used to telling lies this big. As she followed the captain's horse, a chill crawled up her spine and burrowed into the curve of her skull.

Was this an awful mistake?

.7.

The Metal-Plated Girl

As Thorn watched Queen Celestyna walk into her throne room with Princess Orelia at her side, every bone and muscle and speck of whooshing, pounding blood in her body turned to cold iron.

Her thoughts were a jumble, each one screaming that she should run. Brier was right. How could Thorn pretend to be someone she so utterly wasn't?

Beside her, Noro shifted. Even he seemed nervous. It was unusual for a unicorn to enter the queen's castle. But this was an unusual day.

Thorn reminded herself to take slow, even breaths.

Pay attention. Be Brier.

In front of Thorn: the polished marble dais that held the queen's white throne. Behind Thorn: the five guards, including Bartos, who stood tense and frowning. Thorn knew that look; she had seen it when Bartos and her father fussed over sick plants in the garden at home.

Bartos was worried.

The queen settled on her throne. The pale gray and pink folds of her gown floated like clouds about her legs. Princess Orelia fidgeted beside her. Standing in little clumps around the room, the queen's advisers and courtiers fell silent.

"You are Brier Skystone?" The queen's voice was clear and cold.

Brier would not be afraid to speak. Thorn nodded. "I am, Your Majesty."

Her voice came out rather squished. She itched to fiddle with the ends of her sleeves. But Brier would not fiddle with the ends of her sleeves.

The queen glanced at the painted burn on Thorn's chest, still only half dry. "Tell me what happened in the mountains yesterday."

Thorn did, describing everything Brier and Noro had told her—the bolt of lightning waiting for Brier on the plateau. How the bolt had kicked her off Noro's back. The scorching hot pain of the burn. By the time she had finished, Thorn's throat felt completely sucked dry.

Silence filled the throne room.

Then the queen spoke. "Lightning does not attack people."

Brier would have smiled and said something clever and charming, something to sweep the gathered nobles off their feet and put them at ease.

But Brier was at home, in pain and alone.

Thorn tried not to think about that.

Instead she said simply, "This one did."

Whispers and quiet laughter swept through the throne room, sending heat crawling up Thorn's cheeks.

Princess Orelia glanced at her sister, then at Thorn, then back again.

The queen hardly moved. "You saw wrong."

Thorn frowned. That wasn't fair. Brier was at home with some horrible *thing* branded on her skin, and the queen didn't believe the truth? "I didn't see wrong."

Noro shifted from his left hooves to his right hooves. "Your Majesty," he murmured.

"Your Majesty," Thorn added quickly.

The queen waved a hand. "The eyes can play tricks."

Thorn exploded. Words poured out of her. She couldn't stop them.

"What if it was your sister, Orelia, who said she'd been attacked by lightning?" Thorn said. "Would you look at the burn on *her* chest and say *she* was lying?"

Even the mistbirds fell quiet. The lords and ladies of Queen Celestyna's court were no longer laughing.

The queen's eyes narrowed. "*Princess* Orelia, I think you meant to say."

Thorn looked down at her boots—Brier's boots—and tried to keep her face from crumpling.

"Yes, Your Majesty," she whispered after a moment. "Princess Orelia. I'm . . . I'm sorry."

For a moment no one moved. Thorn desperately wanted to grab on to Noro's long mane, or turn around and hide in Bartos's coat. Instead she made herself look up.

The rising sunlight shifted across the queen's mass of silver, color-streaked hair. Cloud-colored, sunset-colored, storm-colored—save for two curls of bright crimson.

"Leave us," commanded the queen. The clean cut of her voice made Thorn jump.

Only after the nobles had hurried out of the room, leaving the queen and her sister, and Bartos and the guards, and Thorn and Noro, and the queen's silent adviser, did the queen speak again.

"You are a bold child, Brier Skystone," she said. "I hope that boldness will serve you well. For your sake, and for ours."

Noro tensed. "Your Majesty, I hope you don't mean to—"

"The storms are fading. You know this."

Thorn hesitated. "Yes, Your Majesty. At least, that's what we all think. The harvesters and I."

"And you know what this means."

Thorn hesitated even longer. "I'm not sure."

The queen laughed. It was a sound with nothing inside it. "But you're the girl with lightning in her veins. The girl who could save the kingdom from the Gulgot."

Thorn wanted so badly to scratch her itchy arms and thighs but bit the inside of her mouth instead. Her thoughts went to her art, which always made her feel better. This time, she imagined *herself* as the art. She had been cut open along the seams, and metal plates were inserted into her body before she was sewn back up again. Instead of veins full of tears and nerves, she had veins of lightning, and skin of secret steel.

It would make a good sculpture. Cut-open tin cans for the

metal skin plates, and thin streaks of silver paint down the arms and legs, and ribbon scraps for the hair, and—

"If our storms are fading," said the queen at last, "then you must find others for us."

Behind Thorn, Bartos cleared his throat urgently.

"Brier Skystone," said the queen, "you will leave Westlin with a squadron of soldiers. You will journey across Estar and scout for lightning in the mountains on our eastern border, where the storms may be healthier and more plentiful than our own. You will bring back proof—a harvest to fill no less than two hundred eldisks." The queen's eyes slid to Noro. "Your horn can handle that, I hope, Norojedzia?"

Noro bowed his head. "Yes, Your Majesty."

The queen nodded, her gaze moving back to Thorn. "You will not be allowed to return to Westlin until you have completed this task. And then you will guide the other harvesters back east, tell them where to hunt, show them where to go, teach them how to handle the eastern lightning, if it is different from our own."

A soft, high-pitched buzz was building between Thorn's ears. To Estar? To the impassable eastern mountains? Past the war and past the Gulgot, and to the farthest border of their country?

To find lightning that might not exist, and *harvest* it?

She opened her mouth to protest. She wasn't the girl with lightning in her veins! She wasn't, she *wasn't*!

"And if there is no lightning in the eastern mountains?" Noro took a step forward, his voice hardening. "What will happen to us then?"

A tiny shadow moved across the queen's face. The ruler of the Vale had power over the unicorns, but that had not always been true. Not when the Old Wild was still strong and everywhere. Maybe the queen knew the same stories Noro did. Maybe she knew that, when the Old Wild was strong, a unicorn would have killed a queen for giving him orders.

"Then you will not be allowed to come home," the queen replied. "You will stay in Estar, use your knowledge of lightning to extend our weapon stores as long as you can, and fight the Gulgot until your very last breath."

All sound in Thorn's world narrowed to the frantic pounding of her own heart.

"You will leave from the Fall Gate at midday," said the queen. "My guards will see that you are properly supplied."

Then the queen retrieved Princess Orelia and glided swiftly out of the room.

.8.

THE WHISPERS DOWN THE MOUNTAIN

Brier awoke from a fevered sleep to hear a bright horn blast cut through the sky.

Her eyes flew open. Curled up on her pillow was Mazby, also wide awake.

"The Fall Gate," he whispered.

Brier was up and running toward the bedroom window on wobbly legs. Her chest smarting with pain, she shoved up the foggy window pane.

A whoosh of wet, green-scented air flooded the room. Brier squinted out into the midday drizzle. A glint of something sparkled in the distance. At the edge of the city, where the great Fall of the Sky raced foaming down to Estar, the towers of Castle Stratiara pierced the clouds.

And there, between the castle and the cliffs, was the Fall Gate, and that familiar blast of horns meant the gate was opening. Either soldiers were going down to war or coming home.

Every time the horns sounded, no matter where she was or what she was doing, Brier would freeze, and wonder, her heart pounding. And she knew, when the horns sounded, that Thorn, wherever she was and whatever *she* was doing, would be frozen just the same.

Someday soon, the horns would mean that their parents' three-month rotation at the Break was over, and that they were at last coming home—until the next rotation, anyway.

Or until the Gulgot crawled free of the Break at last.

Brier waited, listening, but she couldn't see or hear a thundered thing.

She limped down the stairs, then grabbed her father's knobby walking stick from its spot by the front door and leaned hard against it as she hurried down the dirt path to the city, Mazby clinging to her shoulder. She shoved past soaked green fronds, wiped itchy raindrops from her nose.

Hundreds of people rushed through the streets of Aeria, along the outer road that wound along the clifftops toward the Fall Gate. Brier shoved her way through the crowd.

"Move!" she shouted into the din. "Don't you know who I am? I'm—"

Mazby squawked. "You're nobody!"

And that shut Brier up. She clutched her collar shut, hiding the lightning burn from view.

She was Thorn Skystone for now. Not Brier; *Thorn*. A sweep, and not a very good one. A quiet girl, a dreamy girl, a girl who made art out of other people's stinky, grubby trash—

A stupid girl?

Brier pushed down against the bad feelings twisting in her throat. She'd called Thorn stupid yesterday, and it had been such a terrible thing to say—and not true, besides.

Thorn wasn't stupid. Thorn was simply herself. It wasn't *Thorn's* fault that she'd been born without something useful in her blood, like a talent for lightning. Just like it wasn't Brier's fault that she *had* been born with such a thing.

At last the crowd stopped, gathering near the Fall of the Sky. The air roared with the sounds of rushing water. Mist danced in shifting clouds, tugged by the wind racing up the cliffs.

The crowd stood as densely packed as a brick wall. Brier let out a growl of frustration, wiping her clammy forehead, breathing hard through the pain seizing her chest. If Noro were here . . .

"Over here!" Mazby's shrill little voice called.

Brier found Mazby hovering above the chimney of a nearby cottage. He searched past the crowd, wings flapping—and then his yellow eyes widened. He sank onto the chimney and raised one tiny foot, sharp with talons.

"Thorn?" he called out. *"Thorn!"*

Brier's pounding heart dropped to her toes. *Thorn?*

Gritting her teeth, breathing hard, she moved as quickly as she could around the crowd, until she was very nearly at the cliff's edge, where tangled green ferns and twisted black trees trembled in the wind. Leaning against her walking stick to catch her breath, her chest smarting and her legs shaking, Brier squinted through the mist and saw what Mazby had seen.

Where the River of Clouds met the River of Storms, rapids rushed and roiled and then spilled down the cliffs in an enormous waterfall—the Fall of the Sky. Set into the rocky black ridges that flanked the rapids was a giant circle of white stone, cut in half right down the middle, and this was the Fall Gate. When it was closed, it served as something like a cap over the most dangerous thundering rapids and the treacherously slippery riverbanks. When it was pulled open by huge mechanisms of chains and pulleys that only the royal guard could use, each half-moon piece of the Gate rumbled back into slots carved out of the nearby ridges. The twin rivers' rushing water roared without any cover, and mist sprayed everywhere.

The Gate was open now, and a procession of people and horses were walking straight into the waterfall. No, that wasn't right. Brier stared, her heart pounding as loud as the rivers. The people and their horses were in fact starting down a narrow road, slick with water, that zigzagged down the cliffs to Estar. The entrance had been closed off by the Fall Gate, but now the road stood open and waiting. It would take these people behind the Fall of the Sky and down the cliffs.

Brier knew that road. It was one of the only safe cliff roads left; most of the others had crumbled, torn from the cliffs by the Gulgot's spreading darkness. It was the road the Vale's soldiers traveled to get to Estar and the Break. It was the road Brier hoped would soon bring her parents home from the war.

And Thorn and Noro and a team of royal soldiers were marching down this road, through the mist, to Estar.

They were *leaving*.

"I don't understand." Mazby fluttered over and wrapped himself around Brier's walking stick, his feathers pressed flat against his body. "Where are they going?"

The pain in Brier's chest was making her vision black and spotty. She cupped her free hand around her mouth, hoping her voice could be heard over the buzzing crowd, and screamed at the top of her lungs. *"Brier!"*

Thorn, on Noro's back, whipped her head around at the sound of Brier's voice.

For one second, their eyes locked—dark to dark, frightened to frightened.

Thorn raised her hand and shouted something back, but Brier couldn't hear it.

Then the horns blasted again, and the two heavy stone pieces of the Fall Gate slid closed. A grinding noise as the mechanism worked, and then a great slam like thunder, and the rivers' roar grew a little quieter, and the air cleared of mist, and Thorn was gone.

Thorn was *gone*.

Brier stood at the cliff's edge among the soaked ferns and trees for a long time. No one was paying attention to her, and she wouldn't have noticed if they were. She stared and stared at the closed gate until something soft nudged her palm with a miserable bleat.

Unsteadily, she sat down in the bright green ferns and held a trembling Mazby in her hands. The crowd dispersed quickly. A brown-skinned woman soothed her crying child. A ruddy-cheeked man glanced fearfully at the sky. Soon there was only someone's lost cap, abandoned in the mud, and the spray of the roaring waterfall.

Brier closed her eyes. They were dry, but all the same she felt as though the Fall Gate, when it slammed closed, had cut a piece of her deepest self in two.

"I don't know what's happened," she whispered, "or where you're going, but come home soon. Come home safe."

Then Brier imagined that her whisper could travel, and sent it zipping down the cliffs so it could find its place in Thorn's heart.

Standing on the highest terrace of her tower, Queen Celestyna watched as Brier Skystone, her unicorn, Norojedzia, and five of her own best soldiers disappeared through the Fall Gate. A low rumble shook the castle. From below, in the Break, came dim flashes of lightning.

"Do you think she'll do it?" came Orelia's small voice. "That burn on her chest looked so painful, Tyna."

"What?" Celestyna rubbed her aching temples. She hadn't shut her eyes for more than an hour at a time in the past few days.

A stormless sky tended to do that to a child of Westlin.

Especially if that child was a queen.

Especially when everyone expected that queen to somehow bring the storms back, as if that was in her power to do.

Celestyna stared at the eastern horizon, her eyes burning. Orelia was right; the burn *had* looked terrible. And the girl was young, *too* young, hardly older than Orelia.

But Celestyna had no choice. Burn or no burn, Brier Skystone was the girl with lightning in her veins. There was no time to wait for the girl to heal. They needed eldisks, and if anyone could find more lightning, it was her. And when she came back with Norojedzia's crackling horn full of lightning, the people of the Vale would cheer for her—and for the wise queen who had been clever enough to send her in the first place.

Maybe Brier would come back with so much lightning that the Gulgot would die at last, burned by a fresh supply of eldisks, and the Break would close. Those who had fled the country would return, and all would be as it should. The secret anchored in Celestyna's blood would remain secret forever, and Orelia would never have to carry it herself.

And if Brier *didn't* come back . . .

Well, Celestyna knew what she *wouldn't* do, even if Brier Skystone died the moment she set foot in Estar. Celestyna would never, *never* marry anyone. Once, Celestyna had asked her mother if her father had known what he was getting into, when he married the young queen of the Vale. And her mother had smiled, her eyes sharp but sad, and said, "Tyna, darling, love makes a fool out of even the brightest mind."

Celestyna had long ago decided she would never drag another person into her family's awful mess. Some blood should never be touched, and Hightower blood was the foulest of all.

A single word slithered through Celestyna's mind: *Queenie.* She saw the faint image of an old woman wrapped in furs and chains, sitting at the mouth of a cave.

Shuddering, Celestyna remembered the sound of her dying father's voice as he explained the truth: "There is a witch in the mountains, a single witch left alive after the breaking of the Vale. She is called the Fetterwitch, and she crafted a curse to save us all, but she needed flesh and blood to finish it. . . ."

"Tyna, what's wrong with you?" Orelia's voice trembled. "Why aren't you listening to me?"

Celestyna shook herself and knelt before her sister. *Queenie.* The Fetterwitch's voice still whispered in her mind. Her blood tingled, as if she had spent the day in the lightning-charged storm halls, which housed the royal forges. It wanted someone to help carry some of her burden. *It could be a friend,* her pounding blood seemed to suggest in the Fetterwitch's sly voice, *or a partner in love, or a sister. . . .*

Celestyna shoved away those frightened, fretful thoughts and caressed Orelia's cheek with trembling fingers.

"Darling one," she said, "why are you crying?"

Orelia dashed tears from her eyes. "What if Brier dies on the journey? What if she can't find lightning in the eastern mountains? What if there *is* no more lightning?" Orelia drew in a shaky breath. "What will we do then? The Gulgot will crawl out and turn everything to darkness."

Celestyna swallowed all the things she had been longing to say for two years: what the lightning of the Vale *really* was, and how her deepest, most secret fear was that Orelia would find out.

"Brier won't die," Celestyna said firmly. "She will bring home so much lightning that the skies will burn silver, and the

Gulgot will be so frightened, he'll crawl back down to the deep, deep heart of the world, and never come up again."

Orelia gave her a watery smile. "You really think so?"

"Of course. Didn't you hear me before? She has a nose for lightning, that Brier Skystone. The best harvester we've had working for us since Mother and Father died. If anyone can find us the lightning we need, it's her."

Orelia threw her arms around Celestyna's neck, and as the queen hugged her sister, stroking her shining golden hair, her smile disappeared. She stared blearily at the starless eastern skies and thought things she would never have said aloud, not even in the privacy of her empty rooms:

What if the eastern storms cannot save us?

What if the lightning of the Vale is the only of its kind?

What if, soon, it will be gone?

Celestyna closed her weary eyes. Mender of the Break, her parents had named her. Some mender she had turned out to be. So far she'd done nothing but sit idly, waiting for someone else to save the Vale, all while her people fled and her storms died.

But no one was coming. She was alone. And if Brier failed . . . then what?

Queen-ieee, whispered the Fetterwitch, or maybe it was

Celestyna's own mind, and then came a thought so sharp and clear that Celestyna flinched, her eyes snapping open.

"I know what I must do," she whispered. She looked at the gray skies beyond her windows and felt cold all over, for in the murk of the clouds, she could see the Fetterwitch's smiling face.

"What?" asked Orelia, sniffling.

Celestyna stroked her sister's hair. "Nothing."

Travel fast, Brier Skystone, she thought. *Find us new light.*

But she didn't send those thoughts whispering down the mountain, a small blessing for the girl and her guards.

Instead, Celestyna's scattered thoughts turned north, to the high dark mountains some miles away, where a witch sat inside a cave, waiting.

She couldn't wait for Brier to travel all the way to the eastern mountains and back. The Gulgot might escape the Break any day. Brier needed as much time as her queen could give her, she needed someone strong to hold the Vale together until she returned—and there was only one way to make that happen.

Celestyna shivered, holding her sister close.

She would have to visit the Fetterwitch.

.9.

THE LAND RISES UP

The chasm known as the Break—hundreds of miles long, hair-thin in some stretches and wide as lakes in others—shifted like a serpent twisting in its sleep.

A rattling groan drifted up from the darkness, along with an awful hot stink, like the breath of someone who had never minted their teeth, and now had a mouth gone black and soft and sour.

Thorn wound her fingers through Noro's mane. They had ridden through the Fall Gate the day before, and made camp halfway down the cliffs for the night. The narrow switchback trail from Westlin to Estar was long and treacherous. Thorn hadn't slept a wink. She had curled up against Noro and cried into his coat, not even caring if Bartos and the queen's soldiers heard her.

Now it was the next day, and they were crossing the Break by way of a bridge that trembled under the weight of the warhorses. If Noro minded Thorn's tight grip in his mane, he kept quiet about it. He'd said nothing since leaving Aeria, just as she hadn't.

Thorn wanted to ask him if he was all right, but she couldn't find her voice. Her eyes were heavy and her heart even heavier. Her muscles throbbed from riding a unicorn she wasn't supposed to ride.

Of course Noro wasn't all right. Neither of them was.

Maybe they would never be again.

The queen's words trudged through her mind on a never-ending road: *You will not be allowed to return to Westlin until you have completed this task.*

Thorn's throat zipped up tight. The tears that never really left her eyes welled up once more.

A gentle nudge against her arm made her look up. Bartos had come up alongside her on his warhorse. His face was one giant, worried frown. His dark bangs lay damp and curled against his wan skin.

"Do you need to stop and rest?" he asked quietly.

Thorn shook her head. Getting up that morning and leaving their camp had been hard enough. If she stopped again, she might stay there.

The captain brought his horse to a halt and held up his gloved fist.

The other soldiers reached into their saddlebags. Each withdrew a round, ruddy metal disk.

Eldisks.

Thorn's breath caught. She'd never seen one in person. Rimmed with thick, rippled glass, the eldisks crackled quietly in response to the soldiers' bindrock-plated gloves. Small antsy limbs of captured lightning broke through both metal and glass, curled around the soldiers' gloved fingers, then retreated.

Thorn's own plated gloves—*Brier's* gloves—hissed in response. The hair on her arms snapped to attention.

The soldiers waited; the captain's fist remained clenched. Thorn, hardly breathing, watched Bartos scan the Break with narrowed eyes.

The rumbling Break stilled, as did the wet black ground

around it—but the hot stink remained. Thorn breathed thinly through her nose.

The captain lowered his fist. Then he jerked his head at the wooden bridge that stretched across the Break. This crossing was at one of the Break's narrower points.

Bartos had told her quietly the day before, as they inched down the cliffs, that the remaining bridges over the Break wouldn't last long. They might snap in two during a battle with the Gulgot's darkness, or some slimy dark creature that obeyed the Gulgot's command might reach up and drag a bridge down—maybe even while soldiers were traveling on it.

Or a bridge *itself* might decide to fall.

Thorn remembered her parents' letters: *You can't trust anything in Estar now.*

"Forward," commanded the captain.

But when Noro tried to follow orders, Thorn tugged hard on his mane. He hesitated, blowing out an undignified snort.

Behind her, one of the other guards grunted—a slim woman with pale freckled skin and short white hair. "Move, girl," she said.

"Leave her be, eh?" said Bartos, his voice light but his eyes flinty. "She's just scared."

The woman's frown deepened. "I thought she was supposed to be some fearless lightning girl."

"And I thought you were an adult," Noro said smoothly, "and she a child."

Not even this hard-faced woman could bear a unicorn's scolding. She looked away, her cheeks reddening.

Thorn hunched her shoulders and let Noro carry her across the bridge into darkness.

They made camp for the night in a flat stony clearing.

Shallow swamplands surrounded them, smelling like dirty socks that had been soaked in eggs gone rotten. Thick blankets of bright green algae choked the black water. Clumps of white moss wriggled with maggots. Mist shrouded the bulbous trees. Their drooping branches disappeared into the swamp, knotted and leafless.

It was night, according to Bartos, but Thorn's parents had told her there wasn't much difference, in Estar.

Day was dark; night was darker.

Thorn perched on a flat boulder, staring at the bubbling swamp.

The shadows of Estar were heavier than the shadows of

Westlin. They seemed like things of substance—crops you could pluck from the ground, or cloaks you could drape around your shoulders.

Or creatures lying in wait. Creatures that could wrap their fingers around you and *tug*.

Thorn drew her knees to her chest. She decided to ignore the shadows for now, or at least try to.

Instead she looked for lights.

In the distance—two miles away, Bartos had said—amber lights flickered. Candles, lanterns, torches. It was the war front, where the soldiers of the Vale camped. Armed with eldisks, they patrolled the Break that divided the dark ruin of Estar from the high green cliffs of Westlin. They peered down into the Break's endless darkness and shot lightning at anything that moved.

Thorn's parents were among them.

"We can visit them, if you'd like," said Noro. He nibbled at the fuzzy pink lichens lining Thorn's boulder. "I can run faster than any of these warhorses."

"And then what?" Thorn's eyes watered from the smelly sludge crusting her boots. She wondered which of the lights belonged to her parents. The brightest ones, she hoped. "We can't hide from the queen forever. We have to make it home, with all the lightning she asked for. Somehow."

"It was only a suggestion."

Thorn glanced up at the unicorn. Even in Estar, his white coat shone. "I miss Brier too."

Noro sniffed, sounding bored. But Thorn knew better. "Nonsense. We've only been gone a little over a day."

Was that all? Thorn's eyes stung with fresh tears.

Noro nudged her cheek with his nose. "And I'm sure you miss the rat as well."

That made Thorn laugh a little. "We didn't get to say goodbye to them."

"I'm afraid I'm not as cuddly as he is," Noro went on, "but I will try to be—"

A scream cut through the air.

Thorn whirled around just in time to see one of the soldiers being dragged across the clearing toward the water.

It was the freckled woman with the short white hair who had snapped at Thorn to move. The woman clawed at the stone, ripping up ribbons of moss, screaming at her fellow soldiers for help.

Something had her by the ankle—a ropy, dark shape like a long-fingered hand.

Thorn's chest clamped hard around her heart.

The *swamp* was dragging the soldier.

The swamp was *alive*.

Everything her parents had said about Estar was true. Thorn hadn't wanted to believe them.

Now she had no choice.

Bartos threw himself stomach-first onto the stone. "Make a chain!"

The other soldiers jerked out of their slack-jawed terror and obeyed. The captain grabbed Bartos's ankles, and so on, until all four soldiers lay stretched out on the rock. The last one hooked his ankles around Noro's front legs. Noro stood fast, his head bowed and his horn aglow.

"Don't let it get me!" shrieked the white-haired woman, now submerged up to her waist. "Kill it! *Kill it!*"

The swamp crawled up her body like a glistening shell, encasing her in darkness. Muffled moans slithered through the air, as if someone was enjoying a good meal with their mouth stuffed full.

"Pull harder!" Bartos shouted back at the others.

"Put everything you've got into it!" added the captain.

The soldiers heaved, grunting and groaning—but it was no use.

The swamp was at the woman's chin now, crawling up her face and scalp. She screamed once more, and darkness poured into her throat. Her mouth stretched into a gaping lipless maw, covered in a thick film of sludge.

With a great sucking sound, the swamp dragged the soldier under. The water gurgled, popped, and fell silent.

The captain pulled Bartos back to safety. The other soldiers scrambled up the ridge. Thorn rushed to Noro, who aimed his horn at the water. His eyes were dark angry slits.

They all stared, waiting. Overhead, a bird swooping through the low black clouds gave a rattling caw that sounded like croaking laughter.

Then another soldier cried out. Noro reared up with a savage trumpeting cry.

Four huge glistening hands erupted from the swamp, trailing gummy, rotting strands, and raced up the ridge like scuttling spiders.

The soldiers scrambled for their bags. Shrieking and wild-eyed, the warhorses raced away from their masters, galloping clumsily through the sludgy water. More hands thrust up out of the swamp—giant hands, with dozens of fingers and sharp black claws. The hands wrapped around the horses' bellies and yanked them beneath the water, gear and all.

Noro leaped to go after them.

"No, wait!" Thorn grabbed his tail as he streamed past. "Don't leave me!"

Noro skidded to a stop. He looked back over his shoulder to find her, and something behind her made his nostrils flare.

"Look out!" he cried.

Thorn ducked and stumbled, slipping on the slick ground. Her knees slammed into a patch of rocks, and she caught herself from falling into the water by grabbing for a boulder so sharp that it cut right through her left glove. Her palm blazed with pain. She cried out, then heard a loud gulping sound and whirled around.

A monstrous wet hand the size of her bed at home slapped the rock where she'd been standing. Its fingers scraped up clumps of moss before throwing them away in disgust.

"Yah!" Bartos shouted, flinging eldisks left and right, his cloak whirling. Disks of crackling light soared through the air. When they hit their targets, the lightning inside the eldisks detonated. The disk itself crumbled to glinting metal bits. Brilliant angry energy erupted in a flash. At the touch of lightning, the swamp shrieked and dissolved into glittering silver ash.

One of the other soldiers screamed—a brown-skinned man

with a long black braid. Thorn watched the swamp drag him across the ground. He slammed an eldisk onto the glistening muddy hand wrapped around his stomach. The eldisk exploded. Lightning sizzled down the swamp arm and across the soldier's body.

With a piercing shriek, the hand collapsed and released him.

Then four more hands burst out of the swamp and clamped down on the soldier's legs, his chest, his skull.

Smoking and crisped, the soldier gave one last frightened cry.

The hands yanked him under. The swamp rippled, like something huge and hungry was shifting beneath the surface.

A long, loud roar sounded from deep underground.

Thorn's breath caught as she jumped to her feet, holding her hurt hand close to her chest. *The Gulgot?*

The rocky ground quaked and moaned. Two cracks raced across the clearing, splitting it into four jagged sections.

Another scream.

One of the soldiers, fair-haired with a scruffy beard, tried to jump from one section of rock to another. He didn't jump far enough; he fell, knocked his chin against the stone with a choked cry, then disappeared down the crack and into the swamp.

And another shout—

Thorn spun around, shaking. The captain of the guard leaped for a nearby rock. Limbs flailing, he soared—then crashed into the rock chest first, and grabbed hold with all his might.

The swamp crested behind him, huge and dripping. A mouth opened in its center, ropes of mud stretching from top to bottom.

Looking back over his shoulder with wild eyes, the captain screamed.

The swamp swallowed him whole.

Thorn wanted to do something—*anything*—but she couldn't move. Bricks of terror weighed down her feet. Bartos darted between the remaining bags, looking for eldisks and finding none.

They'd used them all.

"Noro?" Thorn whispered.

He shook his head, his beautiful white coat splattered with sludge. "There's a bit of lightning in my horn, but without the royal forgers, I can't get it out."

Thorn swallowed. The world slowed down.

This was it. They were alone—Thorn, Noro, Bartos.

Bartos locked eyes with Thorn. His eyes were bright in his mud-caked face.

"I'm sorry, Thorn," he said, his voice breaking. "I shouldn't have allowed you to come."

"I wanted to come," Thorn whispered, though she wasn't sure that was true. But if she was going to die, she wanted brave words on her lips.

Then a crash sounded from above.

The swamp hands, rising once more from the water, jerked back as if suddenly afraid.

Thorn blinked at the churning dark sky. Her skin tingled.

Was it a storm?

"What the thunder?" Noro murmured, just before a bolt of lightning raced out of the sky and struck the ground at their feet.

Thorn barely dodged it in time. The lightning reared up, then crashed to ground once more. Thorn jumped out of the way, her boot catching on a vein of rock. She stumbled and fell, then looked back and saw the lightning racing toward her like an arrow from a bow.

In a blur of silver and white, his hooves sparking against the stone, Noro darted in front of Thorn, shielding her—and Thorn watched in horror as the lightning knocked into Noro's belly and slammed him to the ground.

The world tilted and boomed.

The bolt hovered over Noro's heaving body, like it was daring Noro to get up and try again.

Goose bumps rose along Thorn's arms. Could this be the same bolt that had attacked Brier?

Tears blurring her vision, Thorn ran toward the lightning, so frightened she could hardly keep her feet moving. At the last moment, the lightning swiveled around as if to face her.

She leaped for it, Brier's bindrock-plated gloves outstretched and buzzing. She crashed into the bolt, gloves first, and wrestled it to the ground.

Even through the protection of her gloves, heat scalded her hands. Her hurt palm stung and burned. The lightning thrashed, trying to escape her grip—she didn't know lightning *could* do things like escape—but the gloves, even torn as they were, shrank the bolt, dimming its light.

Thorn held fast. Tears streamed down her face from the bolt's brilliance, from the sheer breath-stealing heat of it.

And that was when she saw the loveliest, most impossible thing.

Buried in the bolt's twisting white light, staring back up at her, were two wide, pale blue eyes. Thorn saw the curve of a forehead too, and the sharp line of a pointy chin.

There was a *person* inside the bolt of lightning.

Thorn squinted, her heart kicking wildly.

No, not just a person—

A girl.

Very small, and fading.

.10.

THE STORM-TRAPPED GIRL

At first Thorn could only stare at the girl.

She felt as though her body was drifting away from her bones. A *person*, living inside a bolt of lightning?

The girl's face screwed up in anger. She let out a fierce cry. The buzzing lightning warped her voice.

Thorn pressed her hands closer together, gritting her teeth against the sting of her hurt palm. Between her gloves, the bolt sparked and twisted. Brier had many times explained to her how the process worked. If Thorn could get a good grip on the bolt, she could gather up its energy into her bindrock-plated gloves, shrink it into a tight orb, and then Noro would help her trap the lightning in his horn to take to the royal forgers, and—

Noro.

Thorn glanced at him. He lay not far from her, his belly heaving. A charred blackness marred his white coat. His vivid midnight-blue eyes had faded to a milky gray. Thorn felt sick looking at him. That burn on his belly looked just like Brier's.

The bolt thrumming between Thorn's gloved palms suddenly wrenched itself free, so hard that Thorn stumbled and fell.

Her gloves smoking, Thorn stared as the bolt of lightning careened through the air. The light twisted like a knot, then cracked like a whip. Tiny worms of light scattered across the ground. From inside the bolt came faint furious screams that sent chills up Thorn's arms.

Then, with a booming *CRA-ZACK*, and a great bursting pressure in Thorn's ears—as if the air had split apart like glass— the lightning bolt split into a thousand brilliant pieces and disappeared.

A girl with frizzy white hair that fell to her waist hung suspended in the air. She looked not much older than Thorn. Her skin was pale as the far moon. She wore a plain gray gown, the fabric singed at the edges.

The girl locked eyes with Thorn. They were the brightest, clearest blue eyes Thorn had ever seen, rimmed in thick white lashes.

Then the girl dropped to the stone with a heavy thump. She landed on her elbows and backside. *"Ow,"* she muttered, scowling.

"What in all the thundering skies?" Bartos, his swamp-drenched face streaked from tears, gaped at the girl. "How is this possible? What *is* it?"

Sniffling, the girl glared up at Bartos through a net of white hair. "I'm a *girl*, thank you very much."

Thorn's mind spun with questions. But then Noro let out a soft moan of pain, and an idea came to her. *Be Brier*, she thought. Brier would be ruthless and hard. Brier would not hesitate.

Thorn grabbed the long knife hanging from Bartos's belt and lunged. The girl was too slow; when she tried to stand up, her knees wobbled and she fell right over. Thorn pounced on her. The girl let out a muted yelp. Thorn pinned her to the rock and pressed Bartos's knife against her shimmering white throat. Holding the knife made Thorn's wounded palm sting, but she ignored it.

"You hurt my friend Noro," she told the lightning girl. Her voice shook with nerves. "If I let you go, can you help him? Can you fix whatever it was you did?"

The girl glared up at her. "If you let me go, then *maybe* I won't knock you to the stars and back."

Light rippled through the girl's body. A sharp tingling feeling prickled Thorn's skin, like the girl was fire and now Thorn was too.

The girl's mouth twisted in pain. She coughed up sparks. Her pale face suddenly looked a bit green.

Thorn wanted to jump off the girl at once and help her, but Noro was hurt, he was wheezing just behind her, and if the girl didn't help him, who would? And if she *couldn't* help him . . .

Thorn refused to think about that.

"I don't think you can knock me anywhere just now," Thorn said quietly. "I think whatever you did hurt you. So if you want me to put my knife away, you'll promise to help my friend."

The girl's face was stormier than the Westlin skies. Silver tears glimmered at her eyelashes.

"Well?" said Thorn.

"Fine," the girl muttered. "I promise."

"You *can* help him, can't you?"

The girl's gaze flicked to Noro. Thorn thought she saw a little ribbon of sadness move across her face before it disappeared.

"I think so," the girl said.

Thorn held her breath. The whole *world* seemed to hold its breath, even the gurgling black swamp.

At last Thorn stood up and passed the knife back to Bartos. She'd gripped it so hard that her hurt palm throbbed.

The girl knelt beside Noro, examining him.

Bartos joined her, his eyes wide. "Who are you, girl? You were . . . *lightning.*"

"My name is Zaf," said the girl. "And if you bring out any of those nasty metal killers, I won't help your unicorn friend, no matter what I promised."

Bartos stiffened. "I have no more eldisks, but rest assured, Zaf, if you try anything funny or boltish—"

Noro's body seized. He made a horrible rattling sound deep in his throat. "If the girl really can help me, now would be an excellent time."

Thorn's heart ached so fiercely she could hardly breathe. Through a film of tears, she looked desperately at Zaf. Whatever brave things she had made herself feel while holding that awful knife were long gone.

"Please, hurry," she whispered. "Brier will never forgive me if I let anything happen to him. He's like family, really, he keeps us safe while our parents are gone—"

"Wait. You're Brier's sister?" Zaf looked quickly at Thorn, from her head to her toes. "Yes, of course. You look just like her."

Bartos frowned at her. "You know Brier? How?"

Zaf's pale, pointed face was grave. "I struck her, up in the mountains."

Bartos blew out a sharp breath.

Thorn felt as though Zaf had struck *her* in the chest. "But . . . *why?*"

"Because your sister, and all her friends, are hunting my people," Zaf said archly. "Killing us, one by one. We're almost all gone. Soon there will be none of us left. I had almost fought free of my bolt when your sister found me. Bad timing, on her part."

Thorn stared at Zaf. "I don't understand."

"You mean, the lightning isn't . . . lightning?" Bartos asked, sounding like the small boy who had once helped Thorn's father in the gardens. "The lightning is . . . people?"

Zaf's face fell. "We've been trapped in it for years. You really didn't know?"

Noro cried out sharply.

Thorn stroked his neck with trembling fingers. Her hand hurt like thunder, but she didn't care. The thought of traveling through Estar without Noro made her feel like she'd been smashed under a boot.

Zaf, stony-faced, rolled up her gown's sleeves. "All right. This may hurt him. It's been decades since I've been able to use my hands."

She placed her palms against the smoking black wound on Noro's belly, bowed her head, and closed her eyes. Her palms brightened, and her body pulsed with light, as if she carried another bolt deep inside her.

Thorn's tongue tingled. Her skin felt hot and sharp.

"Noro, please, don't leave me," she whispered next to his downy ear. "We have a long way to go still. We have storms to catch and . . ."

She fell quiet and glanced at Zaf.

If Zaf was telling the truth, if all the lightning bolts had people inside them, then that meant . . .

With a sigh, Zaf sat back on her heels. Her paleness looked even paler—watered down and washed out. She shook her frizzy hair over her face.

"Well," she said quietly, "he'll live now."

Thorn, astonished, touched Noro's healed belly. His white coat shone. He grunted, pushed himself to his feet, and shook out his long white mane with a snort.

Thorn bit her lip. Now was not the time to tell him he was acting horsey.

Nor was it the time to ask Zaf to hurry back to Westlin and help Brier next—though Thorn felt the words on her tongue.

"How did you do that?" Bartos asked Zaf. "What did you do to him?"

"All witches of the Vale can heal," said Zaf, glaring at the ground. "Or we *could*, before . . . before everything happened." She traced her fingers across the soles of her feet, her mouth twisting. "I suppose we still can. I just *did*, after all. But it doesn't feel good, like it used to. It makes me feel . . ." Zaf sighed. "It feels like there's only so much of me left. Once, we were wild and powerful. We lived free. Now . . ."

Thorn watched as Zaf shrank into herself, like a small animal hiding from a storm. She pulled off her coat and wrapped it around Zaf's shoulders. Maybe Brier wouldn't have given Zaf her coat. Maybe Brier wouldn't trust Zaf, not even after she saved Noro.

But, Thorn thought, *I'm not Brier.*

"Tell me what happened," Thorn said. She hesitated, then touched Zaf's hand. "Maybe I can help."

Zaf glared at her sidelong. "I've seen you around. My head's buzzing like bees, but I'm starting to remember now. You clean people's trash, right? How would that help me?"

Now Thorn was the one who wanted to wind herself up into a knot and hide.

She scratched her left arm a little too hard, which made her feel better, and said, "If you want to tell me your story, I'm good at listening. You've probably been wanting to tell it for a long time."

Zaf narrowed her eyes. "You won't interrupt me?"

Thorn shook her head.

"You'll believe what I tell you?"

Thorn hesitated. Zaf had used the word "witches." Witches and healing powers and girls trapped in storms were things that belonged to Noro's stories about the Old Wild. Things that had once been, long before the Vale split, but were no longer.

Things it had become hard to believe ever existed.

"I'll listen very hard," Thorn said. "And I will take what you say seriously. That's all I can promise."

Zaf tilted her head. "That's a good answer." She raised an

eyebrow at Bartos. "What about that muddy, floppy-eared boy? Will he interrupt me?"

Bartos was looking out at the swamp that had eaten his friends, his eyes bright. He found the one clean patch on his sleeve and wiped his face.

"I swear to you I won't interrupt." He smiled faintly at Thorn. "I triple swear. Remember?"

Thorn did remember. When Bartos was a boy, and she and Brier were even littler, that was how they promised things. They triple swore them. One, two, three. Thorn, Brier, Bartos.

"In that case," Zaf said, "I'll begin."

She wrapped Thorn's coat tight around her body.

"Once," she said, her voice hushed, "the Vale was full of witches, just like the rest of the world. Then *they* came, and split open the skies. And nothing was ever the same again."

They? Thorn wanted to ask. But she had promised no interruptions. So as the howling swamp winds of Estar swept past them, she watched Zaf's tired, pale face, and listened.

.11.

THE BREAKING OF THE VALE

Cub knew the story too—the story Zaf told Thorn, Noro, and Bartos in that dark and hungry swamp—though Cub's version was a bit different.

All stories change depending on who tells them, but the hearts of Cub's story and Zaf's story shared a nut of truth:

There was a war, long ago. A war of ancient, powerful witches.

And that war killed Cub's mothers, and trapped Zaf and those like her in bolts of lightning, and changed the Vale forever.

৩ ৩ ৩

Cub remembered the day fire split open the skies.

He remembered the fire not being healthy, sunset-colored fire. Instead it was a hundred different colors—all brilliant, all angry. A furious pulsing purple and putrid green and sick vivid orange like the feeling of fear Cub got when he woke up from a nightmare.

He remembered the fire slamming into the storms that covered the Vale like a great swirling fist. That punch of power was so strong that the ground shook and wouldn't stop.

And the fire, when it split open the skies, also split open the earth itself.

The angry-colored fire spat across the stormy skies and spread crackling across the ground. It uprooted trees and turned clear lakes a steaming yellow, and it carried a bitter stench that stung Cub's wet black nose.

"What is that?" Cub cried, cowering between the giant ivy-draped legs of his mothers.

"It's magic," one of his mothers replied, looking gravely toward the eastern mountains, so high and fearsome that even Cub and his mothers didn't like to cross them. "It's witch-magic."

Cub's other mother wore such a deep sadness on her face that Cub felt afraid.

"They've turned on each other at last," she said, her voice heavy and tired.

Cub didn't understand. He knew what magic was—magic was part of the Old Wild, and the Old Wild held the world together. The Old Wild was what pumped through his own mossy veins. He even knew what witches were, for many lived in the mountains of the Vale. They chose to live there, his mothers had said, so they could be near the stars, for the stars were where witches came from, long ago.

But magic didn't smell like this, and neither did witches. At least not the witches Cub knew.

He shoved his snout against his mother's leg in confusion. "But witches are our friends!"

"Not these witches," his mother replied, watching the strange fire race across the Vale. Then his mothers turned toward each other, forming a shield over Cub's quivering body. Fire raced overhead and crashed into their mammoth beastly hides. Their bodies quaked above him and turned searingly hot.

He hid his face in the dirt as the world shook, horrible

colors flashing beyond his squeezed-shut eyes—and the great beasts that were his mothers fell to pieces around him.

And then the Vale—Cub's home, the only place he'd ever known, so green and wild and bursting with life—split in two.

One half of the Vale thrust up into the clouds. This would come to be known as the province of Westlin. The other half dropped low. This would be called Estar.

From a pile of clover-strewn, fur-clumped ashes, Cub watched it happen. A roiling colored storm fell upon the mountains of the Vale like a rushing flood. He heard the cries of the witches who lived there. He saw the angry fire snap them up. Soon there were no witches left in the Vale—only charred spots on the ground where witch mothers and witch fathers and witch children had once stood.

In his old, monstrous wisdom, Cub understood that the witches had been gobbled up. The sky fire had thrown them right into the mouths of all the storms that painted the Vale's sky gray and yellow and green and black. Cub heard the witches howl and shout, trapped inside bolts of lightning. He smelled the storms bleaching their hair and skin white. He watched the unicorns who'd escaped the destruction flee even higher into the mountains, crying out in terror and grief.

Cub thought he saw one particular witch, a tough old thing who was known for being clever, escape the fire. But then he blinked, and whatever he had seen was gone.

With the witches trapped, and the land beaten and burned, and the unicorns fled to the high mountains, magic left the Vale. It was a great loss, a thunderous snap in the air so loud it hurt Cub's teeth. He howled and howled.

He called for his mothers, but they did not answer. He had already forgotten they were gone.

But the angry fire was not finished.

Between the two halves of the Vale opened a great chasm.

As the land split, the chasm opened—wider and wider, faster and faster.

Cub ran.

He ran away from the ashes that had once been his mothers. He ran with sap streaming from his eyes and river mud choking his throat.

With his snout he searched for friendly scents. Maybe he could find other beasts of the Old Wild, and they would lead him to safety.

But the honey-sweet, meadow-sweet scent of the Old Wild

had vanished. It was like even the ancient power inside Cub's own body had gone hiding. Had the other beasts like him died in the fire? Was Cub the only one left?

He searched and sniffed and howled, but the only thing his nose could find was the smell of death, and fire that did not belong in the Vale.

An unfamiliar word came to Cub's mind as he ran: *war*.

Then, because not even a great old beast like Cub could outrun the breaking of the earth, the chasm reached him, and he fell.

He fell for a long time.

He fell through darkness, through layers and old layers and older layers of the world, for the chasm was long and deep, and growing.

Others fell—wild-eyed animals, trees ripped asunder, farmers of the Vale who'd been tending their fields when the sky fire came.

But Cub fell the longest.

When he landed, it was in a damp, close place. Not the good damp, like river mud. Not the good close, like the warm, safe spot between his mothers' bellies while they slept.

Cub hid his face in his bloody, bark-covered paws and cried.

His tears made a new river, narrow and hot at the lonely heart of the world.

Cub awoke, years later, and remembered what had happened.

He went back to sleep in the river he had made, and hoped it would drown him.

Long years passed.

Cub woke up, and slept, and woke up again. He grew while he slept, and was no longer as small a cub as he had once been.

But his heart remained small inside him, and he kept it hidden. He pretended the hurt in his chest was a bad dream.

As he slept, the thin shreds of Old Wild left in Cub's blood told him a story.

From his first day in the world, Cub's mothers had taught him to listen for the Old Wild in his blood.

The Old Wild was even older and wilder than beasts like Cub. It was what had made the world, and everything came from it—beasts and humans, and witches too. If you knew how to listen to it, you could learn much. Cub had never been good at listening, except when it came to his mothers' stories about the Old Wild.

Some creatures—like Cub—were full of the Old Wild, they had told him.

Some creatures—like humans—had none. Their eyes were so simple and small that most of them couldn't even see Cub and the other beasts like him, only hints and shadows, like tricks of light. They would swim in a river and not see the beast that had made it lying on its banks.

"Sweet, plain little foals," Cub's mothers had often said fondly, of humans. "Dull, confused little kittens."

"Kittens," Cub had once pointed out, "taste good."

His mothers had thumped him over the head for that one.

"Neither kittens," they'd told him, "*nor* humans, are to be eaten. What do we eat instead?"

"We eat sunlight," Cub had grumbled. "We eat the wind that whispers through the trees. We eat the nighttime shadows and the silver dew at dawn and the snow on the highest mountains."

"We never eat more than we need. And?"

"And when we eat," Cub would conclude, still grumbling, "we eat only with love and thanks in our hearts."

But some creatures—not beasts, and not humans—had just enough star-flavored Old Wild in them to cause trouble.

These creatures, Cub's mothers had told him, were witches.

Lonely and lonesome, shivering and angry, Cub listened to the story the Old Wild in his blood was telling him.

There was a place beyond the eastern mountains called the Star Lands. This land of seven kingdoms had air thin and clear, and stars so close they shone day and night.

In this place, the first witches had been born, long ago.

Seven of them had fallen from the stars. The First Ones, they came to be known. And as the years went by, and more and more witches were born and left the Star Lands to travel the world, the First Ones stayed in their homeland. They grew powerful, angry, and jealous. They fought often.

And then, the Old Wild in Cub's blood whispered to him at last, *they went to war, and destroyed each other.*

"What is war?" Cub whispered into the deep dark.

War will end us all.

"Even you?" Cub asked.

Even me. It has already begun. Can you feel the Wild, as you once did? Can you smell it?

Cub shivered. No, he could not. He listened and he smelled and he breathed, seeking. But the Old Wild was not what it once was. Even the powerful pieces in his blood felt lost to him—fuzzy, distant, and scattered.

I cannot live, the Old Wild whispered, *in a land of war.*

"You cannot?" Cub dared to ask. "Or you will not?"

The Old Wild did not answer.

So, Cub thought, once he had listened to the Old Wild's story. *So, this is the truth.*

Those First Ones, those seven witches of the eastern Star Lands, had gone to war and now were dead.

But their war had come to the Vale—that fire in the sky, those angry colors that ripped through the clouds and split the land in two. That war had ruined the tender green home Cub had loved, and trapped the witches of the Vale in bolts of lightning. That war had taken away his mothers.

And now . . . now what?

Cub, at last, pushed himself to his feet.

Now, Cub thought, *I will go home.*

"War," he said.

His voice carried through the deep seams of the earth into

which he had fallen. It rumbled all the way up to the mountains of the Vale. There, Queen Celestyna the Sixth woke up sweating in her castle. With the sound of thunder in her ears, she rushed to her window to look down, down, down at the chasm now known as the Break.

"War," growled Cub to himself, far below, "and witches."

He would make the Vale fit for the Old Wild once more.

And he would let no witches set foot in his home. Not again. Not *ever*.

He looked up into the endless darkness and began to climb.

.12.

THE WITCHES, GONE AND BLAZING

Thorn waited for Zaf to say something else.

Maybe Zaf would say that the awful story she had just told had been a joke. Maybe Zaf had hit her head when she broke free of her lightning bolt, so her mind couldn't be trusted.

But Zaf simply watched Thorn, a quiet sadness on her face, until Bartos broke the silence.

"That can't be true," came his voice, shaky and thin. "If that's true, then . . ."

"Then for generations, your queen and her family have

been killing me and my people to fight a monster," Zaf snapped, glaring at him. "The metal killers you throw into the Break carry my people inside them. What did you call them? *Eldisks?*" Zaf's angry eyes were bright with tears. "You're all killers, is what you are."

Bartos dragged his hands over his face, hiding his eyes.

"She wouldn't," Thorn whispered. "Queen Celestyna isn't like that."

Zaf scoffed. "Do you know her? Do you know *anything?*"

Thorn stared at the ground, lost for words—until she thought of something, and turned to stare at Noro.

He was standing very, very still. His coat seemed suddenly dimmer and duller, but his eyes shimmered like jewels.

Thorn's heart sank. "You knew?"

"I did," he said quietly. "All the unicorns know. We saw it happen. The sounds the witches made when the storms caught them . . ."

Noro shuddered. Thorn's throat felt very tight. She could not look at Zaf.

"When the royal family began harvesting lightning and making the eldisks," Noro said, "the witches had been suffering for many years, trapped as they were. We thought . . ." Noro hung his head. "We thought it would be a mercy, for them to die."

Zaf let out a strangled, angry sound.

Thorn's heart pounded in her palms. She could hardly find her voice. "Do the harvesters know? Did *Brier* know?"

"No!" Noro's head shot up. "No, I swear to you, Thorn, Brier doesn't know. She thinks the lightning is simply that. We . . . the unicorns, the harvesters, the queen, all of us, we decided not to tell her until she was older."

"But if she knew, maybe she wouldn't have agreed to be a harvester," Thorn whispered. She felt woozy. The world was changing too quickly, right before her eyes. "She's got a nose for lightning, right? Maybe she would have been able to work out a way to free the witches. Or she could have helped *you* do it."

"The unicorns wouldn't have been able to do a thing," Zaf said, looking coldly at Noro. "You've grown weak since the Vale split. No, I broke free all on my own. It took decades and decades, it was like smashing through a mountain with a tiny hammer, but I did it. Whatever magic trapped us in those storms so long ago, I think it's finally fading." She narrowed her eyes at Noro. "No thanks to *your* kind. Instead of helping us, you've been helping our killers. Letting yourself be bound to humans. Pah!"

Noro looked pained. "Without the Old Wild, we cannot resist them."

"Oh, to the *storms* with the Old Wild." Zaf swiped a hand across her cheeks. "So it got scared away by the sky fire. Well, I've been scared too, and I'm still here. The Old Wild's a coward. Do you hear me?" Zaf jumped to her feet and screamed to the skies. "You're a coward!"

For a long time, no one spoke. Zaf crossed her arms and glared at the ground, biting her bottom lip.

Thorn thought, *Maybe I shouldn't say this.*

Thorn thought, heart pounding, *I wish Brier was here, so she could ask questions instead of me.*

"How many of you are left?" she asked.

"I don't know," Zaf whispered. "The skies are so quiet. Once, there were thousands and thousands of us. Now . . ." She laughed sadly. "I suppose I could be the only one."

Bartos cleared his throat. He held his dirty soldier's cap against his chest. "Maybe they're all just hiding? Maybe some will break free, like you did."

"Maybe." Zaf's voice was shaking. "I don't even know who's alive and who's not. My mama and papa, my grandmum and grandpop. My cousins, my friends . . ."

Zaf turned away, ferociously rubbing her eyes.

Thorn tried to imagine what Zaf was feeling. She remembered seeing Brier on the balcony, afraid and hurting, with that awful black burn on her chest, and thought that whatever Zaf was feeling, it must be at least a hundred times worse.

She blinked hard, waiting until she could speak without crying.

"Queen Celestyna sent us to the impassable mountains to find more lightning," Thorn said slowly.

Zaf nodded sharply. "That's where I'll go, too. I'll help any stormwitches I can find, teach them how to escape their bolts, like I did."

"But then what will we do?" Bartos was very quiet. He was sitting with his hat clutched in his lap, his eyes trained on the ground. "If whatever stormwitches still live start breaking free of their lightning, we'll run out of eldisks. We won't be able to fight the Gulgot. He'll climb out of the Break at last, and darkness will flood over everything, even Westlin."

"You'll find other storms to make your precious metal killers," Zaf said sharply. "Real storms, with real lightning. No witches inside them."

"But what if ordinary lightning isn't enough? What if it's

the magic you carry that does the trick?" Bartos frowned, then looked up carefully. "What if . . . Zaf, what if we help you track storms and free whatever witches you can find, and then we all find a new way to fight the Gulgot *together*?"

Zaf's glare was so sharp it stung. "Witches? Helping *you*, our killers? That's rich. That's worse than rich. It's *stupid*. How dare you even say that?"

"But if the Gulgot escapes the Break, he'll devour us all—including you, and any stormwitches that still live."

Zaf stewed in silence, her pale cheeks coloring pink, and then burst out, "There has to be another way to save the Vale, and I shouldn't have to be the one to figure it out. *You* should do it. We've been helping *you* all this time, after all. We've been *dying* for years to save your miserable skins. Humans and witches, fighting side by side? We can't . . . I *can't* . . ."

Zaf fell quiet, her bright blue eyes sparking silver with tears. Bartos miserably wrung his hat in his hand.

Thorn cleared her throat. Her head felt so heavy that she wanted desperately to lie down in her bed, cover up with a blanket, and think in silence for a good long while.

But her bed was far away. And she had a feeling that finding these answers would take something more than thinking.

She just didn't know what yet.

"None of this matters if we die in a swamp," Thorn said quietly. "We should help each other through this, and we should get moving soon."

Noro shook his head. "The swamp will eat us alive the moment we set foot off this rock."

"No, it won't." Zaf held up her faintly glowing hand. "You saw what my light did to the swamp. There's enough left in me that I bet no monster's shadows will dare come hear me again. For now, anyway. I'm feeling better than I was earlier, but I don't know how long my light will stay." Zaf glanced at Bartos. "And if my light *does* go out, I don't think I'd like to be alone in this rotten place. It would be nice to have Barty's sword to strike things for me, I suppose, and seeing as how we're all going east . . ."

Bartos lowered his head, as if bowing to the queen herself, and held his cap once more to his heart. "We'd be honored, Zaf, if you would join us."

Zaf's mouth scrunched up, as if she was thinking about getting angry again, but then she turned to Thorn, and her grim face softened a little, and she held out her hand. Thorn gently took hold of it with her unhurt right hand, and as Zaf helped her rise, a soft spark of energy zapped from Zaf's palm to her own. Warm and sharp, it settled Thorn's mind enough that two questions formed clearly in her whirling mind:

What would Brier do, if she knew the lightning she harvested carried people inside it? That the work she loved sent witches to their deaths?

And, Thorn thought, her stomach slowly turning over and over like a smooth stone in idle fingers, *what will* I *do, now that I know the truth?*

.13.

The Unexpected Leaving

Far above the swamps of Estar, as her sister and her oldest friend and her beloved unicorn stepped into a swamp with a stormwitch at their side, Brier Skystone lay on her bed surrounded by tear-crusted handkerchiefs.

Downstairs, someone was pounding on the front door and yelling at her.

Well, not yelling at *her*. Yelling at Thorn.

But Thorn, Brier's mind whispered in soft, sad circles, *is gone.*

"Thorn Skystone!" came the voice of Master Tuwain. "If you don't get down here in the next ten seconds, you're fired!

Do you hear me? *Fired.* Finished! Flattened! Thunderstruck! Charred! Burned! Left to crisp and wither away!"

Brier could not abide the note of glee in Master Tuwain's voice. Not to mention the unsettling fact that each of his knocks jolted her body with agony.

It was why she'd been lying in the dark, barely moving, for three days.

Everything hurt. Sounds hurt. Even the faintest light reminded Brier of the bolt that had struck her.

Three days ago, she'd shoved through a crowd and shouted for Thorn over the Fall of the Sky's roar.

Now the mere thought of doing that made her teeth hurt.

She was getting worse—and fast.

She climbed out of bed. The soft blue rug scratched painfully against the tender soles of her feet.

Mazby, bleary-eyed, poked his head out of the pocket of Thorn's sleep-shirt. He'd retreated there three days ago and had only surfaced to listlessly hunt beetles on the windowsill.

"You'll hurt your burn," he warned her.

"Don't care," Brier muttered. Tears stung her eyes as she buttoned Thorn's shirt closed.

For one, the fabric scraped her burn.

For two, the shirt smelled like Thorn—paint and Mazby's feathers and rain from her long hours cleaning the streets.

Brier hobbled downstairs. When she grabbed her sister's patchwork cap and coat, her sensitive fingers felt like they'd been pricked by sharp stickers. She took a deep breath (that hurt too), waited for Mazby to land on her shoulder (that also hurt), and opened the door.

Master Tuwain glowered down at her, then narrowed his eyes, furrowed his brows, and looked closer.

"You look terrible," he declared. "Are you ill?" He pulled his collar up over his nose and mouth. "Great storms. I knew I should've fired you by mail."

"I'm not ill," Brier snapped, "and if you don't stop yelling at me, I'll—"

Mazby chirped a warning.

Master Tuwain's eyebrows shot up in surprise.

Brier swallowed her words. Thorn would not yell at Master Tuwain, though Brier had many times urged her to do so.

"I'm sorry," Brier lied, trying to sound meek. "I . . . Brier left. She may never come home again, is what I've heard people saying. I've been . . ." Suddenly Brier didn't have to pretend. The world blurred hotly. "I miss her."

Mazby's claws gently kneaded Brier's shoulder. The normally soothing sensation felt like someone digging knives into her skin.

Master Tuwain smoothed his shirt back into place. "Yes, well. The whole city misses her, don't we? But that doesn't mean we can skip work three days in a row. If you weren't Brier Skystone's sister, I'd have dismissed you the first morning you didn't show up for your shift."

Brier nodded, fists clenched in Thorn's coat pockets. "I understand."

"Good. Now, get to work, or I really will fire you."

Then Master Tuwain clapped her hard on the back.

Mazby squawked and shot into the air.

And Brier . . . Brier couldn't move.

Fresh pain spiked her chest. Her burn flared to life. Suddenly it felt like a thousand tiny bugs were swarming underneath her skin, desperate for escape.

She gasped, biting back a curse.

Master Tuwain turned at the front gate to glare. "What was that? What did you call me?"

"Nothing, sir," Brier managed. "I . . . had a cough."

"Cover your mouth next time," he said, scowling. "And get to Sixth Street in the next five minutes, or when I fire you, I'll do it in the middle of Center Square, in front of everyone, no matter who your sister is."

Then he turned on his heel and marched away.

Brier waited until he'd disappeared and pushed herself after him, Thorn's broom in hand.

Mazby fluttered beside her head. "What are you doing? Please, you must return to bed. You can't work like this! Brier, you look—"

"I know how I look." She'd seen herself in the mirror early that morning. Her skin looked drained, paler and waxier than usual. The skin under her eyes: shadowed and raw. Her lips: chapped and crusty.

At the end of the path, Brier turned left. She passed through crowded Third Street, then up narrower Half Street, then up even narrower Spare Street, all the while leaning on Thorn's broom and trying hard not to limp.

Normally Brier Skystone wouldn't be able to travel through the streets of Aeria during the crowded mid-morning hours without being stopped for handshakes and questions from worried citizens asking about the latest harvest.

But when she was dressed as Thorn, no one glanced Brier's way. She made it to the city's edge in ten minutes flat, even with her chest burning and her skin crawling and her body aching like it was being pulled between a dozen sharp-toothed clamps.

She leaned against a garden wall, soft and green with moss, and caught her breath. Before her rambled one of the pebbled harvester paths. Past that stood the mountains.

"Brier, talk to me," Mazby whispered, hovering near her cheeks. "Where are we going?"

"*I'm* going to find whoever or whatever did this to me," Brier said, jerking her chin down at her chest, "and figure out how to make it go away. I don't know what *you're* doing."

Mazby's feathers fluffed. "I'm going wherever you're going."

"Fine. Just don't make too much noise."

"I've hardly said a thing!"

Brier was not the sort of girl who melted very often, but Mazby's wounded expression did the trick. "I know, Mazby, it's just . . ."

She looked away. She had spent every day for the last four years harvesting lightning on these slopes. But now, with this strange pain taking over her body, the idea of the mountains felt wild and foreign, like standing on the edge of a vast, unfamiliar forest without a map.

But she had no choice.

"I'm afraid," she whispered. "I think I'm very sick."

"I *know* you're very sick," Mazby replied.

"Can you please not ride on my shoulder?" She shut her eyes in shame. Brier Skystone, unable to bear the weight of a grifflet?

"I'll ride on Thorn's broom when I need a rest," said Mazby gently. "Unless it hurts too much to carry it?"

"No," Brier lied. "I can do this." Another lie. She wasn't sure she *could* do this. Everything hurt. But she truly didn't mind the pain of carrying the broom.

It reminded her of Thorn. And Thorn never complained.

.14.

THE QUEEN IN FLIGHT

Celestyna Hightower the Twelfth, Queen of the Vale, Master of the Realm, Daughter of Westlin, and Mender of the Break, sat at her breakfast table and waited for the moment when she could run.

Her heart pounded at the back of her throat; she could barely swallow her tea. Her untouched, cinnamon-sprinkled porridge sat congealing at her elbow. She had never liked porridge, not since—

She blinked hard until the memory vanished.

At the table across from her sat her sister, Orelia, her long golden curls tied back with a silver ribbon. On Celestyna's left sat gray-haired Lord Dellier, with his gentle smile and his kind brown eyes. On her right was the royal tutor, Madame Berrie, pale and wrinkled, with immaculate white curls.

Lord Dellier and Madame Berrie were important enough to take meals with the queen and the princess, when Celestyna felt like allowing it.

And today she did.

She needed the two of them here, with Orelia, so she could slip out of the castle without one of them finding her, and fussing and scolding and then increasing her guard so it would be even harder to try running away the next time.

No one could know where she was going. Not Lord Dellier, not Madame Berrie, not even Orelia.

Especially not Orelia.

Celestyna lifted her cup of tea to her lips and forced herself to take another sip. Her scalp prickled with sweat.

She did not like high places.

But she would have to crawl out a window and climb down the castle wall.

She did not like witches.

But she had to visit one—an old witch, and so terrifying that her parents had never let Celestyna meet her. The only witch left alive in the Vale, they had said. The witch who haunted Celestyna's dreams.

Even the name was enough to make her shudder. *Fetterwitch*.

And once Celestyna got there, to the old witch's lonely mountain cave . . . she would need to do a terrible thing. It was so terrible she could only think about it sideways, as if it were a shadowy night-creature too frightening to look at with both eyes.

But she had to do it. The people of the Vale depended on her to save them—and so far, she was failing. Brier Skystone might never return, or return too late. Booms from the Break shook the castle day and night. Distant roars from the Gulgot plagued everyone's nightmares.

With shaking fingers, Celestyna carefully placed her cup on the table.

She would not fail her people for much longer.

She glanced at Orelia, who was happily chattering away about the new gowns her ladies-in-waiting had brought back from the city. Lord Dellier listened with a patient smile. Madame Berrie rubbed her temples as if a headache was forming.

There was an awful pang of guilt in Celestyna's chest. Orelia would be beside herself with worry when she realized Celestyna had gone.

But soon the Vale would be saved, and everyone would be cheering Celestyna's name in gratitude, including Orelia.

Celestyna dabbed her mouth with her napkin and folded away the ache in her heart. What had her mother taught her?

Don't yell.

Don't cry.

Don't laugh too hard.

Don't love too much.

Don't fret, don't worry, don't overthink.

"If you'll pardon me for a moment," Celestyna said, rising, "I need to adjust my hairpins."

Orelia wrinkled her nose. "But your hair looks lovely."

"Surely that can wait until you've finished your breakfast," suggested Lord Dellier.

"It could," Celestyna agreed, "but you know how silly we girls can be. I won't be able to eat until I've settled it! The plague of it will eat away at my heart until there's nothing left but ashes!" She staggered a little, hand on her forehead, and fluttered her eyes dramatically.

Orelia giggled. "Tyna, stop it!"

"Oh, the kingdom will fall to pieces should my hair topple! My sister will lose her mind with grief and throw the mightiest tantrum you've ever seen—"

"All right, all right," said Lord Dellier fondly, his mouth twitching.

"Hurry back, dear," said Madame Berrie, fluttering her napkin. "You know Cook's porridge is no good cold."

Celestyna, fake giggling along with Orelia, bowed out the doors to the nearby parlor.

Alone, the smile fell from her face.

Quickly she found the supplies she had stashed under the sofa—boots, cloak, a bit of food. She would have to make it all the way through the castle grounds and into the mountains without the royal guard following her.

Her palms sweating, her heart a fast drum, Celestyna tied her skirts around her knees and hurried to the far window. She pushed open the glass and looked down.

And promptly felt a little sick.

She was high up—*much* higher up than she remembered. Far, far below was the winding green maze of the royal courtyards. If she fell, if she lost her grip, she would do much worse than break a limb.

She gazed down at the castle wall. It was thick with tangled green vines, and through the vines snaked the long metal drainpipe she would hold on to as she climbed. The wall was stony and rough, pocked with holes. She could do this; she could climb down and use the castle itself as a ladder.

A distant clatter from the dining hall made her whirl around. Was someone coming to find her?

From the parlor ceiling, something softly cooed.

Celestyna looked up.

A dozen mistbirds waited in the rafters, their long pale feathers trailing.

Her fingers tingled. Would they start squawking and screeching as she crawled out the window, and give her away?

But then, through the open window came a soft thread of wind. And that wind carried a voice so faint that Celestyna at first thought it was her own mind speaking:

Run, girl.

One of the mistbirds fluttered down from the rafters and blinked up at her with its bright blue eyes.

We won't let them follow.

Celestyna's skin prickled. She recognized that voice now,

from the stories her parents had told her and Orelia, every night before bed.

The Old Wild, they'd said, had gone into hiding after the breaking of the Vale. That was what allowed the royal horse masters to match the unicorns with their harvesters. That was why the Break kept growing and the Gulgot kept coming—because without the Old Wild, the land was brittle and weak.

And why had the Old Wild gone away, leaving only traces of its power behind?

Because of witches.

Witches from the Star Lands, and not the Vale. That was true.

But witches nevertheless.

Celestyna tried not to feel guilty about the stormwitches her soldiers killed every day. Sometimes she stared down at Estar from her tower bedroom and watched the eldisks flash. With every bloom of light, a trapped stormwitch died.

At first, after her parents explained the truth to her, Celestyna had watched the eldisks flash and cried for days.

But now her eyes stayed dry.

It was revenge, her parents had said. Cold and clean and practical. A war between witches broke the Vale and unleashed a monster from the deeps of the world, so Celestyna would use witches to fight that monster. She would use as many as she needed to, just as her parents had done, and her grandparents before them.

Celestyna stood at the open window, the mistbirds' eyes upon her. She stared at the ground so far below and took three deep breaths to find her courage.

Her parents had believed she possessed the brains and strength to end this fight, like they never could—maybe even before Orelia found out the whole truth. Her sister would never need to know what awful things her family had done for their country, and she would never have to do them herself.

So Celestyna listened to that thin Old Wild voice whisper, *Run, girl,* and with one last look at the mistbirds, she climbed out the window, and obeyed.

She didn't stop until she was up in the wet black mountains above Aeria.

The thin air carved up her lungs. A pain in her side made her bend over to catch her breath. Her hair had fallen loose from its shining silver net. Her gown's hem was soaked through, the fine fabric ruined.

She looked back at the gleaming white towers of her family's castle. A bright chorus of horns pierced the cloud-heavy skies. Specks of darkness streamed across the castle bridges—her own soldiers, searching for her.

Celestyna's smile was sharp and proud, and for herself alone.

"Good luck," she said to her soldiers, not meaning it.

She began following the secret rocky path her parents had told her about, hoping the witch who lived at the end of it would be glad for some company. That would make it easier to catch the awful old creature by surprise.

A pang of something sharp and aching seized Celestyna's heart. She shrugged it off, clenching her sweaty fists.

"Witches broke the Vale," Celestyna whispered firmly. "They deserve no kindness."

And since the Fetterwitch was clearly no longer strong enough to protect the Vale, Celestyna would do it herself.

No matter what it cost her.

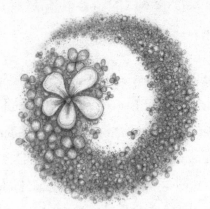

.15.

THE BITTER ELSE-HAND

Climbing up a tremendous crack in the earth for years and years was hard enough for Cub.

But climbing with the else-hand around his neck made everything harder.

He called it the else-hand for two reasons:

The first reason was that it felt like a giant hand clamped around his neck. Sometimes it hung loosely; sometimes it squeezed, which choked off Cub's breathing.

The second reason was that the hand was not made of flesh or bone or blood. It was made of something unseen, something *else*.

Witch-magic.

It had first appeared some years into his climb, and now dangled from his neck, heavy and thumping, like the weight of a dead thing he couldn't shake loose. Over time it had grown crueler and stronger. Every day, more of the else-hand's dark magic trickled free and spilled out into the Break as shadows, and then the shadows climbed up and scuttled out of the Break, faster than Cub could ever go. And every day, Cub thought the world smelled a little more like blood.

As he climbed, Cub dodged lightning being thrown at him from above.

He could not always move quickly enough. Sometimes the crackling bolts struck him like hooves, burning his skin. Sometimes they tore loose boulders that slammed into him and knocked him flat.

Did the people up above know that the lightning they tossed at him contained witches?

Cub didn't know or care.

Witches made the war, and the war had made Cub a motherless beast.

Whenever one of the lightning bolts hit him, he heard the tiny, trapped scream of the witch inside right before it died.

Once, Cub would have wept to hear such fear and pain.

But Cub had kept his lonesome heart small and hidden for so many years that sometimes he forgot it was there at all.

He never forgot the else-hand.

It wouldn't let him forget.

One day, so many years into Cub's climb that he had lost count of them, the else-hand tightened its grip.

Cub lost his footing, and fell for miles. He landed hard on a bed of rocks that pierced his tough furry hide.

"Please stop," Cub begged, but the else-hand never listened.

Instead, its cruel witch-magic hissed, *You will never make it out.*

"I will," Cub cried.

For how long have you climbed? How many crawling years?

Cub buried his face in his mammoth paws, which ached with blisters. "Too many."

The else-hand wriggled in delight around Cub's neck. *Beasts,* it whispered, *belong in darkness.*

But Cub remembered otherwise.

He remembered the kiss of sunlight against the furry crown of his head. He remembered the soft blue world of the ocean floor, where his mothers had taken him on adventures through forests of glowing coral. He remembered his mothers singing in booming voices about the first, oldest beasts, and the earth they had shaped into mountains.

"You're wrong," he told the hand around his neck. "Beasts deserve to see the light."

Cub pushed himself to his feet, pulling against the grip of the else-hand as if it were a rope from which he could snap free. He pulled so hard he saw stars, and whirling colors in the darkness, and then—and *then* . . .

With the else-hand sinking into his neck like a noose, Cub saw a thing of the up-above world:

A witch woman.

Cub knew at once that the else-hand belonged to her. He could smell her rotten-egg stink. He could taste the sour tang of magic moving through her blood. She sat on the edge of a cliff outside a small mountain cave, huddled over a pile of silver chains. She was very old; her veins were full of magic that burned like poison.

The witch peered out from her fur collar and watched a young woman in a pale gown climb up the rocks toward her.

"Queenie comes to say hello," whispered the witch, cradling

a length of chain against her cheek. "Queenie gets knocked back down below."

Cub struggled against the else-hand's grip. It was an old hand, a cursed hand. It belonged to the witch, yes, but there was another chained to it as well—someone newer and younger.

As if it could hear his thoughts, the else-hand tightened its painful magic around Cub's neck, cutting off his air.

The up-above witch vanished. Cub blinked in the sudden darkness and fell back to the rocks onto which he had crashed hours earlier. Or had it been weeks earlier?

Oh, to see the rise and fall of the sun once more! To measure time and watch it pass! These were things that Cub dearly missed.

But he now had a new thing to think about, until the else-hand let him breathe again—its witch and her chains, and the pale-gowned girl climbing the mountain.

What had the witch called her?

Queenie.

Queen.

.16.

THE BLACK AND BLEATING NIGHT

Thorn awoke from dreams of Zaf-shaped flowers and storm clouds that spoke with her father's voice to the sound of someone whispering beside her ear, "Something's hunting us."

Thorn lurched upright.

She saw a shape creeping through the stubby swamp trees toward the patch of stone where they had stopped to rest. Flies of fear buzzed in her ears.

The thing hunting them was tall and slender, like a piece of the night above. It was bigger than Noro, and notched all over, like bits had been chewed out of it.

Thorn's heart raced. *The Gulgot?*

But everyone said the Gulgot was the size of a city, or even a mountain. This thing was big, but not monster big.

Bartos stepped forward, his hand moving slowly for the sword at his belt. His skin gleamed with sweat.

Zaf crouched on Thorn's other side, her pale, glowing hand gripping Thorn's wrist.

"I thought your light would keep the swamp from eating us," Thorn said through her teeth.

"And so it did, for two days." Zaf glared at the approaching night-fiend. "I suppose our luck's gone running."

Thorn drew a quick, thin breath.

Then the thing inching toward them shrieked and pounced.

Thorn didn't have time to scream.

Noro leaped into the air from behind her, his horn flashing, and kicked out with his shining hooves. The creature careened through a clump of moss-draped trees.

And in the soft flare of Noro's horn, Thorn saw what their attacker was.

A unicorn.

A monstrous one.

Instead of a gleaming white like Noro's, this unicorn's

shadow-struck coat was sewn from the swamp. Patches of moss and murk stretched across its jutting bones and jagged spiked spine. Thorn could count its heaving ribs. Its mane and tail were long knots of ropy vines, and when it opened its mouth to scream, Thorn saw a set of gleaming dark fangs and three forked black tongues.

Bartos put himself in front of Thorn and Zaf, raising his sword. "Thundering *skies*. What's happened to it?"

"The Gulgot," Thorn whispered, just as Zaf, beside her, growled the same: *"The Gulgot."*

The monster tearing their kingdom apart, sending darkness flooding out across the Vale, had touched this unicorn and . . . *changed* it.

The unicorn ran at Noro, trumpeting shrill cries that sounded like no words Thorn recognized. Noro dodged its long black horn, skidded around the beast, whirled, kicked out with his hind legs. The other unicorn darted away, then reared up with its own legs flailing.

Noro ducked, then kicked the other unicorn into a boulder. The stone shattered; shards went flying. Bartos pushed Thorn and Zaf to the ground just in time. Thorn heard rock whistling through the air overhead.

The other unicorn pushed itself back up, its foaming mouth snapping like a crocodile's. Horn out, it charged at Noro—but Noro didn't move.

Thorn watched through Zaf's snarled hair as Noro faced his attacker, ears pinned flat.

"Noro!" Thorn cried out.

At the last moment, Noro dodged the unicorn's charge and sliced his horn across its belly.

With a gulping cry, the unicorn staggered and fell.

It was then, as Noro approached the creature, that Thorn saw something curious.

The unicorn was looking not at Noro, but at Thorn, Zaf, and Bartos. Its liquid black eyes, which Thorn had thought so terrifying only moments before, flickered with something small and pained that reminded her of Mazby after he'd broken his wing as a young grifflet.

Thorn's heart clenched tight.

Noro reared up.

Thorn shoved her way past Bartos, too fast for him to stop her. Sudden panic squeezed tears from her eyes. She flung out her arms.

"Noro, wait!"

Noro spun away just before his hooves struck her.

"What are you doing?" cried Bartos. He hurried over, Zaf beside him. "Get away from there, Thorn!"

"It's hurt," Thorn said, feeling stupid, because they were all looking at her as though she'd grown four new heads. But her heart wouldn't budge. She knelt beside the trembling unicorn. "I think we should talk to it before we do anything else."

Bartos reached for her. "It attacked us! Come on, move away from there."

"No, it was walking toward us, and then *Noro* attacked it."

Noro stared at her like all five of her heads had committed the worst imaginable betrayal. Thorn ignored him, her throat tight. She hadn't been able to look at him straight on since learning he knew about the trapped stormwitches, and she couldn't look at him now.

"Thorn," said Bartos, very reasonably, "this creature has been touched by the Gulgot's evil. Killing it will be a mercy. Please, step back. Let Noro finish."

But Thorn ignored him, watching Zaf instead. The stormwitch knelt beside her, and together they faced the fallen unicorn. Half submerged in the shallow swamp, it stared at them with eyes rimmed in pus. Its breathing was fast and uneven. It locked eyes with Thorn and let out a soft cry.

"What did you say?" Thorn leaned closer.

The unicorn strained to lift its head. Thorn couldn't bear the sight. She scooted closer and reached out to touch the beast before she could think better of it.

Noro shouted a warning, but Thorn had already placed her wounded left hand on the unicorn's neck. She'd forgotten—for just a moment—about her own injured palm. Her skin flared hot with pain. The feeling scorched up her arm, then burned her throat, like a too-hot bite of food, then slid down into the pit of her stomach and vanished.

Zaf hissed, "Don't touch it!"

"It's hurt," Thorn insisted, a little shakily. "And I don't think it wanted to hurt us."

"How could you possibly know that?" Bartos asked.

"I don't. But I can't just leave it to die without a word."

Before the others could stop her, Thorn scooted around and settled the unicorn's head on her lap. She smoothed the wet clumps of hair from its eyes.

"Try again," she murmured. "You wanted to tell us something?"

The unicorn squeezed its eyes shut and gnashed its sharp black teeth. Noro rumbled a warning.

"The Gulgot . . . ," the unicorn said at last. Its harsh voice broke open. "The Gulgot . . . is coming. Soon. Sooner."

Zaf whispered, "The Gulgot is coming sooner than we thought?"

The unicorn's eyes snapped open, spotted with milky-white clouds. "Yes. Weeks. Days."

Days?

Thorn swallowed hard, tasting a sour film of terror.

"How do you know this?" Bartos knelt on Thorn's other side. "Are you sure?"

"Came . . . from the Break . . ." The unicorn's voice was fading. "Saw him myself. Fast. Angry."

Zaf slapped the mud. "But what does he want? If he'd just tell us—"

Suddenly the unicorn began to shake. Zaf jumped away with a sharp yelp.

But Thorn held on, cradling the unicorn's shuddering head. "You didn't want to kill us, did you?"

The unicorn coughed up a viscous black liquid that steamed when it hit the swamp. "Was leaving, like the others. To protect the Vale . . . the Star Lands . . . we hide there. We're too dangerous. *Changed.*"

Noro stepped forward. "The unicorns who have been touched by the Gulgot flee to the Star Lands to hide?"

The unicorn nodded, his breathing now a thin, jangling whistle.

Thorn blinked past her tears. "I'm so sorry."

"Listen," the unicorn hissed. "Go east. Go *fast*. Find . . . Quicksilver."

Bartos frowned. "I know that name."

"She is . . . a great witch. She . . . can help."

Thorn stroked the hollow dip between the poor creature's eyes. "She lives in the Star Lands? Where?"

But the unicorn didn't answer. It had gone still in Thorn's arms, its eyes white and wide open.

Thorn looked up at Noro, a sob wedged in her chest.

"I thought he would hurt you," said Noro. He would not meet her eyes. "I didn't know. Thorn, I'm sorry."

"Don't be sorry for that." Gently she lowered the unicorn's head into the swamp. "None of us knew he didn't want to hurt us."

Zaf was watching her closely. "You knew."

"I didn't *know*, I just . . . hoped," Thorn replied. The sight of the unicorn half buried in swamp sludge was so awful that only a small, quiet part of her mind noticed that her cut left hand was no longer hurting.

"Quicksilver, he said." Bartos paced, scratching behind his right ear. "The queen knows of her. There have been stories brought back by our scouts. She fought somebody called the Wolf King."

"Did she win?" asked Zaf.

"Yes. And she has a friend. A boy, a witch named Ari. He's powerful too, I think. I don't know the full story, but maybe they could help us. Star Lands magic has to be at least a little like Vale magic, right?"

Zaf snorted. "And you, Bartos the human soldier, know a lot about magic, do you?"

"Oh, come on." Bartos took off his ruined feathered cap and wrung the swamp muck out of it. "I'm not trying to start trouble, Zaf."

"Funny for somebody who kills innocent grandmum stormwitches to say that."

"We have to do it," Thorn interrupted. "We have to find Quicksilver."

"What if she doesn't want to help us?" Bartos asked. "It was witches from the Star Lands who split the Vale all those years ago, right? Well, she's a witch from the Star Lands. Maybe she'd *like* us all to die."

"Yes, and this isn't her home, after all," Noro pointed out quietly, his head still bowed.

"But the Vale's only so big," said Zaf. "If the Gulgot eats up the Vale, maybe he'll still be hungry. Maybe he'll go east. This Quicksilver, I bet she'll want to protect her own home, even if that means helping us too."

"And if Quicksilver can stop the Gulgot," Thorn said, "then the queen won't make more eldisks to fight him, and . . ." She looked quickly to Zaf. "No more stormwitches will die."

"I like this plan," Zaf said, beaming. She marched over to Thorn and hooked their arms together. "Shall we, Barty?"

Bartos's stern mouth twitched with a smile. "This is not what the queen ordered me to do."

"Do you always do what queens tell you to do?"

"Yes, normally that's how these things work."

"Maybe the queen would like to stop killing stormwitches," Thorn said softly, "but she doesn't know what else to do. Maybe it hurts her every day, to know what she's done."

"You're too nice, Thorn," said Zaf. "Queens don't think about things like that."

"How do you know?"

Zaf shrugged. "You are what you do, and this queen's done nothing but hurt people."

Bartos jammed his cap back onto his head. "Please don't talk ill of our queen in my presence."

"Your murdering queen, you mean?" Zaf snapped.

Bartos sighed, wiped a dirty hand across his forehead. "This is not at all what I thought the future would hold when I helped your father prune his roses, Thorn." He looked west, toward the distant green rise of Westlin. "I wish we were safe in his gardens right now. All of us."

"But we're not," Thorn said wistfully. "We're here."

"We're here," Bartos agreed. Then, with a sad smile, he moved to clean up their camp. Behind him, Noro used his horn to carefully push the dead unicorn's body deeper into the swamp.

Zaf held Thorn's hand as the unicorn disappeared beneath the muddy water. And as awful as it was to watch, as frightened and tired as Thorn felt, as confused as she was by the fact that her left palm no longer hurt even a bit, she was distracted from all of that by the softness of Zaf's hand around her fingers. It turned her stomach wobbly, like an egg fidgeting in its nest. Warm and new and ready to open.

.17.

THE TETHERED CRONE

When Celestyna reached the Fetterwitch's cave, she found the old woman sitting at its mouth with her back to the world. She cradled her chains in her arms and sang to them.

Celestyna looked back at the path she'd traveled, gray and crumbling beneath a murky violet sky. Her tired feet burned in her boots. She shivered with cold and fear.

But if her parents could face their deaths bravely—even *ask* for them—then Celestyna could talk to a crusty old witch with snow in her hair and chains around her belly.

"Fetterwitch," proclaimed Celestyna, standing tall. "I have come to give you a task."

The Fetterwitch burst into rattling laughter. "Have you now, Queenie?"

Celestyna's skin crawled. "That is no way to address your queen."

The cooing Fetterwitch pressed her cheek against a length of chain. "Perhaps you're right about that."

Grunting, she scooted around to face the world.

Celestyna recoiled.

Across the Fetterwitch's pale wrinkled face, thick black veins drifted like drowning worms through a milky-white sea. Her skin bulged, then flattened. Her lips were crusted with dried blood, and her left hand was shriveled and black.

One of the woman's eyes was glassy ebony, the other white as a unicorn's belly. She blinked, and the eyes shifted—black to white, white to black.

"Good evening, Your Majesty," murmured the Fetterwitch. She lifted the hem of her tattered gown. "I'm honored to receive you in my humble home."

Celestyna's stomach flipped over, but she was a queen, and she would sound like one.

"I want you to release yourself from the curse you made," she commanded, "and give it all, in its entirety, to me."

The Fetterwitch blinked in surprise.

"Clearly you're no longer strong enough for it, but I am," Celestyna went on, her heart pounding. "The Gulgot still climbs. You haven't been able to stop him. I can."

A scabbed smile stretched across the Fetterwitch's face.

Celestyna lifted her chin. "You made this curse, you anchored it in my family's blood, but now—"

"Which they agreed to do," interrupted the Fetterwitch. "Your great-great-however-many-times-grandmother was happy to help."

"And you knew what it would do to us," Celestyna snapped, "how it would hurt us and make us sick, generation after generation."

"It was a *spell*, Queenie. It *became* a curse, as I feared it might, because your family and I were meddling in things we shouldn't have."

"And yet you said nothing to warn us, because you're a filthy liar."

"Unwise, to insult your curse maker so blithely," the Fetterwitch murmured. "I have been the thing standing between the Vale and utter destruction all this time, remember."

"Barely. Darkness floods our land. The earth quakes more every day. Soon it will shatter beyond repair."

The Fetterwitch's shifting black-and-white gaze turned cold. "So you trap my people and throw them at the monster."

"What else would you have us do? Let the Gulgot escape the Break and destroy everything?"

"I don't know, I don't know," the Fetterwitch moaned, wringing her hands. She looked out at the mountains for a long time. The gray skies loosed a silent snowfall.

"We should never have done it," she said. "Me, and Celestyna the Sixth. Foolish young girls. A spell to mend the earth and trap a monster? Once the Vale split, that kind of magic fled. Only tatters remained, unstable and unpredictable. We tricked ourselves into thinking this would work." The Fetterwitch closed her eyes. "He's coming fast, Queenie. Haven't you heard? The Gulgot's climbing for us all. Our curse has made him angry, and it won't last much longer."

Celestyna stood. "Then release yourself this instant and give it to me instead."

"You don't know what you ask, girl," said the Fetterwitch, laughing. "Magic isn't as sweet as all your glittering kiddie stories have told you."

"I know it isn't, and I don't care. I'm stronger than you are. *Do it.*"

The Fetterwitch watched her slyly. "Tell me, how did it feel, standing over your parents' bodies? Knowing you killed them?"

Celestyna froze. Shame crawled hotly up her legs and into her throat. "I didn't kill them."

"You did."

"They were already sick!"

"Because the curse was ruining them. You'll face that agony someday yourself, and now you're asking for it sooner?" The Fetterwitch's mismatched eyes gleamed. "And without me to carry the bad parts for you, it'll be even worse for you than it was for them."

The Fetterwitch wagged one mottled finger. "You'd better get married, Queenie, and soon, no matter what. This curse is too much for any one human to bear alone. We knew that from the beginning. Celestyna the Sixth was smart about it. She got married right away to some duke with red hair, if I recall correctly." She shrugged. "With me working the curse, and them anchoring it together, things weren't so bad."

"I'll *never* marry," Celestyna cried. "I'll *never* bind another person to this family, like my mother did to my father."

"Your mother needed help and was wise enough to find it, unlike her fool daughter." The Fetterwitch scratched the side of her mouth, pondering. "Doesn't *have* to be someone you marry, you know. The magic's limber enough for that. A good friend could share the curse with you, if you love each other well and true enough and will it to be so. Or Orelia—"

"Don't you *ever* say my sister's name," Celestyna hissed, so ferociously that the old woman flinched.

After a moment, Celestyna turned away and closed her eyes, remembering her parents' final words. Her coughing mother, struggling to swallow her last mouthful of porridge. Her father, bright crimson blood dotting his lips from the strange sickness eating his insides, had smiled at her. "Thank you, sweetheart," he had whispered.

And then Celestyna had lifted the spoon one last time . . .

"They said I would be the one to stop the Gulgot at last," she whispered. "They believed it, they swore I was strong enough to mend the Break. That Orelia would never have to be a part of this."

The Fetterwitch snorted. "They'd have told you anything. It was the *curse* speaking, girl, don't you see? That's the way it lives on. Me, the witch who made it, having my long, horrible life.

And your family, queen after king after queen. The rulers of the Vale anchor the curse, then their successor kills them and takes it on. Then the next, and the next. For years and years. That's why we're all alive. And the pain of each killing keeps the curse fed. I know your parents told you this."

"I did it to save the Vale." Celestyna stared east, toward the dark skies of Estar. The same words ran in circles through her mind. "They were suffering, and if I hadn't . . ."

"Yes, if they'd died on their own, the curse would have died with them," the Fetterwitch said quietly, "and the Vale would be lost. The Break would widen and widen, and the Gulgot would climb out and devour us all."

She shook her head, dragged her blistered hands over her face. "The time between each of your deaths grows shorter. Since the day your parents died, it's been anchored in you. And you could wake up tomorrow and be in such pain from the curse that you ask your sister to find a knife and help you along. And one of you had better have children quicky-split, by the way, or else this will all end very soon. Curse can't live without a bloodline to feed it."

The Fetterwitch sighed. "So much death, and yet the Fetterwitch lives on and on."

The snowfall was becoming a storm, wind licking across the mountains.

Celestyna sat beside the Fetterwitch, her fingers and toes smarting with cold. "It isn't fair that this burden should lie on my shoulders. I didn't ask for it."

"I understand that, Queenie," said the Fetterwitch. "I didn't ask to be the only witch to live past the breaking of the Vale, and yet here I am." She looked up at the cloudy sky. "What would the world be like, I wonder, if those old witches from the stars had never gone to war, so long ago? Unbroken, the Vale would be. Full of magic too, and the Old Wild still alive and strong. No evil beast. No curse."

The Fetterwitch lifted her chain-wrapped left hand. A knot of shifting black veins crowded her palm, resembling an unblinking dark eye.

Then she squeezed her hand shut and twisted.

From the distant swamps of Estar came low, rolling rumbles and a booming crash. A tremor shook the mountains, followed by a distant, angry roar of pain.

The Fetterwitch cradled her withered left hand against her chest and rocked back and forth, her breath wheezing.

Celestyna watched in horrified silence. So that was what her flesh and blood and bones gave power to. She had never seen the curse work up close.

Dark veins bulged on the Fetterwitch's face, drawing cruel shapes across her sweat-slicked skin.

"Elegant, isn't it?" she rasped. "I tell the curse to seek out the beast and hurt him. I knock him flat. And the Vale lives on for another day." She wagged a gnarled black finger at Celestyna. "And it's your blood that gives it power, only you don't have to feel the icky part, not until the end. For now, only I feel it. Lucky me."

"Lucky you," Celestyna murmured, staring out at the darkening mountains. Her mouth was dry and sour. She found her little bag of supplies, reached inside. Her fingers hit something hard and cold.

"What if *I* killed *you*?" she asked calmly, though her hands shook.

"I don't know what would happen," said the Fetterwitch. She sounded tired—and, Celestyna thought, a little glad. A hungry light came into her eyes. "No one's ever tried to kill me before."

Celestyna's fingers curled around the smooth marble hilt of the blade her parents had given her. She had not been able to stomach the idea of cutting their throats, so she had chosen instead two bowls of poisoned porridge. Not so quick, but less blood, and quieter all around.

Tears gathered behind her eyes. For a moment she imagined running away—but her mother had taught her an important thing: *Don't be scared where people can see.*

"My parents did always tell me," Celestyna said quietly, "to try new things."

When she moved, it was fast, and quiet as the Fetterwitch's lonely cave.

Pain raced through Celestyna's body, dark and swift as the evil flooding out from the Break.

She dropped the bloody knife; it went clattering down the mountain. On her hands and knees, she sucked in air that tore at her lungs. She tried to scream but couldn't.

Queenie, the curse hissed. With no Fetterwitch to protect her, it cut into Celestyna's bones like a thousand gleaming knives.

She rose from the ashes of the Fetterwitch's chains, flexing her blackened left hand. It crisped and smoked, as if lightning had struck it, but it didn't hurt.

It felt *good.*

Power coursed through her, from her skull to her toes. She thrust her charred fist into the air.

Punch him, she thought. *Make him fall.*

From the east came another distant roar. The stone beneath Celestyna's feet quaked.

Oh, how fascinating and cunning this curse was. Celestyna could feel the Gulgot's cracked hide beneath her ruined fingers. She inhaled and tasted the damp walls of the Break on her tongue.

"It's just you and me now, Gulgot," she whispered.

Just a young queen and an old beast, and an else-hand of cursed magic between them.

.18.

THE FAMISHED GRASPERS

Thorn was trying very hard not to scream, but that was difficult to do with monsters crawling across her boots.

And up her legs and arms.

And through her tangled hair.

Something soft plopped onto her neck—another tree slug.

"Don't panic," Noro said quietly. "Nothing has hurt us yet. Maybe, if we stay calm, that will remain true."

But Thorn was long past the point of panic.

Milky-white trees draped in thick spiderwebs arched overhead. The branches glistened black with slugs. They nibbled at the spiderwebs, the sounds of their grinding teeth reminding Thorn of Mazby crunching on scuttle bugs at the kitchen window.

Behind her, Noro cleared his throat. "Why did everyone stop talking?" Thorn wasn't fooled by his calm voice. The last time she'd looked back at him, his coat had shivered with spiders. "We were playing a game, weren't we?"

"Right," said Zaf. She inhaled, slow and shaky. "So. I think this witch Quicksilver probably . . . has warts all over her chin."

On the other side of Zaf, Bartos laughed.

Half-heartedly.

"And frizzy gray hair so long that she could wrap herself up in it," he said, his voice higher than usual, "like a caterpillar in a cocoon."

A six-eyed bird with a gaping, beakless mouth like that of a fish perched on Bartos's shoulder. Another sat on his other shoulder. And another clung to the lapel of his coat, staring blankly up at him. Eighteen filmy black eyes, blinking, blinking.

Bartos swallowed, looking spectacularly ill. But he kept inching his way through the swamp, as they had been for hours. Nearly a day had gone by since Noro's fight with the darkened unicorn, and with every passing moment, the truth became more obvious:

Estar was alive, and hungry.

It liked to climb. And sniff. And chomp. The soles of Thorn's feet burned; the swamp was nibbling at her boots with tiny invisible teeth. Zaf's skin, glowing with whatever lightning remained inside her, seemed to be losing its effect on the swamp and its creatures. They hadn't consumed anyone . . . yet.

But they clung, with grasping fingers.

And slithered.

And groaned ravenous little groans like the hounds that sniffed for scraps along Thorn's sweep route.

Zaf cleared her throat. It was Thorn's turn.

"Maybe Quicksilver has glowing eyes," said Thorn, her voice thin. "Maybe they're such a bright blue that if you saw her in dark woods, you'd think her eyes were fallen stars."

Zaf made a strangled sound. A slime-slicked brown lizard with three bleating heads skittered down the side of her face and into her collar.

Zaf's pale face grew even paler. She stared straight ahead. Her fingers squeezed Thorn's.

Thorn tried not to stare at the lizard-sized lump darting around under Zaf's coat.

Another slug dropped onto Thorn's right arm. And a third,

onto the crown of her head. A fourth, into the swamp at her feet. A fifth, onto the white shell of Zaf's ear. *Plop.* Each landing sent up tiny smoky plumes of darkness.

Thorn watched a tree-shaped shadow peel away from a sagging pine. The shadow swiveled in the air and scraped the branches above, knocking loose a shower of slugs. Then the shadow dropped silently into the water.

Thorn held her breath, waiting.

Ahead of them: a rumble. A gurgle.

The swamp's surface rippled. A cluster of brown bubbles burst on the surface.

Noro's crisp, cold breath was shaky on Thorn's head. "Maybe I was wrong," he said tensely. "Maybe if we start running, they won't mind."

"Or they might mind very much," Thorn whispered, hardly daring to speak. If she spoke wrong, the fat worm bunching across her upper lip might fall into her mouth. Her fingers trembled; never in her life had she so badly wanted to scratch off her skin.

She squinted through the trees at the horizon. She could just make out the towering eastern peaks rising into the distant clouds.

The impassable mountains were still so far away.

Much too far.

Her head spun as she tried to breathe, but it was like someone was sewing her throat closed.

"Thorn?" Zaf was squeezing Thorn's hand again, but Thorn could hardly feel it. A mist was settling over her eyes, and her head was spinning fast. "Thorn, you need to slow down your breathing."

"Can't." Thorn shook her head; a many-legged thing skittered down the back of her neck.

Thorn's strength cracked. She reached back and slapped the thing away.

The swamp . . . *shrieked.*

A shadow slunk out of the water to wrap around the nearest tree. Another followed, and then three more right after. Long limbs of shadows, stretching and reaching.

Dozens of staring eyes—black, yellow, lidless—popped out of the water.

Bartos reached for his sword. With a small, rasping cry, one of the fish-mouthed birds on his hand shot up into the sky. The others clinging to Bartos's clothes rose cawing into the air right behind the leader, their naked wings flapping.

Something in the water circled Thorn. Three ripples chased one another beneath the mud. A long shape brushed past Thorn's legs.

Her vision spotted red and black. She couldn't *breathe*.

Zaf's hand tightened around Thorn's. "I think I can get us there faster."

"What do you mean?" asked Noro.

Zaf jerked her head at the horizon. "I can get us to the mountains. At least, I can get us closer. I think."

Thorn stared at her. *"How?"*

"When I was lightning, I could zip around so quickly," Zaf replied. "I could jump between mountains and skip over rivers. And there's a good bit of lightning left deep down in me. Feels like running, but cooped up in my gut."

"And you think you can access this power?" Noro asked.

Zaf frowned at the rippling swamp, closed her eyes. "Yes, I do."

"Why didn't you say this before?" Bartos asked stiffly, trying to shrug off a wriggling cape of worms.

"I . . . I was afraid it might hurt," mumbled Zaf.

"Will it hurt less than being eaten alive by a swamp?" Bartos pointed out. "I can deal with a lightning shock."

"No, I mean it could hurt . . . *me*."

"Then don't do it," Thorn said at once, her chest tight with sudden fear. "That isn't fair."

"If she doesn't try, then we'll *all* hurt," Bartos yelped, and ducked. The horrible beakless birds were circling around his head. He darted this way and that, dodging their wide mouths. "Zaf, hurry! Do it!"

"We won't make it to the mountains like this," Noro said urgently. "I fear that if any of these creatures bite or claw us, whatever has happened to them may happen to us."

A coil of fear loosed in Thorn's belly. She clenched her left hand, digging her nails into the place where her wound had once burned. She hadn't dared look at it since they had left the dead unicorn.

"Zaf, please!" Bartos shouted, his voice cracking. Thorn's heart quaked to hear him so afraid.

"Everyone grab on tight," Zaf cried, squaring her thin shoulders.

Thorn tugged on her hand. "Zaf, *no*—"

But Zaf plunged into the swarming birds and grabbed Bartos with her free hand, and Bartos seized a fistful of Noro's mane, and the world flared to brilliant life. Heat raced up Thorn's arms and legs.

The swamp crested, a slimy maw stretching higher than the trees. Inside writhed animals trapped in sheets of slime, struggling to break free.

Then the ground tilted beneath Thorn's feet and disappeared.

.19.

THE SILVER SNARE

High in the foothills behind Aeria, Brier stopped at a rocky crest and leaned against Thorn's broom, her breath puffing in the cold air.

Someone was following her.

"Mazby?" she whispered. "Do you see anything?"

"No, but I feel them," he replied, shivering atop Thorn's broom, his feathers frosted white. "They're close."

Brier felt them too.

It had started that morning. She'd been snuggled up with Mazby on a patch of hard black dirt beside a cliff wall, gripped by ill dreams.

Floating up out of sleep, she'd heard it: a twig snapping. A scrape against the ground. A snuffling.

A beast, breathing?

She laid there, listening, waiting for whatever it was to pounce. Certainly she wouldn't be able to fight. She had no Noro (oh, *Noro*). She could hardly stand.

She breathed through the pain of her chest—each inhale a stab, each exhale a punch.

And waited.

But nothing pounced. The thin mountain air remained unbroken.

So she'd shared a breakfast of sour, unripe berries with Mazby, all the while thinking longingly of Thorn's breakfasts back home, and then wondering, with a different, sharper pain in her chest, if Thorn was all right, wherever she was. If she was also eating sad sour meals and being stalked by . . . something. Something unseen.

Then Brier had kept walking.

She was now farther into the mountains than she'd ever gone. There were no paths, no little benches carved into the stone where harvesters took their lunches, no thatch-roofed huts where they could take shelter during storms.

No, these mountains were wild country. All morning, she had crept down tiny pebbled paths that wound between sheer black mountain walls and pulled herself up ledges and skidded down steep declines and edged along canyons with drops that ended in clouds.

Clouds, yes, but no storms. Not even a flash of lightning.

And all the while, as her chest burned and her bones ached, something had followed her.

Branches breaking. Shuffled footsteps stopping when she stopped.

Footsteps?

Paws?

She couldn't tell.

And now she'd reached the top of a rocky rise. Beyond her stretched endless mountains ribboned with snow and dotted with stubby bright green trees. A mountain bird called out. A rock mouse chittered.

Then all sounds disappeared. Even the whistling wind disappeared. Brier and Mazby were alone in stillness.

"Can't we please go home now?" Mazby looked around with wide eyes. "They're close, whoever they are. If we run, maybe they won't catch us!"

Brier clenched her fists. "I'm not going home until I find answers."

"But there's no one out here! No one except us, and . . ."

And *them*. The silent, stalking *them*.

"What kind of answers are you even hoping to find up here?" Mazby hovered before Brier's face. "This was a terrible idea. I'm going to march you straight home and we're going to find a healer."

"Oh? You, a grifflet, are going to march me, a human girl, all the way home, are you?" Brier pushed past him. "You're funny, Mazby."

"You've left me no choice!" Mazby cried out, just before he flung himself onto Brier's left shoulder, dug his claws into her coat, and yanked hard in the opposite direction.

Brier screamed.

Pain erupted in her shoulder and ripped through her body. She crashed to her knees, gulping down air, but her burned chest was on fire, and breathing was like throwing oil on it. Heat climbed up her throat and curled round her skull.

Mazby dropped to the ground, whimpering frantic apologies, but the roar of Brier's blood pulsing through her body pushed away all sound and thought—except for the scrape of something skidding down stone, and a nearby tumble of rocks.

Brier tried to look, but her vision swam and spooled, turning the colors of the world into useless swirls that reminded her, awfully, heart-pangingly, of Thorn's paint.

"Going to show yourself now?" Brier called out. Her voice was in shreds. Tears gathered in her eyes because it hurt to speak, but she wasn't about to let them fall. "Got tired of . . . following me?" She groped for Thorn's fallen broom. "You'd better . . . run . . ."

She looked up just as a long white shape pulled Mazby out of the sky. A squawk, an indignant trilled cry. Feathers went flying. Brier, squinting, saw Mazby being thrown into a cloth sack.

She pushed herself up and swung the broom. "Let him go!" she cried, right before the world turned upside down. Her back slammed hard into the ground.

Watching the sky spin, Brier could not find her breath. The white shape that had grabbed Mazby stood over her.

It was a boy, so pale he seemed spun from silver clouds. His hair sat in a sloppy bun on his head, and his eyes snapped like jewels on fire.

"Got her!" he shouted, a mean grin on his face. Someone nearby whooped in triumph.

Then Brier's world went black.

.20.

THE NOOSE NARROWS

Around Cub's neck, the hand of cursed magic, the hand of *else*, changed.

It felt younger, now. Less mean, but more afraid, which Cub thought might be even more dangerous.

He clung to the wall of the Break, searching the air for clues with his cottage-sized nose.

"Hello?" Cub called out. He hadn't spoken for so long that the word scraped his tongue raw.

Hello, Gulgot, hissed the else-hand, tightening. Its voice was stronger than it had been before. Fresh, and new—a crawling creature stretching its waking-up legs all across Cub's body.

Then the else-hand yanked hard, and Cub fell.

He fell so many times that his skull cracked and swelled.

He fought the else-hand so hard that sores opened on his neck.

He clawed so desperately at the walls of the Break, trying to fight the else-hand's pull, that his blisters burst.

He huddled on a rocky ledge, licking his paws, and slipped into a black and shifting sleep.

Never before had Cub's dreams been so angry.

He had dreamed of his mothers before, and of the day the Vale split. He had dreamed of witches falling into the Break by the hundreds—not witches trapped in lightning, but real flesh-and-blood witches—and of him doing nothing to help them.

He had even dreamed of plowing mountains flat, uprooting forests, running across the sea beds until the waves far above came to a seething boil.

But he had never dreamed of this:

Heaving those toppled mountains into cities full of humans.

Flinging those uprooted trees into bellies and skulls.

Plucking warm bodies from their homes and markets and caves, and tossing them one by one into the sea.

Making sure the waves swallowed them.

Making sure the silt of the oceans dragged them down and buried them.

Of these dark things, Cub had never before dreamed.

Until now—with the one called Queenie living in the hand at his throat.

The hand's wicked witch-magic was too much for one small human body to bear. Cub could feel that clearly. Queenie was no witch with Old Wild in her blood. Inside her, the magic grew darker. It boiled in her body and through the cursed else-hand, all the way down to Cub, alone in the dark, where it burned his bones like fire.

When next he woke, Cub thought one word:

Enough.

He roared it. "Enough!"

This time, when the else-hand pulled, Cub kept climbing. He shook the walls of the Break as he ran, carved canyons into the rock with his claws.

From above came three arcing bolts of lightning.

Cub knocked them aside, uncaring of the charred burns they left on his hide.

He heard the screams of the witches trapped inside the bolts, and he grinned an awful beastly grin.

"Enough," he repeated, crawling faster now.

Enough witches.

Enough darkness.

Enough queens.

He was tired of living in the dark.

He was going to climb free once and for all, even if it killed him.

.21.

THE NEW DARK FLAME

Wherever Thorn had landed, it was different than any place she'd ever seen.

A carpet of grasses stretched across the ground. Some blades were hair-thin, others thick as butcher knives. Some stuck straight up several feet in the air.

The blades of grass were soft and warm, worn satin smooth. And these weren't green and brown and yellow grasses, like Thorn was used to seeing in the Vale. They were lilac colored, orchid colored—pale pink and vibrant violet and brilliant blue smeared with gold.

A forest of bare trees, tall and narrow, stood on all sides. Their smooth white trunks reflected the colors of the sky above.

And the sky above . . .

Thorn gazed at it, not sure she'd ever be able to *stop*.

Such a foreign sight it was, an utterly clear night sky marred by neither storms nor shadows. The sky was as rich and dark a blue as Noro's eyes, glittering with so many bright stars that when Thorn blinked, she saw tiny red spots.

On the eastern horizon, which Thorn could see through the trees, the sun was high in the sky. But even in the sunlight, the stars shone in bold and brilliant colors—sea-foam green and cornflower blue, gentle peach like the soft feathers ringing Mazby's eyes, and a blushing raspberry like Thorn's favorite paint.

"What is this place?" Thorn whispered.

Bartos climbed out of a hollow in the earth, pushing armfuls of grass out of his path. "The ground's full of holes, for one," he replied. Something crunched under his feet; he blanched. "I'm going to pretend I didn't hear that."

Noro shook uprooted blades of grass from his mane. "I think we're in the thick of a mountain range," he murmured.

Thorn followed his gaze up, past the trees, and saw that

he was right. Beyond the forest, to Thorn's left, stretched vast planes of shadow. Starlight illuminated moss-lined cliffs, grinning caves, sprawling veins of snow. As the stars twinkled, the vast towering mountains caught their glow and shimmered.

"But . . . are these the eastern mountains?" Thorn blinked at Noro. "Did Zaf really bring us all the way to . . ."

Zaf. *Zaf.*

Thorn whirled around, searching for Zaf's pale head in the sea of starlit grass. "Zaf? Where are you?"

"Here," came a faint voice.

Thorn's heart lurched into her throat. She trudged through the grass, stumbled into one of those strange hollows (*crunch*, snapped something under her feet), and found Zaf lying in the roots of a leafless white tree. Tiny embers of white light popped around her hands and feet.

And Zaf's body, though it had been pale before, was now even paler still. In Estar, she had glowed. But now that bloom of light had faded. Her luminous pale skin had gone the dull white of old teeth, and looked so paper-thin that Thorn felt tempted to trace the blue map of Zaf's veins with her fingers.

But Thorn was too afraid to touch her.

Bartos, hurrying over to join them, let out a soft, sad sound when he saw Zaf lying there.

Noro immediately knelt beside Zaf and blinked two tears onto her forehead.

"Oh, Zaf." Thorn reached out, hesitated. "What's happened to you?"

Zaf cracked open her eyes. "Lightning moves fast and hot," she said, shifting her body with a wince. "Maybe too fast and hot, now that I'm just little old ordinary me. No bolt to protect me." A tiny hot hiss emitted from all the spots where her skin touched the roots. "I got us out of that horrible swamp, though, didn't I? We're safe?"

"Yes." Thorn glanced around. "At least I think we are."

Noro shook his head. "I'm not sure my tears are helping you, Zaf. Do you feel any better?"

"No, but it's all right." Zaf smiled weakly, patting his muzzle. "I suppose not even unicorns can do everything, eh?"

Bartos knelt beside Zaf, his eyes shining. "Zaf, I'm so sorry. I shouldn't have allowed you to do that."

"Oh, as if you could have stopped me, Barty." Zaf's laughter turned quickly to a cough.

"But I pressured you. I was afraid, and I . . ." He wiped his eyes with his filthy sleeve. "I'm a soldier. I should've been braver. I shouldn't have let you take the risk."

And as Thorn listened to him talk, a veil dropped over her eyes. A swift blink of red and black.

She glared at Bartos, and with those angry colors flooding her eyes, she didn't see her childhood friend anymore. She didn't see a soldier in a uniform.

She saw only a weakling. A gangly, awkward boy crying into his hands like some kind of useless baby.

"Oh, stop crying," said Thorn, the words tumbling out of her before she could stop them. "Zaf was wonderful and brave, even though you were screaming at her and screaming at her, and crying, when all the rest of us—"

Thorn's brain caught up with her tongue, and she stopped talking at once. She blinked in surprise at all of them. The sharp sound of her irritated voice rang in the air, and it frightened her, for she did not recognize it.

Bartos stared at her, color rising fast in his wet cheeks.

It is a rare thing, for a unicorn to look astonished—but Noro looked it, just then. "Thorn," he said, "there's no need to snap at him. We were *all* afraid."

Thorn swallowed hard and looked away. "Yes, you're right. I'm . . . I'm sorry."

And she *was* sorry.

Mostly.

But a small black flame snapping angrily in her chest wasn't sorry at all. The feeling was strange, unlike any Thorn had experienced before. She thought things she dared not say aloud, things she didn't understand because they were so prickly, so *mean*.

No one else had yelled at Zaf to use her magic, like Bartos had.

He was a coward, a pathetic baby.

Thorn clenched her fists. She wished they'd lost Bartos as Zaf sent them blazing through the sky. She wished—

"Thorn?"

At the sound of Zaf's voice, Thorn blinked a few times and tried to swallow, but her throat was dry. The veil over her eyes was gone. The flame in her heart was gone. She felt small and tired and Thorn-y again.

And she could not look at any of her friends. Her heart felt like a heavy stone in her chest.

"I'm really tired," she said after a moment. "Do you think we can stay here awhile and sleep?"

Bartos rose to his feet, straightening his crusty jacket. "A good idea," he said, not meeting Thorn's eyes. "I'll keep watch."

As he moved away, Thorn arranged sheets of grass around Zaf's body. Noro settled beside them; Zaf rested her head on his belly and sighed.

"Are you all right?" Noro asked Thorn. He was watching her in that unsettling, unblinking, unicornish way of his, like he could clearly see all the cruel thoughts stewing in her head. It was the first time he had looked straight at her since telling her he knew about the stormwitches. A lump formed in Thorn's throat. *I miss Brier,* she thought miserably.

I miss home.

"I've never heard you talk like that before," Noro said gently, "not even when Brier teases you."

Thorn glanced at Bartos, who was leaning against a tree several paces away. He ducked his head to wipe his eyes again.

Shame poked Thorn in the hot fragile place between her lungs.

"I don't know," Thorn told Noro. "I just . . . I was grumpy." She fussed with Zaf's coat—*Brier's* coat. "Are you cold? Is the grass too itchy?"

"Are *you* cold?" Zaf watched her through a veil of frizzy white hair. "Is that why you're grumpy?"

Thorn sighed sharply. "I'm not grumpy, really, it's just . . ."

But she couldn't find the end of that sentence. She searched her thoughts and found only scary dark shapes she didn't understand.

Instead she settled down beside Zaf, her head resting on Noro's belly too. She squeezed her eyes shut and thought about the witch Quicksilver, and wondered how in all the storms they were going to find her—wherever in this strange starlit world she was. If they *had*, in fact, reached the eastern mountains, could they climb down from them into the Star Lands without falling to their deaths? And then they would have to navigate another country, which none of them had ever before visited, and what if Quicksilver didn't actually exist?

She worried her thumb along the dip of her left palm, where she had fallen and scraped it not so long ago. She hadn't been brave enough to look at it yet, but now she opened her fist the tiniest bit.

Her hand looked whole and healthy, pale and slightly pink.

She let out a breath of relief. Whatever had happened in that swamp, she would have to believe it was nothing to worry about.

"Stop fretting," said Zaf, nudging Thorn's arm with her elbow. "What does fretting ever do except make you think about things it'll do you no good to think of?"

Despite everything, the idea of Zaf watching her closely enough to see fretting made Thorn smile, and gave her a small piece of courage.

A thought came into her mind. She breathed carefully around it.

"Zaf?" she asked.

"Hmph," answered Zaf, already half asleep.

"Can I hold your hand?"

Zaf made a happy sound that reminded Thorn of waking up on a weekend morning, with nothing to do except paint.

Then Zaf's hand found Thorn's, and Thorn, holding her breath, her heartbeat skipping, grabbed on.

.22.

THE NESTING GIANTS

Thorn awoke when Noro disappeared from beneath her head.

Her skull thumped against a tree root. A muffled yelp came from somewhere close. Zaf?

Thorn pushed herself up onto her elbows, coming face-to-face with . . .

No, face-to-*eye*.

With a *creature*.

Thorn scrambled back into the roots. Zaf, hugging the tree trunk, grabbed her and pulled her close.

The creature crouched in the grass before them was a bird,

Thorn thought—but unlike any birds of the Vale.

This one was even bigger than Noro, with a slick coat of pale pink feathers over stark white skin. It had high, stooped shoulders, and it lumbered closer to Thorn by pulling itself across the ground with its wings' knobby elbows. Its beak was periwinkle and enormous—scooped and gaping, flanked by flaps of feathered flesh.

The bird tilted its head. Its bright black eye blinked curiously at Thorn.

"You are what?" croaked the bird.

Then the bird's head swiveled round. "Seen you, stick head."

Noro, pinned to the ground beneath the bird's left leg, somehow managed to look offended even with his face smashed against the grass.

"Stick head?" he huffed, his voice rumpled.

"Seen you, soldier boy." The bird swiveled around to Bartos, who lay pinned under its right wing.

Bartos gulped, his sweaty dark hair plastered to his forehead. "I'm sorry, er, you . . . bird. We didn't mean to intrude—"

"Seen you, girlie girl." The bird thrust out its neck to consider Thorn closely, then looked at Zaf.

"You are new?" it rasped. When it opened its beak, fetid air blasted Thorn in the face. The smell reminded her of the worm that had crawled across her lip in Estar.

"New?" Zaf laughed nervously. Her skin had regained some of its luster, Thorn was glad to see. "Well, that depends. Do you like new things?"

The bird's head bobbed up and down. "Two more than one. Two for six is one third each, more than one sixth each."

"What is it talking about?" whispered Zaf.

Thorn began inching away from the bird. "If it's all right with you, we'll just . . . be on our way."

Something massive crashed into the ground behind her.

She whirled, taking Zaf with her.

Another gargantuan bird squatted there, leering at them. This one's feathers were blue-green with brown spots, like a jay's egg.

Tree branches swayed overhead.

Thorn looked up . . . and up, and up.

All around them, high in the leafless trees, were at least a dozen mammoth birds, silhouetted by the stars.

"Oh, storms save us," Bartos whispered from beneath the first bird's wing. He struggled to get loose, but doing so turned his face green. "What *is* this place?"

"Star Lands," said the first bird, sounding almost cheerful. "Where go?"

The Star Lands.

Thorn's arms tingled. Zaf had really done it, then.

Thorn scanned the forest and saw several paths snaking off through the trees. But the birds would catch them as soon as they tried to run.

Unless Noro got free of the bird, and they all jumped on his back, and he sped away faster than he'd ever run before.

She needed to stall.

"We search for the witch named Quicksilver," she blurted.

Noro hissed, "Thorn, no!"

"Ah!" The bird slapped its wings against the ground. The others, high up in the trees, thumped their branches. "Foxheart's the thing."

Zaf blew out sharp air. "No, you dum-dum. *Quicksilver.*"

"Maybe don't call the giant scary bird a dum-dum," Thorn muttered.

"Quicksilver," said the bird, scooting forward. As it moved, it dragged Noro and Bartos along with it. "Foxheart. Same one, same the other."

"Quicksilver Foxheart," the birds overhead whispered. "Quicksilver Foxheart."

"You know this witch?" Bartos spat a clump of grass from his lips.

"They may just be speaking nonsense," Noro pointed out, squirming angrily beneath the bird's claw. Thorn watched nervously. If Noro could just free himself enough to stab the creature's leg . . .

Thump. Ka-thump.

Thorn glanced up. Three of the birds had jumped down to lower branches and hung there, necks drooping like snakes.

"The city there," said the first bird, jerking its head east. "Lots of girlie girls and dum-dums and monsters."

"Do his dum-dum and my dum-dum mean the same thing?" Zaf whispered.

Thorn ignored her, peering east. Then she turned back to the bird. "You'll show me?"

The bird let out a sharp cawing sound, over and over, like it was trying to make itself sick. The other birds echoed the call, and soon the entire forest was quaking with the noise.

"Funny girlie," said the bird at last. "Katsom help for nothing?"

"That was *laughing*?" Zaf whispered.

"Katsom." Thorn inched closer, despite Zaf's squeaky

protests, and placed her hand on the bird's oily wing. "Is Katsom your name?"

"Katsom." The bird lowered its head to stare. "You?"

"Thorn Skystone."

"Thorn," whispered the bird.

"Thorn, Thorn," echoed the other birds. Another dropped from the trees to waddle closer.

Thorn's throat was dry as sand. "If we help you with . . . something you need help with, will you tell us how to find Quicksilver?"

"Thorn!" Zaf hissed, slightly frantic.

"Do not bargain with them," Noro said sharply. Katsom whacked him with his feathers.

"Will do this thing," Katsom replied. Then the bird opened and closed its beak three times. *Click-click-click.* "You here." Katsom slapped the ground, then flung its wing east. "Quicksilver there."

Thorn squinted through the starlit forest. "I can't see anything but trees."

Katsom waddled forward. Just before it dove, Noro shouted Thorn's name in fear—but it was too late. The bird used its beak to grab Thorn and Zaf by their collars, and threw them up into the trees.

Bartos shouted after them, and Noro trumpeted furiously, thrashing beneath Katsom's foot, but Thorn and Zaf were already spinning fast through the air.

Another bird, high in the trees, snagged them as they started to drop and tossed them up, and again and again they were thrown toward the stars, bird by bird, until the last bird flapped laboriously to deposit Thorn and Zaf in the uppermost treetops.

Wedged between several slender white branches, Thorn grabbed on to Zaf, and Zaf grabbed on to Thorn. They huddled together, faces buried in each other's necks and wild hearts pounding chest to chest, until Thorn, then Zaf, found the courage to look around.

Below, nestled in trees and grass, Thorn hadn't felt the mountain winds. But above the forest canopy, the winds cut like paring knives. Thorn shivered in the cloud of Zaf's white hair; Zaf shuddered beside her.

Thorn looked east.

Her breath caught. So did Zaf's.

A vast country stretched out before them. To Thorn's left—north—was a massive, sprawling woodland that grew darker and thicker the farther it went, and a distant castle squashed onto a narrow hill glimmering silver with rivers. Beyond that was a far-flung snowy landscape capped with white mountains.

Mountains. Rivers. Woodlands. Thorn knew of these things. The Vale had them by the hundreds.

But the *color* of the Star Lands was like nothing Thorn had ever seen.

It was as if someone had emptied a chest of jewels onto the world. Amethyst fields and coral forests, bright crimson roads and rivers that rippled a hundred different iridescent shades— opal and obsidian and milky-pink pearl. The cities that scattered the countryside boasted polished rooftops that winked with starlight. Thorn watched a flock of gleaming turquoise birds, bright as stars, spin past on a mountain wind.

An ache grew in Thorn's heart. Tears burned behind her nose. The jumbled colors reminded her of her father's gardens, and her own collection of paints—but the colors were so bright that she soon had to cover her eyes.

Zaf, though, stared dreamily at the world.

"Have you ever seen anything quite so lovely?" she whispered.

"I don't know what we're supposed to look at," Thorn called down to Katsom. "There's so much out there!"

"City on edge!" Katsom called. "Girlie, can't you see?"

Thorn squinted through her fingers at the pink eastern

border, her eyes watering from the glare of stars above and land below.

Then—*there*. A glint of a city, so tiny on the far horizon that it could have belonged to ants rather than people. It bordered a thin black line. An ocean?

"A city on the sea?" she called down to Katsom. "Is that what you mean?"

"City on sea!" Katsom answered. "City on sea!"

The birds scattered throughout the trees slapped their wings together, wet and thunderous, so loud that Thorn's ears rang.

"Is that a yes?" Zaf muttered.

But Thorn could no longer keep her eyes open. She squeezed them shut against the blinding world; tears slipped down her cheeks.

"Hey there. You all right?" Zaf's hand was soft on Thorn's arm. "You're crying."

"My eyes keep watering. It's so bright!"

"Oh, I think it's just right. The Vale seems so dingy and gray compared—"

Before Zaf could finish, Katsom shot up into the air before them—Noro wrapped in one set of talons, Bartos in the other.

"Time for the help," said Katsom. His wide black eyes gleamed, turning Thorn's stomach.

Then Katsom used his beak to grab Thorn and Zaf by their collars and swooped down from the treetops, back to the forest floor, to drop them all unceremoniously into a soft grassy hollow in the ground.

They landed hard on a carpet of eggshells.

Giant, shattered white eggshells, still warm and sticky, speckled with a blue that matched Katsom's beak.

"Thorn," said Zaf, carefully calm. "Turn around. Slowly."

Thorn obeyed.

Six Zaf-sized birds—their skin pink and gleaming, their eyes bleary and white—stared from the shadows.

One tilted its head and squawked, "Seen you."

Another squawked, "Bite you."

Two more than one, Katsom had said.

Six birds. Six pairs of unblinking eyes.

A shadow fell across the nest. "New girl, you and stick head go. Too much food. Too much magic." Katsom stretched out a wing. "You climb. Bye, girlie girl. Bye, soldier boy. Two for six is one third each."

Bartos scrambled away from the birds and shoved Thorn

and Zaf behind him. Noro surged forward with his head bowed and his horn flashing.

"They've only just been born, looks like," Bartos said grimly. "Bet you can outrun them on Noro. I'll hold them off."

Thorn thought quickly, her heart dropping with each passing second. "Can you use your magic one more time, Zaf?"

Bartos spun around. "No. *No.* She can't."

"We may not have a choice if we want to survive this," Noro said quietly.

Zaf's body deflated. "Thorn, I don't know if I have it in me."

"I won't ever ask you to do it again." Thorn looked Zaf in the eye, trying to smile even though she felt like crying. "I promise."

Zaf held her face very still. "I'll not forget that promise, once we get out of here."

"And I won't forget it either," Thorn replied.

Zaf grabbed Thorn's arm. "Barty?" she said, her voice thin and shaky.

Bartos grabbed on to Zaf's other hand, and then clutched Noro's shining silver mane.

"You are a brave girl," Bartos said solemnly, "and a strong one."

"Right you are I am," said Zaf, her sharp pale chin jutting in the air, and then three things happened so quickly it seemed to Thorn that they crashed together into the same frenzied moment:

The six baby birds screeched and lunged forward—sharp blue beaks open wide, bright purple tongues reaching.

Zaf's grip tightened on Thorn's hand, and then, with a defiant little cry, Zaf lit up like the bolt she had once been.

The world blazed white, knocked Thorn's head against an unseen wall, and pulled her, hard, into the cold mountain air.

When Thorn next opened her eyes, she smelled salt in the air. A warm breeze kissed her skin.

Woozy, she saw that she stood on a winding road of pale stone, beside a body of water so brilliant with the rising sun that it made her head pound.

She sank to the ground, rubbing the light from her eyes. Zaf had done it again. She had brought them . . . well, somewhere.

All the way to the city by the sea?

She'd certainly gotten them out of that nest—even if the going had felt a bit rougher.

Because Zaf was still in pain from the first time? Thorn wondered.

She forced her eyes open a crack.

Beside her lay Bartos, moaning, his pale face tinged a nauseated green. He smiled weakly at her.

Noro was picking himself up from the stack of crates he'd crashed into, shaking splinters of wood from his shimmering mane.

And Zaf . . . ?

Thorn searched, her heart thump-thumping.

There. Zaf lay on the ground, not far from Bartos.

And she wasn't moving.

Her washed-out skin was so dull compared to the vivid world around them that she seemed hardly more than a pale smudge on the ground.

Thorn crawled across the warm stone road, but Noro got there first. He lowered his head to drop two tears on Zaf's still, still face.

"Zaf?" Thorn cradled Zaf's hand against her cheek. The bright world shimmered past her tears. "Zaf, say something, *please.*"

"Unicorn!" a high voice called out from down the road.

And the voice sounded . . . frightened.

Thorn squinted through the dazzling light, despite how awfully it made her head hurt. A clutch of small figures—

children?—stood at a curve in the road, near the shoreline. Vibrant shapes in canary yellow, emerald green, sapphire blue flitted about the children's heads. First the colored shapes were the size of sparrows, and then they ballooned larger, big as eagles. They spiraled down to land on the ground and galloped along the road toward Thorn, ears pricked and tails low, like cats on the prowl.

Thorn's head spun. How could animals change forms like that?

"It's a unicorn!" called out one of the children. "Quicksilver, hurry!"

Quicksilver?

Thorn whirled around and saw two blurry shapes hurrying toward them. One was a little taller than Thorn. The other was short, and dark, and . . . barking.

A dog?

"It's all right!" cried the taller shape, its voice clear and strong. "Stand down, witches! This unicorn is not our enemy."

Noro blew out an indignant, unbecoming, horsey puff of air. "Are other unicorns your enemy?"

"The shadow-struck unicorn, remember?" Thorn said. "It said they came to the Star Lands to hide." Then she shielded her eyes and called out, "Please, don't hurt us! We're lost, and my friends are hurt!"

"I've no intention of hurting you." Suddenly the shape came into focus: a pale young woman, a few years older than Thorn, with a long braid of brilliant red hair streaked with silver, wearing a patchwork coat of a hundred colors that fell past her knees. When she knelt at Thorn's side, her face was kind, but curious.

"What's your name, child?" the young woman asked.

"I'm Thorn Skystone of the Vale," Thorn replied, trying not to think about how cold Zaf's hand felt, "and I seek the witch named Quicksilver Foxheart."

The woman's eyebrows shot up. "Well, Thorn of the Vale, it's a lucky day for you, and a thoroughly strange one for me. I'm Quicksilver Foxheart, and you and your friends dropped right into the middle of my class, which—"

Thorn let out a small cry. Her relief was so great it nearly knocked her flat. This woman didn't look like an evil witch who would want to help the Gulgot destroy the Vale. She looked kind, and clever, and had a brave, warm face that made Thorn think of her mother.

Forgetting she was in a land so far from home and so strange that she couldn't even properly open her eyes to look at it, Thorn launched herself into Quicksilver's arms and held on tight.

"Can you help my friends?" Thorn whispered. Something warm and wet licked her hand. She cracked open her eyes and saw an enormous shaggy black dog with white paws panting happily at her.

"I can't," said Quicksilver, plucking grass from Thorn's hair, "but worry not. I know someone who can."

.23.

THE MOUNTAIN CHILDREN

When Brier awoke, she was lying in the middle of a grassy, snow-dusted clearing. Above her rose cloud-covered mountains.

And surrounding Brier were four unicorns, their horns—each crackling softly with lightning—aimed right at her heart.

Brier's mouth dried.

These were *wild* unicorns, not like Noro at all. They were unbound. Free, and dangerous. Their stormy eyes held neither kindness nor warmth.

The pale white-haired boy with the mean grin crouched beside Brier, smiling smugly.

"Good morning, Thorn Skystone," he said. "I do hope you're feeling better."

Brier opened her mouth to reply that, no, she wasn't feeling better, and where was Mazby, and she didn't appreciate being surrounded like this. Didn't they know she was Brier Skystone, the most valued harvester in Westlin?

But then she realized, with a jolt of shock, that she *was* feeling better.

The pain she had lived with since being struck by lightning had vanished. When she shifted her weight, placing her palms on the crunchy frosted grass, no agony shot up her arms. Instead, a simple dull ache ballooned through her muscles, like the soreness before a fever.

Hope fluttering in her throat, Brier pushed aside her collar, looked down at her chest, and cried out.

The lightning burn hadn't vanished entirely, but it was small and faded. No longer an angry glistening charcoal, but a muted, tired-looking gray.

"It'll come back," said the boy, "and I'll let it, if you don't obey us."

Brier glared at the boy, but the absence of pain was such a relief that she could only ask, "How did you do this?"

Grinning, the boy held up his hands and wiggled his fingers. A faint white light flashed along the lines of his palms.

"Stormwitch," he said.

A tiny tremor dropped down Brier's backbone. Some of Noro's stories about the Old Wild, and the Vale as it had been long ago, were about witches. The idea of witches had always fascinated Brier: like humans, but with powerful pieces of Old Wild in their blood, which gave them the ability to heal and weave spells.

Brier lifted her chin, determined to look unimpressed. "Where's Mazby?"

"The little flying rat?"

It required all of Brier's self-control to not slap the boy. It was one thing for Noro to insult Mazby. He was family; that was allowed.

"He's a grifflet," said Brier, turning her right hand into a fist. "And his name is Mazby."

Grinning, the boy gestured over his shoulder. "Don't worry. We haven't cooked him and eaten him. Yet."

Brier looked beyond him. Two pale, white-haired children crouched behind a ridge of rock covered in brown fuzzy moss. One held a squirming Mazby in his hand. Twine bound the grifflet's wings, legs, and beak.

"If you hurt him," said Brier through her teeth, "by the storms, I'll—"

"You'll what?" The boy shook back his wild white bangs. "We outnumber you, sweep."

Sweep. *Sweep.*

Because she wasn't Brier; she was Thorn. And Thorn wouldn't threaten her captors. She would . . . what?

Brier lowered her gaze, let her shoulders slump. "How do you know who I am?"

"Lightning sees far, and stormwitches pay attention. I'd wager we know Westlin better than even you do." He paused. "You're a curious one, you know. Always rooting about in the gutter for whatever people have thrown out and forgotten. What do you do with it all? And how did you get that burn? It's a grisly one."

Brier didn't answer. "How many of you are there?"

"Enough."

A sharp snowbird's whistle sounded from Brier's left. The boy turned narrowed eyes onto the rocky slope below them. Then he echoed the whistle and gestured at the unicorns. Swift and silent, they fanned out to hide behind the rocks that framed the clearing.

"All right, sweep," the boy muttered to Brier, "listen closely.

Your sister's murderous little friends are getting close."

Brier frowned. "Murderous?"

"Not a nice enough word for your delicate city-girl ears?"
He bowed, hand on his heart. "Your sister's *harvester* friends, the
ones we've watched do their killings for years and years? They're
heading this way. You'll sit here, pretend your leg is hurt, pretend
you can't move. You'll shout for them, ask for help. You'll cry and
sniffle and look pathetic—shouldn't be hard—until they're right
on top of you."

"And then?" Brier's heart thudded fast.

The boy's eyes held a wicked gleam. "You'll stay as still and
flat as you can until it's all over. Unless you want to watch your
rat's feathers get plucked out one by one."

Brier swung hard at his chin with her fist—but the boy
caught it easily.

"Careful, sweep," he said. "That won't help you."

"My name is Thorn," she growled, yanking her arm back.

"And mine's Zino. Thank you for helping us out. It's awfully
kind."

With a smirk, he dashed away to crouch behind a cluster of
boulders.

Brier licked her dry lips. Pale figures shifted, flanking her.

She glanced behind her and found a dozen children, hiding and waiting in the rocks. The four unicorns ducked low to cloak their flashing horns.

Brier looked back down the mountain.

Three harvesters were climbing up the slope. No unicorns accompanied them. Judging by the sunlight, it was around midday. Lunchtime. Their unicorns would have run off on their own for a while, to stretch the bonds to their riders as far as they could go.

Another snowbird whistle.

Zino peered out from behind a boulder. Beside him, a second stormwitch held Mazby. Zino mimed the action of plucking a feather from Mazby's wing.

Brier could hardly swallow. Her mind raced for a solution, but nothing was coming to her, and . . . what was a *stormwitch*, anyway? Noro had only ever talked about ordinary witches. And had Zino really done something to ease the burn on her chest? And *would* it return if she disobeyed them?

If she cooperated, could Zino heal the burn entirely?

Her stomach pitching, Brier clutched her leg and waved.

"Help!" she cried. "Please, help me! Over here!"

The harvesters whirled around to search the slope.

One of them cursed. "Thorn?"

Brier's throat constricted. She recognized that voice. That was Farver Pickery, and now she could see the two others were Gert Goldfuss and Eldon Pye.

"I've hurt my leg," she called out. "I . . . I can't walk!"

Immediately Farver, Gert, and Eldon hurried up the slope.

"Don't move!" Farver called out, already huffing and puffing. Really, he was too old to be hiking up into the mountains every day, but Queen Celestyna wouldn't allow her harvesters to retire, not with the eldisk stores so low and the skies so quiet.

Stop spiraling, Brier scolded herself. *Focus.*

Farver and the others were running toward her across the clearing, and if she just had a bit more time to think—

Then, to Brier's right, a furious series of squawks exploded.

Brier spun around just as Mazby shot up into the air, his bindings dropping to the ground. He'd sliced himself loose, bitten and clawed right through the twine. Chirping and shrieking, he zoomed around the clearing, tugging at the stormwitches' hair with his talons, evading the unicorns as they swiped their horns.

Brier dashed across the clearing. Her healing chest pinched with each breath.

"Run!" she cried. *"Go!"*

She grabbed the astonished Farver Pickery's hand and raced with her friends down the mountain.

They couldn't run long; Farver's breath turned thin, and Brier's squeezed out of her lungs in sharp little bursts.

She imagined a horrible vision: the burn on her chest darkening, and spreading, even meaner and hotter than it had once been. It would bleed across her torso and down her limbs and around her skull until she was a charred crisp of a girl, glittering and black.

"There!" Gert Goldfuss gestured at a nearby hill spotted with patchy green grass, where one of the harvester's huts stood. "Inside!"

Three of the hut's walls were made of the mountain itself. The fourth was a jumble of stones, patched together to resemble a natural formation.

Eldon Pye wrenched open the door, Brier and the others close behind. Dry and plain, the hut contained two narrow beds, a tiny stove, bundles of firewood, and a few sealed crates of goods, in case a harvester got stuck during a snowstorm.

Farver sank onto one of the beds and wiped his brow. He had lost his cap as they ran; his gray hair was wild from the wind.

"Thorn, what are you doing up here?" he rasped. "My dear girl, these mountains are no place for an untrained sweep."

"Forget that," Gert snapped. She crossed her muscly arms over her chest. "Who were those *people*? There must have been a dozen of them up there—and all of them white as snow from head to foot!"

Brier perched on the other bed, clutching her collar closed. She wanted desperately to look down her shirt and see if the burn had worsened.

And Mazby . . . oh, *Mazby*. He'd gotten loose and thrown himself at those awful people. What would they do to him?

Brier gritted her teeth against her fear and said tightly, "They call themselves stormwitches. Though I don't know what that's supposed to mean."

Then Brier remembered Zino's words, and felt a chill that was neither from her burn nor the howling wind outside, which had begun to rattle the hut's wooden door.

"One of them said . . ." But they were difficult words for Brier to say. "He called you my murderous friends. *Murderous*."

The word dropped like a hammer.

Brier waited, expecting Farver or Gert or Eldon to protest. "Murderous" was not the proper word to describe the queen's harvesters. A proper word would be "courageous" or "talented" or "irreplaceable."

Eldon shifted from his left foot to his right foot, absently rubbing his wind-bitten brown cheek.

Gert glared at the floor.

And Farver leaned forward, elbows on knees, and lifted weary eyes to Brier's own.

"What is it?" Brier glanced from Farver to Gert to Eldon to Farver, searching their faces for some reassurance and seeing only terrible exhaustion. Farver's shoulders slumped, as though something heavy had just landed on his back.

"He's not . . ." A hot sour taste climbed up Brier's throat. "That boy. The stormwitch. He was lying, wasn't he? He's got it wrong. None of you have killed anybody."

"No, Thorn." Farver dragged a hand down his face. "He hasn't got it wrong."

"We decided not to tell Brier," Gert said sharply, still glaring at the floor. "She was so talented, right from the start. Too talented not to recruit her, even though she's so young."

"Too young," Eldon mumbled, from the door. His black curls fell over his eyes. "We should never have let her enlist."

"Well, we did," snapped Gert, "and we decided—all of us—

not to tell her the truth." She glanced at Brier. "Usually we do." Gert's mouth twisted around like she was chewing on something rotten. "But we needed Brier."

"To help us find lightning," Farver continued reasonably. "That's the most important thing. That's why we do what we do."

"Even though with each bolt we capture," said Eldon slowly, "we send a witch to their death."

The silence in the room grew, and grew, until it was so heavy and thick that Brier felt like she was breathing in water. A blast of wind hit the door. She gripped the bed's stiff, scratchy blanket.

"You're lying," she whispered.

"I wish I was," Farver replied. "Every bolt of lightning in the Vale has a witch inside it. They've been trapped in storms since the breaking of the Vale. And their power, which we harness inside our eldisks, is what keeps the Gulgot at bay—and keeps the Vale from shattering."

Brier listened to the wind howl and the door rattle as her own blood surged and rolled. Farver and Gert and Eldon watched her, their eyes tired and angry and sad, and she wanted to kick each of them in their soft, lying guts.

But instead she clutched her blanket, remembered that she

was supposed to be her sister, and kept her voice soft.

"And you knew this whole time?" she asked at last.

Farver nodded. "Every harvester's told when they're matched with their unicorn."

Brier looked sharply at him. "Every harvester except Brier."

Farver closed his eyes. "Every harvester except Brier."

"And now she's fighting her way across Estar, risking her life for all of us, to find more lightning in the eastern mountains. More witches to kill."

"If there are even any witches left at all," Gert muttered.

Brier drew in a shaky breath, remembering the anger burning hot and blue in Zino's eyes.

Stormwitches. Lightning.

"Those children who tried to attack you," she said. "Those children who have . . ." But she couldn't say Mazby's name. "If they're stormwitches, how did they get out of their lightning? Has that ever happened before?"

"Not once," Gert said. "Far as we knew, they *couldn't.*"

"Maybe not all the witches were trapped in storms when the Vale broke," Eldon answered. "Or maybe whatever magic trapped them is finally wearing off, after all these years."

Brier forgot her Thorn self, and snapped, "So it's possible for them to get free, then, only most of them can't, because you've killed them."

She paused, her voice giving out as the last piece of truth finally became clear.

"And because *Brier* has killed them too," she whispered, a numb feeling spreading through her body. Her feet and hands were cold and heavy as stones.

Eldon turned away to gaze sadly out the tiny window beside the door.

"The queen has no choice, Thorn," said Gert. "It's them or us."

Brier's mind whirled to keep up. So Queen Celestyna knew too. She knew, and the harvesters knew, and, probably the queen's soldiers knew, or at least some of them.

Everyone knew except for her.

A terrible, cold thought fell into her heart.

"The unicorns know too," she whispered. "Don't they?"

Farver wouldn't meet her eyes, and Brier was glad. She didn't want any of them to look at her, ever again, and she didn't want to see them, either, and she didn't want to think about Noro, her dearest friend, knowing this horrible thing and keeping it from her.

How could friendship with a liar be anything but a lie?

"I'm tired," Brier said faintly, which was true, and then, "I need some time to think," which was also true.

She turned away on the bed, curled up into a tight knot, and when Farver tucked the blanket around her, she whispered two lies: "I understand why you did it. And don't worry. I won't tell my sister."

When Brier awoke an hour later, her mind felt a little less fuzzy, and carried a plan.

.24.

THE WITCH WITHOUT A MONSTER

Through a pair of tinted goggles set in brass frames, Thorn watched Quicksilver's friend work.

For protection, the witch had given goggles to Thorn and Bartos, until their decidedly ordinary eyes adjusted to the radiance of the Star Lands. It was such a bright country, Quicksilver had told them, because since the War of the Wolves, witches had come out of hiding, and magic was returning to the land.

The Thorn of the past, who had not yet seen her sister burned, nor been sent off to Estar, might already have begun sketching a picture of the place in her mind, and planning what paints she could use to color it.

But the Thorn of now worried her hands in her lap, as if she were molding a shape out of clay, and tried to ignore the strange twists of her gut.

The twists felt almost like nervousness, the kind of nervousness that made her want to scratch and scratch at her legs and arms, but it also felt like something different. Something new.

She'd felt it in the nests of those awful giant birds, when she'd snapped at Bartos—a nugget of something unfamiliar in her belly. A little like hunger, a little like fear, a lot like anger. Hot and snapping and pinching and snaking—and growing.

Now, it felt like not just a nugget, not just a spark, but a fist.

A fist that shifted and burned.

When the fist opened, fingers all sharp and splayed out, the sensation nauseated her.

But when the fist closed, as though ready to punch, Thorn felt . . .

What was it?

She pressed her hands flat against her legs, struggled to smooth her breathing into steady ins and outs, and thought about it.

When the fist closed, Thorn felt ready to punch too. She felt clearer, and sharper, like all her life she had been a scratchy Thorn sketch dusted in pencil shavings, and suddenly someone had shaken free her page. Now she stood out in stark relief against the world—clean and outlined and impossible to ignore.

No, if anyone ignored Thorn when she felt like this, if anyone tossed trash at her while she was sweeping, she'd chase them down the street with her broom, and they'd try to run, but they wouldn't be fast enough, not for this Thorn with the fist living in her belly—

A pained cough interrupted Thorn's tumbling thoughts.

Thorn shook her head, blinked, and as the fist in her gut relaxed its clutching fingers, her mind cleared and focused.

Zaf.

Zaf, lying on the bed in front of her, eyes closed, breathing thin and soft, a sheen of sweat painting her pale skin silver.

A young man with fair hair and freckled skin who looked about Quicksilver's age sat beside Zaf's bed. His name was Sly Boots—a healer, Quicksilver had said, one of the best in the Star Lands. Thorn sat in a chair beside him, and Noro watched over her shoulder, fitting neatly into the small room in his strange, unicornish way.

On the other side of the bed stood Quicksilver, arms crossed. Her shaggy black dog, Bear, sat on the floor at her feet. Against the far wall, on another bed, lay Bartos, watching through his goggles as Sly Boots funneled a thick grass-green liquid into a cup and brought it to Zaf's lips.

"Poison her," said Bartos sharply, "and it will be the last thing you ever do."

Sly Boots glanced over his shoulder. "I don't know what life is like in the Vale, but here in the Star Lands, we don't march about poisoning children."

Quicksilver's mouth quirked. "Now, Boots. Let's not be rude to our guests."

Sly Boots looked up at her with a soft smile on his face that made Thorn think of her parents, and Brier, and Mazby, and Flower House, and all of the sweet, warm things she had left behind in the Vale.

Tears filled her eyes, which didn't surprise her. It didn't matter what emotion it was—happiness, sadness, fear, anger. They all turned into crying. Thorn felt a thing, and the tears came at once. Brier was always teasing her about it.

This time, her gut lurched and cramped, like it had ingested something poisonous. And up from that sick, knotted feeling shot a surge of anger.

It was so immense, so sudden, that it made Thorn gasp. Heat jolted from her left palm down to her stomach. She jumped up from her chair, her limbs vibrating with the urge to punch the wall, to kick her chair and send it flying.

Instead she stood with her fists clenched—two at the ends of her arms; another, throbbing and furious in her belly—and snapped, "Will she be all right, or won't she?"

Sly Boots looked up at her in surprise. Everyone did. Zaf's eyes fluttered open.

"I think so." Sly Boots wiped the corners of Zaf's mouth with a cloth. "But I'm not exactly sure what's wrong with her. I've never met a witch like her."

"I'll be *fine*." Zaf struggled to sit up. "I've just never done this sort of thing before. It takes a lot out of a girl."

"What sort of thing is that?"

"I used the lightning lingering inside my body to zap myself and my friends across the world." Zaf batted her lashes. "What have *you* done today, Mr. Boots?"

"Treated an infant suffering from the coughing fever, set two broken bones, and cut out an infectious lesion that, had it been allowed to fester, would have made the girl lose her leg."

Zaf frowned. "Fine. You're impressive enough, I suppose."

Regally, Sly Boots inclined his head. "As are you."

Quicksilver hid a smile behind her hand. "What kind of witch are you, Zaf?"

Zaf started to answer, but soon erupted into a fit of coughing that shook her tiny frame.

Thorn looked away and began to pace. The angry jagged fist in her gut punched up her legs and arms, made her skin crawl and her blood thrum. Ferociously, she rubbed her right thumb against her left palm. If only she could kick something, she might feel better.

"She's a stormwitch," Noro answered, glancing curiously at Thorn.

Sly Boots pressed a damp cloth to Zaf's forehead. "I've never heard of a stormwitch. Witches here in the Star Lands are quite different from you, Zaf."

"I noticed that," said Noro. "Your witches work their magic through animal companions?"

"They're called monsters," Quicksilver explained, an odd hollow note in her voice. "They can take different forms and use magic in many ways, depending upon the will of the witch."

Bear butted his nose against Quicksilver's palm. She scratched behind his floppy ears.

"What kinds of things can you do with your monster?" Zaf stared awestruck at Quicksilver, little coughs shaking her every few seconds.

"All kinds of things. A monster can cloak his witch so she can't be seen, or hit an enemy with pure energy if his witch is in danger." That strange note returned to Quicksilver's voice, like a shadow passing through sunlight. "If he has the right tools, a monster can send his witch through time. But that is knowledge I hope dies with me."

Sly Boots reached across Zaf's bed and squeezed Quicksilver's fingers.

"Can you heal people with your monster?" Zaf asked. "Can you travel with your monster, like I did with my lightning?"

"I've never tried, but I suppose it's possible. Unless the power of witches is simply different here than it is in the Vale. . . ." Quicksilver's voice trailed off. "Are you all right, Thorn? You seem agitated."

Thorn stopped pacing.

Only then did she realize how out of breath she was, and

how her cheeks felt so hot it was like she'd been sitting too close to a fire, when in fact the little room Quicksilver had brought them to was made of cool stone.

"Agitated? No, I'm not agitated." Thorn's words tripped over themselves, but she didn't think she could have slowed them down if she'd wanted to. It felt like a match had been lit inside her, and now everything was sparking out of control.

And Thorn realized, with a little thrill, that she didn't mind the feeling.

In fact, she rather liked it.

You're not stupid, Thorn, no matter what everyone says. Brier's words from eight days before lingered in Thorn's mind like nasty burrs she couldn't pull free. But Brier and everyone else could say what they liked about her—that she was stupid, or dirty, or unimpressive. The shadow sister compared to Brier's sun. They could say that, and if she heard them, if she ever saw for herself their smirking, scornful faces . . .

She flexed her fingers, itching to slam them against something.

"We're wasting time," she spat. "Every moment we stand here talking means the Gulgot's getting that much closer to escaping."

Noro pressed his muzzle against her neck. "Thorn, why don't you sit down?"

"I don't want to sit down!" Thorn shoved past him and marched over to Quicksilver. Tears were standing hot in her eyes again—of *course* they were—and the feeling of them disgusted her, made her stomach turn like she was going to be sick.

Why couldn't she ever think or feel or say *anything* without crying about it?

"We came here to find you," Thorn said to Quicksilver, her voice tight and trembling, "so you could travel back to the Vale with us and seal the Break, or stop the Gulgot from escaping, or maybe kill the Gulgot, I don't know what the best way to help us is, but you should know, you're a witch, and you can do magic—"

"All right, Thorn." Quicksilver gently touched Thorn's shoulders. "Slow down and breathe."

Thorn jerked free. "Don't touch me!"

"Thorn, what's wrong with you?" scolded Bartos. "Just ask her not to touch you, if you don't want her to."

"Don't yell at her, Barty," came Zaf's sharp voice.

Quicksilver stepped back, hands raised. "I'm sorry, I shouldn't have assumed it was all right."

"Nothing's wrong with Thorn," said Noro, though he didn't sound convinced.

Thorn turned away from his sharp blue gaze. She didn't know what he was looking for, but she didn't want him to find it.

"I'm just . . . I don't know." She shook her head. She felt like her skin might burst, and something new and frightening would come out. She closed her eyes and took a deep breath, then a second, then a third.

"I'm scared," she said at last, and moved the goggles so she could wipe her eyes. "I'm scared for the Vale."

Which was true, but not the whole truth.

This angry fist in her gut, this restlessness, like her body was roiling and crawling—she was also scared of that.

Zaf touched Thorn's wrist. "I'm frightened too, and that's why we're here, remember? To ask for help."

Zaf's soft hand washed Thorn's thoughts clean like a fresh breeze, and for a moment, she felt like herself again—familiar and small, wretchedly unremarkable.

How awful it was, to know the feeling of yourself so well, and be so thoroughly unimpressed by every inch of it.

Thorn stepped away from her friends. She ignored Zaf's

hurt expression, and Noro's worried dark blue gaze, and Bartos's bewildered frown.

Instead she asked Quicksilver briskly, "Well? What do you think? Can you help us or not?"

And the look on Quicksilver's face made Thorn's heart plummet to her toes.

"I wish I could," Quicksilver replied. "Truly, I do. But though I'm a witch in blood, I'm no longer a witch in practice."

She touched Bear's shaggy black coat. Sly Boots watched her sadly.

"My monster died years ago," said Quicksilver, after a moment thick with silence. "I can therefore no longer work magic, and so I'm afraid I have none left to offer you."

.25.

THE QUEEN, TRIUMPHANT

Even though the Fetterwitch's curse sawed at her bones, Celestyna strode back into Castle Stratiara with her head held high.

She had hidden in the wild for as long as she dared, testing how to speak and move and breathe with the entire curse now living inside her. Her soldiers had combed the mountains, searching for her, but the curse kept her hidden, the clever thing.

Now it was time to return home. It was time to show them all what their queen could do.

A small crowd met Celestyna at the rear entrance, near the

courtyards—Lord Dellier, Madame Berrie. Her personal guard. Her ladies-in-waiting, all clutching their handkerchiefs.

"Where have you been, child?" asked Madame Berrie, her white curls bouncing.

"We've been quite worried about you, Your Majesty," added one of her ladies-in-waiting breathlessly. Her eyes were red from crying. "No one could find you, they've been searching for three days straight!"

Lord Dellier was the first one to notice Celestyna's curse-blackened hand. His gray eyebrows shot up. He said nothing.

But the Fetterwitch's curse was cunning, and through it Celestyna could feel every crack and fissure in the Break. They echoed the paths of her freshly darkened veins. And the Gulgot, forever climbing. Celestyna could feel him too.

As if the sensing hairs of her arms and her ears and her mind had been spliced open and multiplied, Celestyna could taste the fear of the people gathered before her.

She had snuck out of the castle, right under their noses. She had *run away* and disappeared into the mountains for three days. And she had come back with a charred left hand.

"It isn't polite to stare at your queen," she told them coldly, taking in the sight of them with her new, all-seeing eyes. How small and weak they looked to her now. Her knees bloomed hot with pain. Her hands twitched at her sides.

But as Celestyna glided past her people and entered her castle, she kept her face serene.

What had her mother taught her?

Don't laugh too hard.

Don't be too nice.

Don't let them see you cry.

Don't let them see you get angry.

Not even when your blood is boiling black with magic.

Celestyna hurried upstairs. A lopsided weight tugged at her legs. She had the unshakable feeling that if she glanced over her shoulder, she would see the Fetterwitch's corpse being dragged along behind her, chained to her ankles and smearing red across the polished floor.

She did not look back.

"And then Lady Valestia took me to the rose market," Orelia said, burrowing into her nest of pillows, "and we picked out new bouquets for the evening hall, and they're so pretty, Tyna! We bought the speckled tea-moss kind you like so much, and west hill sunnies too, the blue-and-yellow ones."

Celestyna tucked blankets around Orelia, barely listening. It was difficult to concentrate with this strange new pain lodged in her throat—like she needed to swallow past a lump of sickness, but couldn't.

She turned her face into her silk-gloved left hand and coughed. Nothing came up.

Restlessly, she sat on the cushioned chair beside Orelia's bed.

Orelia had started a new book in her piano lessons.

Orelia had practiced her figures for two straight hours yesterday, and had even managed to stump Madame Berrie with a particularly challenging equation.

Orelia had explored the gardens and discovered a strange yellow toad with blue eyes, which now lived in her room. She named him Thonk, for that was the sound he made when he hopped about her carpet.

Celestyna couldn't get comfortable. Every bone in her body jabbed toothily into the next. She stretched, her joints popping and cracking in ways they had never popped and cracked before.

Then Orelia fixed Celestyna with a keen look. She crawled out of bed, put her ear to the door, and turned down all the lamps.

When she returned to her bed, she said, "All right, I've been talking for nearly an hour. Everyone must have gone to bed by now. We can speak freely." Orelia leaned closer, her brow furrowed. "You look awful. Where the thunder did you go? What happened to you?"

Celestyna blinked at her sister. "I beg your pardon?"

"You ran away, and you didn't tell me where you were going, or why." Orelia's jaw was set, but her eyes were bright. "Do you not trust me? We've kept secrets from everyone before, and I've never said a word, not to anyone. Tyna." Orelia's face was grave. "I wouldn't even tell Thonk."

For a moment, Celestyna considered it. She could tell Orelia everything—the Fetterwitch, the curse, the real reason their parents had gotten sick.

And how they had actually died.

Immediately, the curse awoke. It reared up, ravenous. If a curse could have a mouth, this one would have opened wide, tongue wagging.

Yes, it hissed. *You could tell her. Such a burden to bear alone. Let her take it from you.*

Celestyna's heart thundered like the storms her people wished for every day.

The curse was an old thing.

It was so old that it had grown a mind of its own, and it was endlessly hungry.

For years it had been bound to an old, crusty witch, and now it was bound to a young, not-crusty queen, but what was younger and even not-crustier than a queen?

A princess.

The curse stretched and purred in Celestyna's blood, and as it stretched, it whispered a word.

Orelia.

Celestyna sat very still, hardly breathing. Orelia was speaking, but Celestyna could only hear the curse's whispers.

If Celestyna would just find her sister a knife—any knife would do, the curse assured her—and tell her the whole truth, surely sweet, tenderhearted Orelia would want to give her sister an escape from the burden she carried, just as Celestyna had relieved her parents of theirs.

"No!" Celestyna shoved herself away from the bed, knocking over her chair.

The curse lashed against Celestyna's bones, from her skull to the tips of her toes.

Orelia scrambled upright. "Tyna?"

"Get away from me!" Celestyna snarled. "Where I have gone, and what I have done, are not your concern."

Orelia's worried gaze dropped to Celestyna's gloved hand. "Tell me what's wrong. I've heard people saying . . . *Please,* Tyna tell me."

Celestyna twisted the lace trim of her silk glove. Past the lace, a slim band of charred skin stood out starkly against the rest of her wrist.

"Tyna . . ." Orelia crept closer. "What have you done?"

Celestyna spun away from her. "Nothing! I'm perfectly well."

"You're lying to me. You're hurt!"

Celestyna whirled back around, flinging out her unhurt arm. Her hand hit Orelia's cheek with a loud *thwack.*

Orelia staggered back and fell to the carpet.

The sisters stared at each other—one breathing hard, the other with the breath knocked clean out of her.

Orelia, eyes shimmering with tears, cradled her cheek in one hand.

"Tyna?" she whispered, her mouth trembling.

Celestyna fled—out of Orelia's bedroom and down the hallway. Windows full of night on one side, portraits of queens on the other. She flew down the stairs and through her castle's silent halls. Pain shot through her like arrows, but that didn't stop her. She clenched her blackened fist and punched the air.

Hurt him, she instructed the grinning curse. *Punch him. Make him fall.*

The polished floor beneath her feet shuddered—as did the castle, the quiet wet streets of Aeria, the lonely green-and-gray slopes of Westlin.

And so did the Break, far below.

And the monster living inside it.

Celestyna heard the distant angry roar of the Gulgot, felt the crash of his body against the rocks as he fell—down, and down, losing all the ground he'd gained that day.

She ran, thrusting her ruined fist into the air again, and again, and again, and smiled past her tears.

.26.

THE SHARPENING TWIN

Tavarik was the name of the colorful city by the sea. Thorn now knew that much.

She also knew that the room in which Zaf was currently sleeping was one of several rooms given to the witch Quicksilver and her friend Sly Boots whenever they visited Lord Vilmar.

She knew Lord Vilmar ruled the country of Koreva, and the roof Thorn was lying on was part of his castle. Lord Vilmar was a jovial brown-skinned man, with bouncy black curls and a generous smile. His husband was a witch, as were his five children. Quicksilver was teaching them, and Lord Vilmar's newest witch knights, how to work more effectively with their monsters. That entire day, they had all been experimenting with using their monsters to travel, like Zaf had done.

Thorn knew all of that.

But this Thorn knew most vividly and horribly of all:

The witch Quicksilver hardly deserved the name.

A witch who could not perform magic? Pah!

Lying on the cool slate roof, wearing her goggles, Thorn glared up at the brilliant stars.

As far as she was concerned, Quicksilver might as well have been a mere human—useless and small, just like Thorn was.

She flattened her left palm against her belly. Since arriving in the Star Lands, her stomach had been off-and-on upset, and it was getting worse by the hour. It was now upset more often than not. Perhaps all the magic in the air disagreed with her not-magic blood.

Or maybe . . .

She swallowed hard, scratched the inside of her left elbow, and tried to push the thought out of her mind. But in the middle of the night, while everyone she loved slept, it was much harder not to think terrible things.

Maybe, back when they'd been in that swamp—and she'd

touched that shadow-struck unicorn with her hurt left hand—something had gotten inside her, and was starting to change *her* as well.

"You can't sleep either?" came a voice.

Thorn peered over the roof's edge.

Noro stood on the terrace between a set of wide doors thrown open to the night. The stars cast colored lights across the glowing canvas of his coat, making him look like one of the painted tin creatures Thorn used to decorate Flower House's windowsills—although he was ever so much finer than anything her own stupid fingers could have crafted.

What was the point of spending time fashioning figurines when she could be occupying herself with some much more impressive activity?

Like harvesting lightning, perhaps?

Thorn's heart twinged, which brought more thoughts she couldn't push away:

Is Brier all right? Where is she, this very moment?

How will I tell her the truth about the stormwitches?

If, that is, I ever get home.

But did she even *want* to get home? Back home, she would wear her sweep's cap and assemble her figurines out of trash and return to her small, unexceptional life in the shadow of her not-small, exceptional sister.

Noro was watching her curiously.

"No, I can sleep," said Thorn. A thousand other answers sat on her tongue. "I'm just afraid to."

Noro blinked. His lashes sparkled with moonlight. "What are you afraid of? The Gulgot?"

Anger sparked inside her, sudden and sharp. It was like she'd stepped off a stair she didn't know was there, her whole body jolting hot-cold and startled.

Thorn clenched her fists and bit her tongue. Her chest felt sharp and prickly, and deep in her gut, something churned restlessly, something dark and hot. If she opened her mouth, she would say something nasty, though she didn't quite know why.

Noro turned around and looked back over his shoulder.

"Would you like to go on a walk with me?" he asked gently.

Once, the thought of walking alone with Noro would have cowed Thorn. But now Thorn only grinned and shimmied down the copper drainpipe onto Noro's back.

He was the only unicorn in Lord Vilmar's castle, and he had sought *her* out, and no one else.

The new angry fist in Thorn's belly preened.

They found a winding pebbled path that ambled alongside the Bay of the Moons.

That was one comforting thing: in the Star Lands, Thorn could look up past the boundless wash of stars and see the same two moons that lived behind the clouds of the Vale—one near and violet tinged, the other distant and white.

"Are you sure you don't want to walk next to me?" asked Noro.

Thorn gritted her teeth. Yes, every point at which her legs and hands came into contact with Noro's coat smarted like needles were pricking her skin. All this time with Noro, and his bond with Brier still didn't like Thorn being so near.

But Thorn pressed her palms and legs closer to Noro and let the pain smart and sting.

She was growing tired of Noro's constant worried questions. Would he worry so much about Brier? No, he would know Brier could handle herself. He would trust her to let him know if she needed help.

"Stop asking me that," Thorn snapped. "I told you I'm fine, and I mean it."

They walked in silence.

Then Noro said, "I couldn't sleep because I keep thinking about Brier."

The sudden ache in Thorn's chest felt like trying to breathe through ice.

"Miss her, do you?" she managed, her voice brambly. "Wish she was here instead of boring old sniveling me?"

Noro stopped in his tracks and peered back at her. "That's an awful thing to say about yourself."

Thorn looked away to the diamond sea. Her eyes filled with tears. Of *course* they did. She hated Noro for making her cry, and she hated herself for allowing it, like she always did. She was a hundred knots of hate, shaped into a torso and a belly and a skull.

"Isn't it true, though?" she snapped. "Wouldn't you rather Brier was here instead?"

"I do miss her," said Noro, "but I don't wish she was here instead. I rather like spending time with you, which we've not done much before now, just the two of us. That's what I was going to say."

Noro resumed walking.

Thorn's cheeks flushed, but she set her jaw. What was there to apologize for, anyway? She'd spoken her mind, that was all, like normal people did. People who *didn't* cry at everything and mumble through their lives. Usually she swallowed her complaints and kept her head low to the ground, swept from dawn till dusk, and came home reeking of the gutters.

I will never do any of those things again, vowed Thorn. *Not a single one of them.*

The fist in her belly squeezed with pleasure.

She scratched her forearm so hard it hurt.

"May I tell you something honestly?" Noro asked. "It might make you angry."

The fist inside her fractured, stretched, became a web. From belly wall to belly wall, it elongated. It climbed up her throat and clung to the back of her tongue, dark and sticky.

Thorn swallowed, smiling to herself. Whatever the web was, she didn't mind it. It had been silly, to be afraid of this new feeling and worry about that dead unicorn. This fist-turned-web was reinforcing her insides, rebuilding her. Why should she be afraid of a thing that made her so much stronger than she had been before?

"Fine," she muttered to Noro. "What is it?"

"You've been acting strangely since we arrived in the Star Lands."

Thorn's heartbeat thudded in her ears.

The web in her belly stretched taut. Had the unicorn detected the truth?

Was he sniffing it out?

Thorn made sure to sound bored. Her heart thumped in her ears. She rubbed the dip of her left palm. "Strangely how?"

"Sharper. Snappish." Noro hesitated. "Unkind, on occasion."

"Am I not allowed to be unkind?"

"I only meant that the Thorn I know doesn't often have such storms brewing behind her eyes."

"Yes, well," replied Thorn, her voice dripping with venom. "The Thorn you know is—"

Gone.

That was the word wavering on the tip of her tongue.

Thorn clamped her mouth shut. She hadn't meant to say those words, and certainly not with a voice like *that*, so mean and cutting. She had never before considered herself ferocious. What a tasty feeling it was. Ferocious people were not ignored. Ferocious people did not live their lives in quiet shadows.

But that voice . . . it had not belonged to her. It was almost like something had taken over her throat and tugged out another person's words.

"Thorn," said Noro quietly, "is there something you want to talk to me about?"

Yes. *Yes.* Thorn gripped Noro's mane so hard that she expected to see fresh red cuts carved into her hands.

The voice had frightened her—almost like her own, but not quite. Feeling like her own words, and yet not.

She opened her mouth: *I think I might be ill.*

There's something inside me—something new and strong, and growing, and terrifying, but also wonderful.

But if she confessed to Noro, what then?

Would he think her mad?

Or worse, would he take her to Sly Boots, and ask the healer for a tonic that would wipe her belly clean?

"I'm worried about you," Noro said. "I've been thinking that maybe, in the swamp, when—"

"So, what will we do now?" Thorn asked loudly, forcing cheer into her voice. She had to distract Noro, make him forget what he was thinking. "You know, since Quicksilver's turned out to be useless."

"I'm not sure I'd describe her quite that way," Noro replied tensely, "but, to answer your question, I don't know. We came here for a witch. Perhaps there's another one who might be able to help us."

Thorn snorted. "So we'll just go hunting around the Star Lands, for storms know how long, until we find someone who wants to leave their home behind to come to a strange land of shadows and darkness and monsters? Someone powerful enough to actually be of use to us?"

Thorn slid off Noro's back, marched to the bay's edge, and glared out across the water. Starlit waves, amber and lavender and coral pink, lapped at her toes.

"We should just *take* someone back with us, and as soon as possible," she muttered. "Doing things the proper way will waste too much time."

Noro went very still, in that cold, stony, ancient way he took on when he was too tired or angry to pretend he was tame. "Are you suggesting we take someone to the Vale against their will?"

"I'm suggesting we do whatever is required to save the Vale, instead of lingering for however long in Lord Vilmar's castle, being polite and saying please and begging for our lives like a bunch of babies."

"Well," said a hard voice behind Noro, "that's certainly an alarming thing to overhear."

Thorn spun around.

Quicksilver stood there, arms crossed over her chest and a growling Bear beside her.

Flanking them were six of Lord Vilmar's witch guards—and their crouched, glowing monsters, all of them ready to pounce.

Quicksilver didn't allow Thorn to speak until they'd returned to Lord Vilmar's castle.

They gathered in a sitting room in the east wing and waited in tense silence until Bartos, Sly Boots, and Zaf arrived.

The moment she stepped into the room, Zaf darted to Thorn, clasped her hand, and faced Quicksilver with a defiant gleam in her eye.

"Whatever she did," Zaf said, "she didn't mean it. And if you want to hurt her, you'll have to go through me."

Thorn decided to ignore the slight lingering wheeze in Zaf's voice, which somewhat diminished the weight of her threat, and instead concentrate on how sweet it felt to have Zaf standing a little in front of her, as if to protect Thorn. Maybe the only stormwitch alive in the whole world, and she had chosen *Thorn* to be her friend.

Thorn stifled a smug smile. That was as it should be.

"No one's hurting anyone," said Sly Boots, looking quickly between Thorn and Quicksilver. "I've had a long day, and I don't feel like bandaging up any of you."

Thorn noticed the stormy expression on Quicksilver's face, and then, all of a sudden, began to speak. The words spilled out of her mouth, faster and faster, shoved up through her throat on the sticky, clever cords of her belly's web.

"Zaf's right," Thorn said, pouting delicately. "I didn't mean what I said. I've just been . . . well, I'm tired, and I'm worried about my home, and I'm in a strange place where I have to wear goggles on my head all the time, and they've given me a constant rotten headache—though I am thankful that you gave them to us, of course." She smiled a little. She scrunched up her face to illustrate the words "rotten headache."

The hard line of Quicksilver's mouth softened.

Thorn's heart pounded gleefully. Was this what it was like for Brier, every day? To know exactly what to say, and what people wanted to hear?

Thorn breathed in and out. The web in her stomach expanded and contracted, dark and sprawling.

"I was rambling to Noro," she went on, "because I couldn't sleep, and I was just saying aloud any thought that came into my head, no matter how stupid or wrong or mean."

Thorn took a deep breath, looked Quicksilver right in her sharp gray eyes. "Of course I wouldn't take anyone to the Vale against their will. I wouldn't even if I had the ability for it."

Quicksilver's gaze cut to Zaf, then back to Thorn. Her face was unreadable plaster.

Then she withdrew a folded piece of paper from her pocket and passed it to Sly Boots. He read it, then closed his eyes.

"Oh, Quicksilver . . . ," came his soft voice.

Quicksilver flinched.

A war raged inside Thorn's belly.

On one side: an ache of pity. The urge to reach for Quicksilver. Perhaps a warm touch would comfort her.

On the other side: the web holding her fast with a slight growl. Not a growl that Thorn heard, but one she *felt*.

Don't be a weakling, it said.

She froze. She wavered, teetering.

Yes, the web was right. Of course it was right.

Comforting Quicksilver was a thing the Thorn of the past would have done. The soppy, soft Thorn who hid her face in her tangled hair and clung to her broom like a baby.

Thorn stayed put.

The web sighed, content.

"My friend Ari has been abducted," said Quicksilver softly. "He is a prince of Valteya, the northernmost country of the Star Lands. He was coming here to visit us when a company of masked soldiers attacked his entourage. When his guards came to, he was gone."

Quicksilver closed her eyes briefly. "They did manage, however, to capture one of the attackers. They didn't get much out of him before his wounds claimed him, but he told them one crucial thing, and they passed it on to me. It would have meant nothing to me, before your arrival."

Quicksilver took the note from Sly Boots, held it up, and looked calmly at Thorn. "He said, 'I fight to save the Vale, and I am not ashamed.'"

The chill that swept through Thorn's body nearly buckled her knees. It silenced every other thought. It silenced the web.

"I don't understand," Zaf said, her hand still clamped around Thorn's. "Why would soldiers from the Vale want some Star Lands prince?"

"Because he's not just a prince," Quicksilver said, her eyes bright. "He's a witch."

Zaf inhaled sharply.

Thorn's stomach, web and all, turned over. Thinking, just like her mind was turning over and thinking.

"They want him for something," she said. "Something to do with the Break. Just like we thought you could help us, Quicksilver." She turned to Bartos. "You don't know anything about this, do you? Could the queen have secretly sent people to bring back a witch to the Vale?"

Bartos shook his head, his pale face drawn and angry. "Maybe. I didn't even know it was *possible* to get past the eastern mountains."

"Unless you're a stormwitch," Zaf said proudly.

"Unless you're a stormwitch," Bartos agreed, rubbing his forehead. "But as we've discovered, apparently there are many things I was never told."

"I doubt soldiers of the Vale would have risked their lives to cross Estar and the eastern mountains unless the queen had ordered them to," said Noro thoughtfully.

"Maybe she wants to use the Star Lands witches just like she's used us," Zaf muttered.

The part of Thorn that was still herself ached to hear the pain in Zaf's voice.

But the webbed part of her was cold and felt nothing, and spun her mind quickly.

"Take us with you to find Ari," she said to Quicksilver. "We can help."

When Quicksilver did not reply, Thorn pressed on. "Who better to help you track down soldiers from the Vale than actual people from the Vale?"

Bartos cleared his throat. "I do know how these soldiers will cover their tracks. The tricks they'll use to stay hidden." He tugged his jacket straight and squared his skinny shoulders. "Having me on their trail can only help you, Madame Quicksilver."

Sly Boots snorted.

Quicksilver, straight-faced, elbowed him in the ribs.

Thorn saw her opportunity.

"But if we help you find Ari," she said, "then both of you have to come back with us to the Vale. You may not be able to work magic anymore, but you *know* about magic, and Ari—"

"Ari's monsters are dead too," said Quicksilver flatly. "If you're hoping he can help you instead of me—"

"Well, so we'll have two witch minds helping us, then. You can give the queen and her advisers ideas. Solutions they may not have thought about."

Quicksilver frowned. "Perhaps."

Thorn hesitated. The dark web inside her curled like a grin. "Maybe you can bring along some of your witch students—"

"Absolutely not." Quicksilver's eyes flashed. "Grown witches who volunteer to come with us, fine. But not my students."

Anger stirred in Thorn's pulse points—her wrists, her neck, the cage of her heart. *But young magic tastes so much nicer,* whispered a voice inside her.

Thorn bit the inside of her mouth. A tiny fear skipped up her throat and then was gone.

Quicksilver glanced at Sly Boots. He nodded, and Quicksilver's posture relaxed, and Thorn swallowed a smile, because she had won.

"All right, Thorn," Quicksilver said briskly. "Help me find Ari, and we'll come back with you to the Vale, assess the situation, see what we can do. Which," she added, with a stern look, "may not be anything. You understand that."

"I understand," said Thorn, "and thank you."

As she clasped hands with Quicksilver, Thorn felt Noro's eyes upon her face. She avoided looking at him. What did she care if he looked at her? He could look all he wanted to look.

There was nothing wrong with her. The hot angry web coating her bones was *clarifying* her. It made her mind move faster and sharper. Her muscles felt stronger, more agile.

She liked this bold new Thorn, who made deals with witches and didn't take no for an answer.

This Thorn who was so much better than the Thorn she used to be.

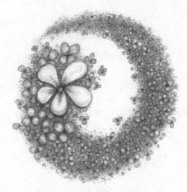

.27.

THE QUESTION IN THE DARK

The Break was a jagged country of rises and valleys, and craters smashed into its walls like the footprints of mountains, and long snaking canyons, and forests of rocks, sharp and knobby as a growing boy's knees.

Maybe, at the beginning, when the magic of those ancient warring witches had slammed into the Vale, the Break had been a simple gash cut from the world by magic. A chasm of sheer walls and a smooth, forever drop. Cub couldn't remember much from the day he first fell.

Most of what he could remember were all the years after—

years of climbing and roaring, and being knocked down and yanked down and *pushed* down by the wicked else-hand clamped around his throat.

Wicked.

Wicked.

Yes, the else-hand was wicked. It carried dark power inside it. It did not belong in a place where the Old Wild had once lived.

If I don't belong in this world, the else-hand's cruel magic often whispered to Cub, *then neither do you, beast.*

Cub tried not to listen to the else-hand when it spoke. Not listening was difficult. The else-hand was clever and knew just the right awful things to say.

But Cub had survived the breaking of the Vale. He had survived the deaths of his mothers. If he could do that, then he could do this.

So he told himself, every long and sunless day.

The else-hand was full of angry magic, but that was all right.

Cub was angry too.

As he climbed furiously skyward—sky, oh, *sky*, it had been too long since Cub had laid his eyes upon it!—the else-hand punched and kicked him.

The cursed magic inside it felt desperate. The small human queen at the other end, up above, was not as strong as the old witch had been. The else-hand was fraying, like ancient rope. It was brittle, like thin glass. Its dark power had been leaking for years, and now it spilled out fast as darting shadows, racing over Cub's body and up the Break and out into the world like a million skittering spiders.

But Cub kept climbing. He was only a tiny bit afraid. His anger gave him strength. So did the things he could remember.

He told himself the story his mothers had given him, about the birth of the stars.

Once there had been two worlds: one of light, brilliant and jubilant, and one of darkness, lonesome and lacking.

The world of light had so pitied its twin that it had carved out pieces of its own self with a cold silver knife fashioned from a comet's tail. When the world of light shook loose its wounds, a thousand thousand brilliant embers cascaded down and stuck there, spangling the velvet dark.

Thus, whispered the world of light to its sister, *you shall never be truly alone, for I will always be with you.*

This, Cub's mothers had taught him, was how the stars were made—a gift from one sister to another.

Cub liked this story. His anger was bright in the darkness too.

The else-hand punched him. He fell, slammed his chin against a rock, then scrambled up and kept climbing. His huge paws were thunder.

Die, the else-hand hissed. *Fall. Never get up. Stay forever in darkness, foul beast.*

But Cub didn't listen. Brilliant stars of anger showed him the way up.

One morning—or maybe it was night, Cub couldn't say—he awoke from a restless sleep and thrust his cold, cracked snout into the endless dank air of the Break, preparing himself to climb.

Then he sniffed, and realized something:

He was no longer alone in this miserable dark place of shadows and rocks that had become his home.

Someone was nearby.

Someone new.

He heaved his great body off the slab of stone he'd claimed for his bed and followed the sweaty scent in the air. He knew that smell; he had smelled it on his own crusty skin for as long as he could remember.

It was fear.

Cub paused.

He sniffed.

Two someones.

This new creature was not alone. It had brought a friend.

And, Cub thought, this particular flavor of fear tasted familiar.

It belonged to humans.

Two humans. Humans, *here*.

Fury swelled in Cub's chest like the crashing waves of the oceans he had once loved.

He would find these humans, these creatures who tossed stormwitches into the Break. As if witches could ever possibly be enough to knock down a beast like Cub for good!

He would smash the humans beneath his paws, squash and grind until they were twin flattened puddles drying around shattered bits of bone. Maybe that would make him feel better. Maybe hurting them would make him climb faster.

But first he would ask the humans a question. A single question that had been swimming along the currents of his mind for as long as he had lived in darkness:

Why?

Why did the ancient eastern witches go to war, so long ago?

Why did his mothers have to die, and why did humans hurt witches, and why did witches hurt with their magic?

Why had Cub been punished by the world he had so dearly loved?

Why were there so many awful, lonesome things about being alive that Cub could not understand?

He howled it, his voice bursting:

Why?

.28.

THE COLLAR'S HUSH

The next morning Celestyna entered her throne room, prepared for a day at court. Eyes dry and itchy from a sleepless night. Face painted, but not *too* painted. Smile on, but not *too* on. Gloves tied tightly at her wrists.

Curse quiet. For now.

But once inside the great gleaming room, she froze.

It was empty, save for Lord Dellier and the members of her personal guard. Two of them quietly locked the doors behind her.

Celestyna's body went hot-cold with rage. She opened her mouth to scream.

The guards lunged at her. One grabbed her left arm, one her right.

"I'm sorry, Your Majesty," one of them whispered, his voice trembling. "He says this will help your pain."

Celestyna hardly heard him. She kicked her legs, flung out her arms.

Bleed them! The curse howled up her spine. *Make them pay!*

And Celestyna tried, she *tried*. The curse was a bludgeon in her belly, and when it struck, so did Celestyna. Her knuckles hit a soldier's jaw with a crack. Another soldier took his place. They held Celestyna fast.

Lord Dellier came forward. In his hands lay a flat golden band. The sight of it filled Celestyna with dread so sharp she saw black.

"I'm sorry, child," said Lord Dellier, his voice gentle and cracking, his weary eyes ringed with shadows.

Then the cold metal band settled around her neck and snapped shut.

Immediately the world dimmed, like someone had stuffed wool in Celestyna's ears and drawn a veil over her eyes.

It wasn't such a bad veil. And the wool, scratchy as it was, felt almost pleasant, if you liked that sort of thing.

Celestyna found that she did.

୭ ୭ ୭

She could still feel the curse binding her will to the Gulgot, but it was not so eager now, and not so near.

Celestyna listened for the curse's whispers, and heard them, faintly, but the words were gibberish to her ears.

Lord Dellier helped her stand. He and Madame Berrie escorted Celestyna to her rooms. Madame Berrie was crying. Lord Dellier's voice was an exhausted thread.

"I know everything, Celestyna," he said. "*Everything*. I have watched over you, and I watched over your parents, and before me it was my father, and before him it was my grandmother. For generations we have guarded your family."

He drew a breath, rubbed his face. They were in her rooms, now. Madame Berrie helped Celestyna sit in her favorite blue chair. Celestyna stared at Lord Dellier. She was tired. She wished he would let her sleep.

"The Fetterwitch made the collar long ago, in the case of her death," Lord Dellier said. "She told my family what signs to look for. How to recognize the curse. We have kept this collar under close guard. I think it will help you sleep. Your other advisers and I, we sent soldiers on a mission to the Star Lands to bring you another witch. One to bear the weight of the curse, as the

Fetterwitch did. We sent them weeks ago. She was growing frail. We thought it was time to try for a replacement, and then—"

"And then I killed her," Celestyna concluded.

A pause. "Then you killed her," Lord Dellier agreed.

"It hurts less now, with the collar," she said curiously. "The curse, I mean. It's quieter."

Madame Berrie wept into her hands.

Lord Dellier looked ten years older than he had only that morning. "Yes, my queen."

Celestyna didn't understand why they looked so upset. Then she caught a glimpse of herself in the mirror, saw her face branched with black veins and her cheeks hollowed with hunger.

A ripple of something passed through her, but she was too numb to feel afraid. She touched two fingers to the metal band at her neck, blinked up at Lord Dellier, and whispered, "Thank you."

The Fetterwitch's collar sat cold and smooth around Celestyna's neck, like a snake pressed flat and gilded.

The queen of the Vale laid her head on her pillow and stared at the ceiling. She didn't care that Orelia had been hysterical since finding the collar around her sister's neck and seeing her sister's cursed hand. That Orelia had been confined to her room with the nurses until she'd calmed down. That she hadn't come close to calming down.

Celestyna heard Orelia crying from inside her rooms. She heard, and she didn't care.

The important thing, she knew, was for her to remain calm, so the curse could function properly, so she would not endanger herself or others or the Vale. And the collar would help her with that.

"Don't show them you're afraid," she whispered to the darkness of her lovely rooms. Mistbirds watched from the rafters, cooing their soft trills. Their eyes followed the trails of their queen's floating black veins, drifting like thin malevolent clouds beneath her skin.

"Don't smile too much," whispered Celestyna.

"Don't talk too loudly."

"Don't . . ."

Sleep snatched her quietly, like a thief.

.29.

THE LIAR'S TRICK

"Just a little farther!" Brier called over her shoulder. "I think I dropped it over here!"

She climbed up the steep grassy path, her eyes trained on the clearing ahead of her—the very same clearing from which she and the harvesters had run for their lives, only a few hours earlier.

Brier's stomach knotted itself so tightly she worried she might never untangle it. The thin mountain air felt sharp in her lungs.

While safe and warm in the hut, her plan had felt like the

best idea in the world. Now she worried if she breathed too hard, the whole thing would shatter.

Behind her, crunching through dry tufts of grass, Gert muttered, "Is this really necessary? Brier will understand if you leave her necklace behind."

The lies Brier had told clogged her throat.

But if Farver, and Gert, and Eldon, and Noro, and all her other friends could lie to her face every day, then she could do it this once, couldn't she?

Brier's side pinched. Her chest was starting to ache again. But she forced words out of her stiff mouth.

"My sister may never make it home again," she declared. "You'd really force me to leave it behind, when Brier, the hero of the Vale, is out there in the dangerous wild, saving all of us?"

An image came to Brier's mind—Thorn, frightened and alone, lost in the swamps of Estar, fighting the same shadows as their parents. Feeling the world quake under her feet. Hearing the Gulgot's not-so-distant roars.

Except Thorn wasn't entirely alone.

Oh, *Noro*.

Brier blinked the sting from her eyes. *Noro, Noro. How could you have kept such a horrible truth from me?*

But she couldn't think about that now—not the countless bolts of lightning she'd helped guide into Noro's horn for safekeeping. Not the eldisks being forged in the queen's storm halls.

She couldn't think about Thorn, maybe out there in the impassable eastern mountains, capturing stormwitches with Noro's help and not knowing it.

Part of Brier hoped they had never made it to the mountains, that they were still wandering lost in Estar, maybe turned around for good. At least if they were stuck in the Estar swamps, where the darkness was too thick for storms, they would not be killing any stormwitches.

Brier stamped her feet hard as she walked. She could not think about any of those awful things. She pushed them out of her mind with each step.

At last they reached the clearing—but when Brier searched the surrounding rocks, her heart dropped.

No stormwitches. The clearing was empty. She'd hoped they would still be lingering, waiting to try again—

Ah. There they were: two pale shapes, shifting quickly beyond that far line of boulders.

Behind Brier, Farver Pickery stopped to catch his breath.

"Where is it, Thorn, my dear? What does the necklace look like again?"

Then, a third pale flash.

Brier squinted through a narrow crevice between two tall boulders—and locked eyes with Zino.

Her skin prickling with nerves, she started jogging toward the boulders. "Right over here! I think I see it!"

Farver and the others followed her, their footsteps crunching. Brier's eyes blurred. They were so eager to trust her. And why shouldn't they? They trusted Brier, and Thorn was Brier's softer half.

She nearly spun around and stopped them. She nearly told them to run.

But they were liars.

Brier's chest constricted. Even knowing what she had done, part of her longed to parade down the streets of Aeria on Noro's back, her hair crackling with static and her bindrock gloves buzzing with all the lightning she'd caught that day.

What a happy girl that Brier had been.

A swift blur of white: Zino, hiding beyond the boulders, disappeared.

Brier, swallowing hard, followed him.

"This way!" she told the harvesters.

Slipping through the crevice between the boulders, her skin crawled. She emerged into a smaller clearing, sheltered from the wind. The tall rocks surrounding them leaned against each other like elders in conference.

Brier turned back just in time to see six stormwitches jump down from the rocks and tackle her friends to the ground.

"Don't hurt them!" she cried. She hid her face against a boulder soft with brown moss. It smelled of snow. "Be kind to them, *please*!"

A moment passed. Then a few more.

Something soft touched Brier's shoulder.

Brier looked back through her fingers.

Zino was watching her, his blue eyes sharp as ice. Beyond him, Farver, Gert, and Reston lay on the ground, cloth sacks over their faces, wrists bound. A dozen stormwitch children heaved them onto the backs of three kneeling unicorns.

"Why did you do this?" Zino asked.

Brier opened her mouth to respond, and couldn't. She was crying and shivering, like some weak city girl who couldn't handle the mountain air she so loved. Sometimes, after a long day of harvesting, she had come home to Flower House and felt that the warm stillness of their house was not cozy, but sweltering.

On those nights, Thorn had been the one to suggest sleeping with the windows open, even though that meant sharing a bed, sleeping squashed together under a pile of all the blankets they could find.

"You don't mind it?" Brier had once asked, nose to nose with her twin. "The cold?"

Thorn had smiled, her dark hair in tangles against her cheeks. "I like that you like it."

Staring at Zino, Brier's tears spilled over. She wasn't used to the feeling. Thorn was the weepy one. Brier was . . . Brier was . . .

But she didn't know what or who she was, not anymore. Not now that everything had changed.

"I didn't know what they were doing," she said, her voice hoarse and small. "I didn't know what *we* were doing. They didn't tell me."

Zino's eyes widened. He looked her over, then whispered, "Brier Skystone?"

Miserably, Brier nodded. "My sister took my place, because of this."

She placed her palm against her chest. The faded burn sizzled slightly. She winced and bit her lip.

Zino was watching her closely. "You didn't know?"

Brier shook her head. "And now that I do . . ."

She couldn't finish.

Zino nodded, his sharp face no longer quite so sharp. "Now that you do."

Brier looked down at her two snow-crusted boots. "I can help you find the rest of the harvesters. They're all out working on the mountain trails." She hardly recognized her voice. "We'll hold them somewhere, so no more lightning will be trapped until we come up with some kind of plan to . . ."

To what? Ask the queen to, if she wouldn't mind, please stop harvesting lightning and let the Gulgot come and destroy them all? What an idea. Brier might as well ask Thorn to stop painting, or Mazby to—

Mazby.

Brier gasped and looked up, but Zino had already whistled like a snowbird. One of the other stormwitches hurried over, a girl with her white hair in messy knots all over her head. In her hands she held a bundle of cloth.

"We rather like the little fellow," admitted Zino, "though I don't think he likes us very much. He banged up his wing a bit helping you escape before, but I don't think it's too bad."

Brier reached for Mazby, all bundled up in a ratty red scarf, his crown feathers askew but whole. She cradled him against her chest, kissed his head.

"Brier," purred Mazby, his eyes heavy with sleep, or maybe pain, or maybe from missing Thorn. He trilled softly. "I hurt my wing."

She pressed her face against his silky feathers. "I know, and I'm sorry. You're so brave, Mazby."

"The bravest grifflet there ever was?"

"And ever will be."

With Mazby in her arms, Brier found it easier to speak. She looked at the harvesters she had betrayed. "Do you have a warm place to keep them, until we decide what to do? And food?"

Zino shrugged off his fraying coat and wrapped it around Brier's shoulders.

"I promise you, Brier Skystone," he said solemnly, "that your friends will be warm and safe."

Brier nodded. The warmth of Mazby against her chest was not nearly enough to soothe her troubled heart.

"Follow me," she said. "I'll help you find the others."

.30.

THE STOLEN PRINCE

Thorn crouched in a cluster of shimmering iridescent ferns and searched the forest for her prey.

They'd been walking west from the city of Tavarik for three days. There was no time to waste; Prince Ari Tarkalia and his abductors would already be far ahead of them.

Thorn had closed her eyes whenever they stopped to make camp, pretending to rest just like the others, but she didn't see the point of resting. Instead she would lie in a tight knot, hands bunched into fists, jaw clenched. If they could just keep going, keep pushing onward, instead of stopping every few hours to nap like a passel of weaklings, maybe they'd have caught up with Ari by now, and then—

"There," whispered Bartos, who knelt nearby, hand at his sword. "I see them."

Tracking the Vale soldiers had made Bartos seem like himself again. His eyes were clear. His washed cap was bright and clean atop his big ears.

Thorn followed his gaze. A group of five huddled a few hundred feet away in a small copse of trees boasting heavy crimson leaves the size of Thorn's torso.

The five people wore brown jackets, long and hooded, and carried small packs slung round their shoulders.

One of them—a stout, fair-skinned woman with cropped brown hair—threw back her hood, took a swig of water from a leather canteen.

Bartos sucked in a sharp breath.

"That's Emmi," he murmured. "She trained me in sword work."

The web in Thorn's belly stretched fast, climbed rough and hot up into her lungs.

Curling her fingers into the mud beside her boots, Thorn gazed hungrily at Emmi's throat. The woman was part of whatever secret plan Queen Celestyna had concocted to sneak into the Star Lands and steal a prince.

But if anyone was going to bring a witch back to the Vale and save everyone from the Gulgot, it should be Thorn.

She was the brave one. *She* was the one with real power inside her. Anyone else would just muck things up.

Thorn could imagine it: her hands, wrapping around Emmi's throat. First Emmi, then the other four soldiers. Then *Thorn* would be the one to bring Prince Ari and Quicksilver to the Vale. They would think she had saved them, they would think her their friend, and then she would give them to the queen, and the royal healers could carve them open and find whatever magic they were hiding. Because surely they were lying. So what if their monsters were dead? They just didn't want to share their magic!

And then she, Thorn, would be given jewels and titles and a great glittering sash, because *she* would have been the one to capture the witches of the Star Lands and save the Vale.

Or maybe, whispered a hungry, cruel voice in Thorn's mind, *maybe we don't give the witches to the queen.*

Maybe we throw them in the Break. Give them to the Gulgot.

Wouldn't they taste nice?

"Where's Ari?" whispered Zaf, beside Thorn.

One of the five people burst out of the group, running fast. His hood fell back, revealing a boy around Quicksilver's age—fair skinned, black haired.

Emmi chased after him, threw a sloppy punch. The boy dodged her fist, dropped, and rolled. Two of the other soldiers tackled him to the ground. They wrenched dark cloth around his eyes and mouth, stifling his furious cries. A third soldier, brown skinned with short white hair, slowly scanned the forest, his sword drawn.

Quicksilver came up softly beside Thorn. Bear followed, his bright black eyes trained on the flattened boy.

"Ari's the fellow on the ground," said Quicksilver, her eyes blazing. "Your tracking skills came through after all, Bartos."

Despite everything, Bartos looked ever so slightly pleased with himself. "All right," he muttered, "here's the plan. There aren't many of them, but more might be on patrol. We'll take a look, stay quiet, and once these four have made camp—"

Bear yelped in distress, cutting him off, and tore out into the forest, right for where Prince Ari lay in the dirt. Ari turned in the grip of his captors, called out Bear's name.

Quicksilver shouted an angry command, but Bear ignored her, barking at Ari's captors.

Thorn grinned. Here was her opportunity.

She twisted free of Zaf's grip and took off after Bear. She heard Zaf call her name and kept running.

Sit around waiting for these soldiers to fall asleep? And *then* get Ari away? No.

What *really* needed to happen was for these soldiers' faces to be pounded into the ground. If they were dead, they couldn't steal the glory that rightfully belonged to her.

With every running step, Thorn's heart drummed a vicious song. The web inside her climbed merrily up her rib cage, tugged on the back of her tongue, whispered, *Faster. Strike them. Hurt them.*

Again, Thorn saw her hands around Emmi's throat. Her fingers itched and curled.

Bear leaped onto one of the soldiers holding down Ari, knocking the man flat.

And Thorn flung her body against Emmi's, grabbed the woman's neck with both hands, and squeezed.

It felt good to pinch and twist Emmi's tender neck flesh. It felt *right*.

She heard distant shouts and ignored them all. She squeezed and squeezed, and the web inside her whispered its congratulations. She had moved boldly, and swiftly, instead of standing there twisting her hands together, worrying and waiting and wondering, like Thorn of the past would have done.

Through a haze of fuzzy gray, Thorn watched Emmi's face swelling red, then purple. She heard an ugly gagging noise.

A hand grabbed Thorn's coat and yanked her loose.

Legs thrashing, Thorn fought to get free, but whoever had grabbed her pinned her arms to her sides.

A sharp cry: *"Thorn!"*

Zaf's voice cut through Thorn's thoughts and squashed the web flat.

She blinked, the storm in her eyes clearing.

Zaf, a few yards away, clung to Noro, her eyes wide with horror.

Bartos was helping Emmi sit up and breathe.

Thorn's blood thumped dully in her ears. She looked around at all of them: Sly Boots. Noro and Zaf. The soldiers from the Vale. Ari, still on the ground, holding a whining Bear.

They all stared at Thorn with expressions that sent her stomach plunging.

Noro was the only one who didn't look terrified of her. Instead he said firmly, "Thorn, listen to my voice. Look at me. You are Thorn Skystone of the Vale."

"Are you going to fight me anymore?" asked the person holding Thorn close—Quicksilver, her voice thin and tense.

Emmi, leaning against Bartos, coughed a horrible, racking cough. Ugly bruises bloomed on her pale throat. They were shaped like Thorn's fingers.

"I'm all right," Thorn said quietly, her tongue too big for her mouth, her head fuzzy and aching. "I won't hurt her."

Quicksilver released Thorn, and Thorn, hearing Emmi's rasping breaths, felt sure she was going to be sick.

She turned and ran.

On a soft pile of yellow moss, beside a shallow brook in a bed of tiny lavender rocks, Thorn sat in silence, knees pulled to her chest. She scratched her forearms and shins until it hurt.

Her goggles sat atop her head. Her eyes had been adjusting to the brightness of the Star Lands, but it still smarted to look directly at any color, even the soft lavender river rocks. That was a good thing.

She had hurt Emmi, and now she deserved to hurt.

As she stared at the brook, her eyes watering, Thorn realized it had felt *good* to hurt Emmi, though she didn't know why. Looking back, it was like seeing someone else—a Thorn who was not *really* Thorn, leaping out of the bushes and knocking Emmi flat.

Thorn wiped her nose. The Thorn of the past would never have hurt someone, would never have *dreamed* of it. Past-Thorn would have cowered in the ferns and done what everyone told her to do. Maybe they would have ignored her altogether. Maybe they would have forgotten she was there.

No one could ignore a girl who'd strangled a grown woman she'd never even met before.

Thorn pressed her cheek harder into her knee, watching the sparkling water slip and trickle and rush. She felt the familiar start of tears—the hateful, hot tingling in her nose, her tightening throat—and shut her eyes, willing the feeling away.

A quiet moment passed. Then a soft weight pressed into the moss beside Thorn. Without opening her eyes, Thorn knew who it was from the slight stormy charge in the air.

Zaf.

Zaf, *Zaf.* Thorn said the name over and over in her mind. Each time made it easier to breathe.

Zaf hooked her arm through Thorn's and pressed her cheek against Thorn's shoulder. "I still like you, Thorn. I hope you know that. I like you very much."

Thorn squeezed her eyes shut. Zaf's voice rasped, her breathing was thin and wheezing, and it got worse every day, even with the tonic Sly Boots kept giving her.

Then Thorn thought of something.

The shadow-struck unicorn in the swamp had touched her.

And now she was touching *Zaf*. . .

Panic exploded inside her. Why had she never thought of this before?

"Don't touch me!" Thorn cried, shoving Zaf away.

But Zaf did not look afraid, even though her breath rattled and her hands hardly glowed, her skin wan and dull.

"Me being weak has nothing to do with you," Zaf said firmly. "It's only because I used too much magic to get us here. And besides, I've already touched you, and so has Quicksilver, and Bartos, and everyone. We've all talked about it and decided. If we're infected by the Gulgot too, then we're infected. We're not going to hold our noses around you."

"So . . . you all know?" Thorn whispered.

"Noro told us," said Zaf. "He said he wasn't sure until what just happened. He said he was trying to convince himself it wasn't true."

Thorn closed her eyes and looked away. So they knew. They

all knew about this *thing* inside her, this dark, grinning web.

Would they try to take it from her?

Did she *want* them to?

"My hand got scraped when I fell before," she whispered, "so it was hurt when I touched that shadow-struck unicorn, and I think that's when . . ."

She couldn't say anything more.

"They're all talking about what to do," Zaf said quietly. "You really scared everyone, Thorn. You scared *me*."

A curtain of nearby leaves parted, revealing a frowning Bartos. He marched over and flung himself down onto the moss beside Zaf.

"Noro told me what's happened," said Bartos, "but I'd like to hear you say it yourself."

"She doesn't want to talk right now, thank you," said Zaf.

"Well, that's just too bad," Bartos replied. "Because the woman who trained me now has Thorn-sized handprints on her throat. Some people back there think you ought to be taken to Tavarik and put in a cell."

A taut cord snapped, somewhere deep in Thorn's chest—the dark web, lashing out like a frog's hungry tongue.

"Your plan was too slow!" she snarled.

Zaf looked sadly up at her. "Thorn, this isn't you."

"But it *is* me! It's who I am now. I'm strong, and I'm not afraid, not of anything." Thorn's voice broke. "I get angry when I want to, and I say what I want to, loud and mean if I want to, and no one ignores me, and no one wishes I was Brier, and—" Choking a little, she backed slowly away from Zaf and Bartos. "I don't cry, I never cry, not anymore, not *ever*—"

"That," said Bartos calmly, "is not the Thorn I know."

"The Thorn you know is worthless."

"Not true."

"She's small and skinny and she smells like trash," Thorn continued, her eyes filling up.

"She works hard keeping our city clean," Bartos argued, "and she makes beautiful art that fills her house with color." He smiled a little. "And my house too. Vases and figurines, paintings and wind chimes."

"She's a shadow. She'll be forgotten when she dies." Thorn let out a little sob and viciously wiped her face. "She cries too much."

"Oh, Thorn," he said with a sigh. "It is no small thing, to have a gentle heart."

Thorn stared at him, a slight calm falling over her.

"My mother said that to me once," she whispered.

Bartos smiled. "I know. She said it to me too."

Zaf reached for Thorn's hand and held on tight. She stared at Thorn with her huge blue eyes, so bright and beautiful that for a moment, Thorn forgot everything else.

"Maybe the Gulgot's darkness hurt you," Zaf said, her voice thin but fierce, "because, when you comforted that unicorn, you showed so much light to grab on to. The darkness couldn't resist it. It was a kind thing you did, Thorn. A brave thing."

Thorn looked away into the forest, trying to find her breathing once more. Zaf was being nice, but she was wrong.

The truth was she was weak, small, and less than ordinary. She had known it all her life, and now the Gulgot's darkness knew it too. It had found her, and was changing her, because it sensed that it *could*.

"Come," Bartos said, rising to his feet. "We'll have some food. I'll introduce you to Emmi, properly."

"You should just leave me here and go home," Thorn said dully, stepping back from Zaf. "I'll hurt someone again. I'll go hide, like the shadow-struck unicorns. I'm not . . ."

Her throat closed up. She couldn't say the words she wanted to say: *I'm not worth saving.*

Bartos took her gently by the shoulders.

"You are worth saving, Thorn of the Vale," he said, his voice leaving no room for argument. "And that's what we're all going to do."

"How?" Thorn whispered.

"By saving the Vale," Zaf said, hands on her hips. She grinned, tilting her head. Her eyes sparkled. "Haven't you been paying attention?"

Thorn let them both wrap her into a hug so warm and tight she could hear nothing of the nasty whispers in her head. She hid her face in Bartos's coat and smiled into the wild white fall of Zaf's hair.

Later that night, Thorn awoke to whispers.

She left Zaf in their little bed of moss and crept across the camp. Where Thorn stepped, the moss shifted—sunset orange under her feet, then deep vermilion, then back to a cool aquamarine once she'd passed.

She followed the whispers to a glittering patch of pearl-colored sand beside one of the brook's shallow tributaries. In the sand crouched Quicksilver, Ari, Sly Boots, and Bartos. Behind them stood Noro.

Thorn sat gingerly in front of Noro's legs and stared at what they were all looking at.

Someone had drawn in the sand a map of the Star Lands, and now Bartos was finishing up another map, joining it to the first. A map of the Vale.

Thorn's tired heart warmed to see the familiar lines—rivers and valleys, Estari cities that had once stood tall and proud, and now lay empty and ruined. Touched by the Gulgot. Shadow-struck.

Just like her.

She clutched her stomach with one hand and found the long line that cut Bartos's map of the Vale in two:

The Break.

"Once we get here," said Bartos, pointing to the lines beyond the Break, "to the Westlin cliffs, we'll be safe. There's a hidden trail that will take us right up into the basement levels of Castle Stratiara."

Quicksilver nodded, frowning at the maps. Absently she patted Thorn's shoulder. Noro pressed his muzzle to Thorn's neck. Just like Zaf, they weren't afraid to touch her.

Thorn, too tired to smile, nevertheless felt a bit warmer.

"It will take three weeks to travel the rest of the Star Lands," murmured Quicksilver. "We could go much faster if we recruit witches to help us and try traveling by monster. Willow-on-the-River isn't far from here."

Ari made a skeptical sound: *puh!*

Quicksilver rolled her eyes. "Ari thinks I'm mad for even suggesting that traveling by monster could work."

"Caution," said Ari, a bit loftily, "is a virtue."

"So is courage, *Your Highness*. I'm telling you, I think it could be done, with some more experimenting. I made decent progress with Lord Vilmar's knights before we left Tavarik."

Ari raised an eyebrow. "Or we could just *walk* to the mountains, instead of wasting time trying to craft a spell that might not even work."

Sly Boots glanced at Thorn with a rueful smile. "They're fun, aren't they?"

Quicksilver thwacked Sly Boots on his arm.

Ari looked at Bartos. "Traveling by foot from the mountains, how long will it take us to get through Estar to the Westlin cliffs?"

Bartos scratched his chin. "Three weeks, maybe. That's if the land doesn't turn on us, which it very well might."

"By then," said Ari, "the Vale could be lost, if what you've told me is true."

"Zaf could get us there faster."

Silence fell at Thorn's words—words she hadn't meant to say. The cruel web inside her had been quiet, maybe scared away by her friends, but now it was back. And it was angry.

"Zaf is the stormwitch, right?" Ari asked.

Bartos frowned. "Thorn, you know we can't ask Zaf to do that."

"Another trip like the one that brought you here might finish her," added Sly Boots.

"No, it won't. I can do it."

Thorn turned around and found Zaf. Framed by gargantuan gleaming black leaves, she looked narrow and small. She leaned against a tree, breathing thinly. The wind ruffled her frizzy white hair.

Quicksilver spoke first. "Zaf, really, we don't need you to—"

"If it's what Thorn wants," Zaf said, bright blue eyes fixed on Thorn's face, "then I'll do it."

As she locked eyes with Zaf, Past-Thorn cried out that Zaf couldn't, she *couldn't*. It was awful to ask. Zaf wasn't strong enough. And Thorn had promised: never again. No more travel by lightning. No more Zaf exhausting herself nearly to death.

But what about Brier, and her mother and father forever at war, and the ruined plains of Estar?

The Thorn of now thought cuttingly, clear-eyed, web-voiced, *What good is a gentle heart, if your home is torn apart before you can save it?*

Thorn's insides roiled with impatience. She couldn't stop the feeling. She spoke through a clenched jaw.

"If we travel home any other way," she said, her voice clear and flat, "the Vale might be lost by the time we get there."

The look on Zaf's face punched Thorn in the softest part of her belly, where the web couldn't reach.

It was obvious now. Zaf had been hoping Thorn would say, "No, never, not you, not again. Stay safe. I *promised.*"

But the moment had passed. The words had been said, the promise broken. And no one was speaking up to argue.

Zaf lifted her pointy chin in the air and said quietly, "Then I'll do it."

.31.

THE LAST LONELY BEAST

Cub watched the humans from the dark.

He had forgotten how big he was. Looking at them, he remembered.

There were two: one with long brown hair tied in a knot at the back of her neck, the other with short brown hair. They wore the same gray clothes with gold buttons and blue belts, and they were sleeping.

Cub tilted his mammoth head and sniffed them. His snout quivered in the air. They were stinky, all right. Two words came into Cub's head: *man. Woman.* Maybe they had been climbing for a very long time, just like Cub had.

But why would humans come down into the Break? He had never seen any down here before. They stayed up above, where the sky was, and the meadows and the oceans.

Cub raised one of his scabbed front paws, clumps of clover dangling from it. He should smash these humans. He should grind them to nothing under his huge tough feet.

But he couldn't stop looking at them. The words of his mothers floated through his thoughts on sweet tides of memory.

Neither kittens, nor humans, are to be eaten.

Did that mean they weren't to be stomped, either?

Cub growled. He shook his great shaggy head and moaned. It was so confusing, to be Cub! His anger was brilliant inside him, but so were the things his mothers had told him.

He wasn't sure which bright light he should follow.

As Cub blinked at the tiny humans, one of them, the man with the short brown hair, awoke. He stretched and looked up into the darkness.

He grew very still. So did Cub. He blinked and stared at the human man. He whuffed a breath out of his snout. Clumps of brittle grass dropped from his cracked lips.

The man touched the woman sleeping beside him. "Fern,

wake up please. Slowly. And don't scream."

Light sparked at the man's waist. The pack he wore buzzed with lightning.

Cub heard the faint screams of the trapped witches and stamped his feet. *"Why?"* he howled quietly.

The human woman was awake now, and as Cub watched, she reached for him with her tiny hand.

Cub jerked away and roared.

The woman's hands flew up to cover her ears, but Cub's roar was loud enough to shake the Break. The ground bucked the woman's body, sent her tumbling over the edge.

The man screamed and grabbed the hood of her coat. She scrambled back up onto the rock, and the man pulled hard on her arms. Then they held each other, making strange broken sounds, so soft and sad.

Cub stared at them. He heard the rush of blood through their frightened bodies. Pounding heart to pounding heart. These humans, they could *see* him. His mothers had told him that humans held none of the Old Wild inside them. Their eyes were too simple and small to glimpse great beasts like Cub.

But maybe something was changing, after so many long years.

Maybe, Cub thought, a shiver prickling his hide, the Old Wild had decided to help.

The man whispered, "If this is the end, know that I have loved you deeply and happily, my darling."

"I love you, Ford," said the woman. "I love you, I love you."

Cub forgot he was angry. His tired old heart ached as it hadn't in years and years. Maybe ever since his mothers died. *Love.* He knew that word.

He leaned over and sniffed the humans' tiny dark heads. They stared up at him, holding each other and trembling like leaves blown off their limbs.

And suddenly Cub remembered something from the day the eastern witches' angry fire tore open the Vale's skies.

His mothers had looked so frightened. Scared and small and lost.

These humans' faces looked just the same.

The woman sat up tall and asked, "Why?"

At the same time, Cub rumbled that very question. "Why?"

The woman crept toward the edge of her cliff. The man whispered, "Fern, no!"

But the woman was brave. Cub knew then that she must be a mother.

He lowered his head to stare at her. His eye was as tall as her whole body.

The woman said, "Why do you hurt us, Gulgot?"

Cub was confused. "Gulgot" was a word he had heard the else-hand use, but he did not know what it meant. And now this human was talking to him like *he* was Gulgot.

He blew hot air out of his snout. "Why?" he asked again. "Who?"

"You are turning our land into one of darkness," the woman said. "The higher you climb, the faster your shadows spill out into the world. They're turning swamps into monsters, animals into vicious beasts. Fog sits heavy across the land, choking the trees and stinking up the rivers. And every day, the Break widens. The Vale will shatter."

The woman began to cry, and as Cub watched her, he began to cry too, mammoth tears that splashed onto the rock.

"Why do you do this?" the woman asked. "Why do you hurt us?"

"Why?" asked Cub, his words grinding like rough metal plates, for he was not used to speaking to anyone but himself. "Why did my mothers die?"

The human man gasped.

The woman stared at Cub, her face gone scrunched. She was confused, just as Cub was!

"Your mothers?" she asked.

Cub groaned in frustration. He shook his massive head back and forth, back and forth. That made a wind that nearly blew the humans away into the darkness.

The man scooted closer and held the woman tight. "You are a child?" he asked. His voice was gentle and warm, like what Cub remembered of sunlight.

"No mothers," Cub rumbled, and then he felt so lonely that he could not hold his head up any longer. He lowered his snout onto the rock where the humans sat.

They were afraid. Cub could smell that.

But they came to him anyway and put their tiny hands on his snout. They petted him like his mothers used to do with their paws when it was time to sleep, and that felt so sweet and strange to Cub that he whimpered in the dark and closed his eyes. His tears ran down the Break like waterfalls.

"Tell us what happened to you," whispered the woman. She sat beside his nose and plucked old brambly burrs from his coat. "Would you, please? We would like to understand."

And with those words, something in Cub's heart opened up, a

soft, secret place he had kept guarded for so many years he'd forgotten it was there. He couldn't hear the else-hand. He could only hear the Old Wild, whispering its stories from deep in his blood.

"Listen," Cub said, letting the power of the Old Wild rise up inside him, right into the humans' tiny hands. He was a beast, after all. Older than the stars.

And as he breathed in and out of his huge mossy lungs, the Old Wild told the humans a story.

Afterward, Cub blinked in the darkness, listening to the humans breathe.

The man was crying.

The woman hugged Cub's snout with her skinny little arms. "You poor thing. I'm sorry. I'm so sorry. Cub. It's very nice to meet you. My name is Fern. Fern Skystone. And this is Ford Skystone. Fern and Ford."

"Fern Skystone," Cub murmured, his tired eyes fluttering shut. He pressed his snout gently against Fern's tiny body. "Ford Skystone."

But then something tight and sharp slithered against Cub's neck. Fear jolted him, sharper than any lightning bolt. He pulled away hard, swinging his head.

"No," he moaned. "Bad. *Run.*"

He clawed at the matted fur around his neck. His massive paws scraped open old wounds. In his ears, the else-hand's cursed voice cackled.

"It hurts," Cub mumbled. "It *hurts.*"

Ford said quietly, "If you touch him, you may get infected. Whatever he's doing to the land, he might do to us."

But Fern shook her head. "I don't think it's *him* infecting the land. It's that hand he talked about. The hand made of witch-magic. Isn't that right, Cub?"

Cub grunted and nodded, then wiped his snout on his leg. He loved hearing Fern's gentle voice and hoped she would keep talking.

"We can't see the hand," Fern said, "but he can certainly feel it, and I can see where it rests. *Look*, Ford."

She pointed. Cub whimpered and bowed his head, and when Fern stroked beneath his chin, he closed his great tired eyes. A light feeling like furry seeds on the wind was floating through him. Humans, he decided, were far superior to kittens, if only because they knew the proper way to scratch chins.

Ford stretched up on his toes to look and gasped. "His neck

is bleeding! Like he's wearing a collar that's cutting into his skin."

"Only you can't see the collar," Fern said grimly. "We came down here to find answers. Well, here's our answer. If we help him, maybe that will help everyone."

Cub blinked at both of them. They were using so many words, and so quickly. Cub had to work hard to understand. "Help?" he rumbled.

"If he can get to the surface," said Ford, "and we can all explain what's happening, maybe the queen and her advisers will help us find a solution."

Fern stared up at Cub. Her face looked very serious—at least Cub thought so. He was not used to humans and their strange little foal faces.

Cub trembled as he listened to them. What if the else-hand let him go and grabbed on to them instead?

But he was tired of being lonely, and their tiny hands were so warm on his cold nose.

He held very still as Fern reached for the knot of clover hanging from his jaw. She touched a bright yellow flower that bloomed there.

"Are you afraid, Cub?" Fern asked quietly.

Cub's howl was soft. "Always afraid."

"Us too," said Ford with that kind voice, gentle as flowers. "We're also afraid."

"Cub," said Fern, "I have two daughters. Little girls, not much older than you, maybe. They're twins. Would you like to hear about them? And then maybe you can start climbing again. Only you won't be alone now. All right?"

Cub looked at her, then at Ford, then at her again.

"Mothers?" Cub asked.

Fern thumped her hand against her chest. "Mother."

Ford did the same, his smile as tired as Cub felt. "Father."

Then Fern, her words so soft, so full of warmth, told Cub the story of her daughters.

.32.

THE SPOTTED KNIFE

Deep in the mountains, farther than she had ever explored with Noro, Brier Skystone sat on the cold floor of a dead stormwitch's kitchen.

Wind whistled down the chimney. It rapped its sharp knuckles across Brier's arms, made the door of shabby rags shudder and snap.

Brier tried not to think about the eleven harvesters held captive in the rooms below her feet—the bedroom of Zino's dead parents; the washroom, with a drain drilled through the stone that spat water off the side of the mountain; and the smaller room, painted with faded murals of witches and unicorns, that had once belonged to Zino's grandpop.

There were little secret villages like this one throughout the Westlin Mountains, Brier had learned over the past two days. The villages sat in caves and tunnels and clustered along winding stone paths, cleverly carved out of stone and nestled between sheer, sharp cliffs.

Zino had told her the villages had once teemed with stormwitches.

Now, only a handful of children lived there. They had been trying to escape their lightning bolts ever since getting trapped inside them years and years ago, and over the past few weeks they had finally broken free. Zino described their escape as feeling like digging a hole through a mountain with only a little knife.

So far, only the children had managed to break free. Alone, they were scratching out a wild, lonely existence without their mothers and fathers, without their uncles and aunts and neighbors and grandparents.

Some of them were still trapped. Some of them, long gone. Harvested. Shoved into eldisks. Thrown into the Break.

Sometimes, when she grew angry with them, Brier had wished her parents away. To be able to roam Aeria without them breathing down her neck! To run around Flower House at all hours of the night without anyone yelling at her or telling her what to do!

Then her parents had gone to Estar for their war rotation, and Brier had gotten her wish.

Sitting in this empty room where Zino had once eaten breakfast with his family, Brier felt heavy and sick with sadness. All these mothers and fathers gone, and all these parentless children—because Brier had been killing . . .

She had been *killing* . . .

A net of cold sweat beaded her forehead. She squeezed her eyes shut.

At least the other harvesters were safe and bound downstairs, and couldn't hurt anyone else.

Because I betrayed them, thought Brier. She touched her chest, which was whole and well. In exchange for her help capturing the harvesters, Zino had healed her burn completely.

But Brier could not even feel glad about it.

"You did the right thing, Brier," whispered Mazby. He lay in Brier's lap, swaddled in a threadbare cloth to hold his hurt wing still. "Until we can talk to the queen, we have to do what we can to protect whatever stormwitches are left. You said so yourself."

"I know," whispered Brier, shaking her head, "but I still feel awful. Those are my *friends* I helped capture."

Soft cries sounded from outside. Boots scraped stone.

Mazby chirped softly, his feathered ears perking up. "Something's happened. Someone's *crying*."

Brier carefully tucked Mazby into her coat pocket and hurried through the rag door.

Outside, Zino and four other stormwitches huddled a few paces away from the house. Zino was hugging a small sobbing stormwitch boy named Erko, whose hair fell down his back in a messy white braid.

Brier couldn't be sure what these witches really thought of her. Was she a friend, or was she simply a temporary ally? Now that she'd caught her harvester friends for them, would they turn on her?

She stepped forward, through her nerves. "What is it? What's happened?"

Zino looked over Erko's shoulders, his face stretched thin. "We found someone."

He stopped. He glanced at the stormwitch girl with her hair in five messy buns. Talla was her name.

Brier's stomach dropped at the expressions on their faces,

like they'd seen something so terrible they didn't know what words to use for it.

Mazby poked his head out of her pocket. "Who? Not a stormwitch?"

Zino said nothing and stepped out of the way so Brier could see. All the air left her lungs. Mazby shrank into her pocket, only his eyes and the top of his blanket peeking out.

A few paces away, at the edge of the cliff outside Zino's home, lay a large pile of bloody rags.

"She used to be a witch," Zino said, his voice small and strange, "though she doesn't smell of lightning."

Erko pressed his face into Zino's stomach, wailing softly.

"Her magic smells sour. And very old. It almost smells to me like . . ."

Zino trailed off, jaw clenching. Gently he passed Erko to Talla and approached the pile of rags, arms crossed over his chest.

Brier took a deep breath and followed him. Near the rags, the air smelled sour, yes, and strangely sweet, like rotting flowers. She breathed shallowly and touched the pocket holding Mazby. He nuzzled his head softly against her fingers.

"What does it smell like to you?" Brier asked Zino. If he were a friend, she would have given his shoulder an awkward pat. That was how she handled such moments, when they happened, which wasn't often. Thorn had always been better at this sort of thing.

A small pain stretched between Brier's chest and her gut like a thrumming string.

Oh, Thorn, she thought. *I miss you.*

"Her magic smells like a tether," Zino answered. "Like sweat and rot. Like something binding one thing to another."

Zino didn't speak for several long moments. Too horribly curious to resist, Brier reached for the rags.

"Let her rest," Zino said sharply. "We've already dragged her all the way back here, to bury her properly. And besides, you don't want to see. Trust me."

Brier nodded, stepped back.

"She'd fallen, I think," said Zino. "From a great height."

Brier swallowed several times against her rising stomach. Mazby cooed sadly.

"We found this beside her," Zino added.

From his coat Zino pulled a small bundle wrapped in a tattered rag. With shaking hands, Brier unfolded the fabric, expecting gruesome remains—and saw, instead, a knife.

A lovely one too, despite the blood staining the blade:

slender but solid, the hilt inlaid with small pale blue jewels. Carved into the hilt were familiar shapes: a tall tower, five long-tailed mistbirds flying around it.

"I don't know what those markings mean," Zino said quietly, "but the knife lay very near the . . . the body. It had fallen with her, perhaps. And her chest, it . . . she had a wound . . ."

Zino's voice failed him.

Brier considered biting her tongue and saying nothing. She had spent four years as a harvester, as the famous lightning girl of Aeria. For four years she had reported to the castle every week, occasionally even visiting the young queen in her throne room.

"I know what the markings are," Brier said at last. She wrapped the rag around the blade, then held up the knife so the gathered stormwitches could clearly see the engraved hilt.

"This is the Hightower crest," she said. "The queen's crest. Only a member of the queen's family would own a knife like this. And the only members of the queen's family still alive are the queen, and her little sister."

Silence followed her words.

Then Talla said hopefully, "Maybe someone stole it from her? Brought it into the mountains?"

"Or maybe the queen came into the mountains herself,"

said Brier, her voice hard, "and has decided harvesting lightning isn't the only way she'd like to kill witches."

The stormwitches shifted, shook their heads, hunched their shoulders miserably. Talla's mouth trembled.

"Tell me," said Brier, looking at each of the gathered stormwitches one by one, "would any of you be interested in a little sneaking around? I know of many doors that lead into the castle, and I think the queen owes us all some answers. But I can't do it alone."

"Brier!" Mazby whispered. "What if we just *go* to the queen and ask to talk? There's no need to sneak around anywhere!"

"I have a feeling she won't want to talk to us at all once she sees that most of us are stormwitches," muttered Brier. "She'll want to silence us so we can't spill her secrets. No, we've got to surprise her."

Zino, grinning a little, glanced at Talla, then back at Brier. "I like this idea. What's your plan, Brier Skystone?"

She hesitated. "I'm not sure yet." Which was true. But Brier wasn't worried. Brier had spent four years bossing around old men and grumpy women and a strong-willed unicorn. A crew of stormwitches couldn't be harder to wrangle than that.

"Take Erko inside, get him some food," she instructed. "By the time I join you, I'll have a plan."

Brier didn't wait for them to acknowledge her. She could see, in the sparkling, wide-eyed looks on their faces, that they couldn't quite believe their luck: the famous Brier Skystone turning traitor for them, offering them a path into the queen's own castle?

Lucky indeed, Brier thought bitterly, turning away. *They'd be luckier, maybe, if I'd never been born.*

Not so many witches would have died, if there hadn't been a Brier to catch them.

She sat on the cliff's edge, legs crossed. She used a rag to scrub hard at the blade in her hands. But the blood had long dried, and didn't wipe clean easily.

"You don't have to do this," Mazby whispered, watching forlornly from her pocket.

Brier scrubbed harder.

Zino sat down beside her.

"It's a brave thing to turn on your queen," he said quietly, "and to turn on your friends too. You must be . . ." He scratched the back of his neck.

Brier didn't help him find his words. She bore down hard on the blade, scrubbing and scrubbing, careful to avoid the sharp edge.

"You must be worried about them," Zino said at last. "Your friends, I mean." He paused. "I found more blankets for them in my grandpop's chest. And my guards are being quite kind. I promise."

Brier nodded tightly, watching through glazed eyes as the blade began to shine.

Zino tapped her boot with his. "You should rest before we go."

Brier held up the knife, examining the blade. She had made good progress, and in so little time. Though some stains remained, the rest of the blade shone a clean silver.

"We'll leave tomorrow morning, I think," she said sharply. "That should get us to the castle by nightfall. The queen won't see us coming."

.33.
THE MIDNIGHT BREACH

The curse was too powerful for a simple collar to defeat. Even quiet, even far from Celestyna, it whispered.

It woke her in the middle of the night with a *tap, tap, tap* against the rungs of her spine.

Celestyna's eyes opened. She felt the wrongness in the air at once. The curse sent its thousand tiny tongues out into the castle and brought back information.

There were people in Castle Stratiara who did not belong there.

Fifteen people, in fact.

Running, slipping around corners, whispering warnings: *quiet. Hurry.*

This way.

Celestyna unfolded herself from her bed, hair falling down her back in silver and gray and lavender and sky-blue curls.

Cursed hair.

She passed the mirror on the wall and saw the two thick crimson curls that fell against her cheek. They'd started growing the day she'd stood at her parents' bedside, her hands trembling around an empty bowl.

At first she'd tried cutting the curls. They reminded her of things she did not wish to remember. She would cut them every night before bed, right down to their roots, but when she hurried to the mirror the next morning, there they would be—bold and cascading once more.

Now Celestyna found that she liked the sight of them. They were a marker of her strength. The collar around her neck allowed her mind to see things clearly. What a delight it was, this collar. And the curse too. One to give her power, the other to calm her mind so she could use it. A pair of delights, like candies she could roll around her mouth.

Regrettable, that the Fetterwitch was dead. Celestyna wished she could thank her.

She padded barefoot down the hall, past Orelia's bedroom.

A pang of something poked Celestyna's ribs. She hesitated, listening to Orelia cry.

But then the curse whispered up her arms, raising all the fine hairs at her elbows and shoulders and nape.

Hurry. The children are here.

Celestyna continued down the hall and the first set of stairs, past the guards standing at the bottom step, into the corridor just outside the royal wing.

She grabbed a sword from the wall. It had been welded to a fixture for display, but came away easily, because the curse, oh, it was a clever thing, and it had clever, sly fingers, and a clever, sly will.

Her guards flinched and gazed at her in wonder.

Sword in hand, Celestyna knocked on Lord Dellier's door. He opened it after a moment, wrapped in a dressing gown, a nightcap on his head, a pink mark on his cheek from the press of his pillow. He blinked in surprise.

"There are invaders in the castle," Celestyna said. Her words unfurled, slow and toneless. "Follow me. I can show you right where they are."

Lord Dellier frowned. "Who?"

She tilted her head. "The children I'm going to kill."

Lord Dellier's tired eyes fell to Celestyna's withered hand. "Your Majesty, how are you feeling? Is the collar helping?"

For an instant, it felt like someone had ripped the rug out from under Celestyna. Her knees knocked together. She swayed a little and wished she was back in her bed, with Orelia safe beside her.

But then the feeling passed. The curse whispered faintly, *Focus, Queenie.* Celestyna stroked her blackened wrist.

"I'm quite well, thank you," she replied, "though I'm perturbed that a group of children have come into my home without invitation—"

Celestyna froze, listening. The curse was speaking to her. There were ants running fast along her bones, black and hard shelled, and they told her, in a thousand tiny whispering voices:

The children are stormwitches.

Except one.

Heat flared inside Celestyna like a forest going up in flames. The collar was no match for the curse's growing anger.

The little liars, hissed the curse.

"The little liars," said Celestyna.

"Who?" asked Lord Dellier. "What children are you talking about?"

She stalked away from him and flew down the main stairs. Lord Dellier followed, his midnight-blue dressing gown glittering with torchlight.

At the bottom of the stairs, Celestyna faced four more bewildered guards and showed them her ruined black fist.

She clenched it, tugged it down sharply through the air.

Punch the beast. Pound him and kick him and shove him down, down, down.

Keep us safe.

The castle quaked; the framed portraits of her ancestors rattled against the walls.

Down from the night air drifted a furious, faint roar.

The curse carved a smile across Celestyna's face.

Her guards stepped away from her.

"There are fourteen stormwitches and one lying human girl running through the basement of my castle," Celestyna snapped. "Somehow they got past your idiot compatriots at the perimeter of the castle grounds—and don't think I won't punish you for that." She stared them down. "The more quickly you bring these children to my throne room, the less severe your punishment will be. Go."

Without a word, the guards unsheathed their swords and

hurried away. Celestyna, watching them go, felt Lord Dellier's worried gaze upon her.

He's confused, informed the curse, in that slick feathery voice. *And afraid. Ignore him.*

Celestyna's glee tugged a laugh from her throat. She could hardly feel the collar anymore. How funny, that her old, dotty adviser thought this little necklace could stop a curse. She touched the back of the collar with her blackened hand, and the collar fell to the floor, singed and half melted.

Celestyna closed her eyes and took a deep breath. The curse flooded back through her veins, even stronger and sharper than before. Shivering, she kicked the ruined collar into the shadows.

Lord Dellier was aghast. "Your Majesty, why did you do that?"

"Wait," she called out to her guards.

They turned, eyes wide.

"I don't care about the witches," Celestyna told them. "Hurt them if you must. But the girl, the liar—Brier Skystone. Bring her to me unharmed."

"Brier Skystone?" Lord Dellier approached her slowly. "But, Your Majesty, you sent Brier to Estar—"

She whirled around and struck his face with the back of

her ruined hand. The curse bumped up her throat with a slight sizzling burn. Without the collar, there was nothing left to obstruct it. Celestyna smiled widely, her eyes full of shadows.

"Don't speak of what you don't understand," Celestyna told him. "And never question me in front of my soldiers again, or I'll tear out your tongue and throw it into the Break."

Sword in hand, she hurried down the hidden stairs to her throne room. Lord Dellier stumbled after her. Maybe he was having trouble keeping up with her.

Or maybe, Celestyna thought, delighted, he was afraid of what would happen to him, should he fall too far behind.

.34.

The Climb to the Castle

Quicksilver showed them out of the forest to a wooded hill. From the top they could see across the Star Lands to the distant towering shapes of the mountains that divided the Star Lands from the Vale.

The mountains that pointed the way home.

Thorn squeezed her eyes shut. It was so much farther than Zaf had taken them before, and with more people too.

But you have no choice, whispered the dark, hungry voice in Thorn's head. *You've been gone for nearly two weeks now. You're so slow. Move faster, Thorn. Hurry. The queen needs you. Only you can save the Vale, remember?*

Noro, standing beside Thorn, blew out a long, cold breath. At the bottom of the hill waited Emmi and the other soldiers from the Vale. They had agreed to stay in the Star Lands for a time. Thorn, Bartos, Ari, Quicksilver, Noro—it was already so many for Zaf to carry. Any more would be too risky.

Thorn was glad to leave the soldiers behind. Mostly.

But every few seconds, her hungry fingers twitched.

The web in her belly stretched its limbs, climbing ever higher, coating her ribs in shiny hard black.

And Thorn wondered: if the web grew, and grew, and kept growing, until it was all she could hear or feel or think, would she too become a monster like the Gulgot? Like the unicorn Noro had killed?

Where would she live? Who would be her friends?

Thorn stared at the star-touched horizon, her stupid eyes filling up. She wiped her face, and her fingers came away wet with cloudy gray tears.

She stared at her hand.

"Well, I suppose this is it," said Noro, his breath cool against her itchy scalp. "The end of our journey, one way or another."

Thorn wiped her fingers on her coat and bit down until her jaw ached.

One way or another.

She knew this was the right thing to do—for the Vale, for the other stormwitches who might still live trapped in the skies. The web had told her so, in its dark, clever voice that was so much cleverer than her own.

She shook her head, clenched her fists. "No," she whispered, "you are *not* clever. And you're not right."

But the web only laughed, cutting its teeth on her bones, and Thorn's doubts slithered right out of her head.

She looked up as Bartos finished climbing the hill. A stone-faced Zaf walked beside him, her palms faintly glowing. Her cheeks glittered with soft light.

Zaf's eyes cut quickly to Thorn, then looked away.

Words formed on Thorn's tongue: *I wish I was strong enough, Zaf, to carry you myself.*

But the web's black whispers were louder, slithering like shadows through Thorn's mind. *One stormwitch,* the darkness hissed, *is worth the sacrifice. To save the Vale? To show them you're more than just a meek little sweep?*

"Be safe," murmured a quiet voice behind Thorn, lower on the hill. "Do you hear me?"

Thorn turned, saw Sly Boots hugging Quicksilver goodbye. His face mashed into Quicksilver's messy red-and-silver braid, and his fingers dug into her shoulders. Beside them, Bear whined and wagged his tail.

Quicksilver pulled away and ruffled Sly Boots's pale blond bangs. "I always hear you, Boots," she replied with a smile. "I just don't always choose to listen."

Sly Boots laughed quietly. He pressed a glass vial into Quicksilver's hand. "Here's the last of Zaf's tonic. It should help her with the pain."

"You'll watch over Bear?"

"I'll guard him with my life."

Quicksilver smiled fondly at him. "So dramatic."

Sly Boots's eyes shone in the starlight. "And Quicksilver—"

"I'll be as safe as I can." Quicksilver touched his cheek. "I promise."

"And I'll be safe too, of course," said Ari, with a wounded sniff. He stood a little apart from them, a tiny smile at the corner of his mouth. "If anyone cares."

"Shut up, Ari," said Sly Boots, pulling the prince into a tight hug.

Thorn stepped back, her knees rocky. She almost said quietly to Zaf, "Can I please give you a hug, Zaf, before we go?"

But before she could, Quicksilver joined them, eyes bright. Bear, sitting beside Sly Boots, watched her walk away and whined, his tail wagging uncertainly.

"Let's do this before I change my mind," Quicksilver muttered.

Yes, exactly! Thorn wanted to cry out. *I've changed my mind!*

But she couldn't find her voice, and suddenly Zaf was instructing everyone, "Hold on to each other, and don't let go." A sharp stormy charge was building in the air, and it was too late for changing minds.

Thorn swallowed hard, her hand sweaty around Quicksilver's. She looked up just as Zaf grabbed Bartos's hand and pressed her face into his arm.

"One," whispered Zaf, trembling, her skin brightening like the rising sun, "two . . . three."

Thorn heard Bear's mournful howl.

The world turned white.

They landed on a sheet of black stone, so hard the impact hurt Thorn's knees.

Someone shoved past her, then someone else right after them. A flailing hand knocked her in the chest. She lost her footing and stumbled. Quicksilver caught her by the elbow.

Thorn pushed her goggles into her hair. Her vision shimmered, bright and colorful around the edges like she'd looked at a fire for too long. She blinked hard and looked around.

They were on a narrow path of stone that wound in long zigzags up the tall Westlin cliffs. The air was dark and damp. It smelled of rain and black soil and the electric burn of eldisks.

They were *home*.

Screaming soldiers ran past them, their dirty faces streaked with sweat. They were running up from Estar to Westlin, carrying supplies on their backs. Some rode their warhorses; others tugged them blindfolded up the cliffs.

Bartos stared at them as they rushed past. "Hey! Where are you going?" He waved his arms. "The war's *that* way!"

"War's over," a soldier hollered, racing past on her horse. "The Break is lost!"

Thorn flattened herself against the cliff wall, Quicksilver and Noro on either side of her. The stone path quaked under her feet. Waves of black dust rained down from above, clogging her nose and mouth. A clattering boulder tumbled past. Quicksilver yanked Thorn out of the way.

The stone crashed into a running soldier and knocked him screaming off the path.

Thorn ran to the edge and looked down.

She followed the man's spinning, screaming form until he disappeared into the gaping black maw of the Break.

And the Break . . . the Break was widening.

As Thorn watched, new fingers of the Break raced across the plains of Estar, as if someone had stepped onto a melting frozen lake, and now the ice was ready to shatter. Howls split the air, drowning out the shaking cliffs and the splitting ground and the frightened cries of the fleeing people.

Thorn's blood rushed hot and loud in her ears.

Those howls . . .

The Gulgot.

An explosive bang shook the world, and then another, throwing Thorn back from the cliff's edge. A third bang threw the fleeing soldiers off their feet, sent boulders flying down the cliff sides.

Behind Thorn, someone called out her name—Quicksilver, maybe? Noro?

But Thorn had to see for herself. Did those loud booms mean the Gulgot was falling, again and again?

If the Gulgot was falling that many times, and so near together, then that must mean . . .

Thorn swallowed, her throat closing up.

That must mean the Gulgot was close to escaping, and any soldiers left at the Break were trying everything they could to knock him back down.

Thorn peered down through the smoke and dust to scan the Break. Noro grabbed her coat with his teeth to keep her from falling. Yes, *there*—flashes of light, far away in the gloom of Estar. Each flash meant a dead stormwitch.

And each flash might be an eldisk thrown by Thorn's parents, fighting the Gulgot.

A low moan came from Thorn's left.

She scrambled back around, all her insides fighting for breath, and saw Zaf, trembling in the dirt. Bartos helped the stormwitch drink the last of the tonic from Sly Boots, then scooped her up into his arms, and Zaf shifted to look down into the Break. She was *alive*, Thorn thought, feeling a little faint and shaky. Zaf had brought them home, and she was *alive*! But her skin, flaking and thin, stretched too tightly over her bones. It was as though something had sucked the last one hundred meals out of her body. Thorn could see every line of Zaf's skeleton beneath her brittle flesh.

Her heart swelling until she felt it thumping even in her toes, Thorn thought, *And yet she is still the most beautiful girl I've ever seen.*

"They're killing them," Zaf moaned, watching the Break flash with light. "They're *killing* them!"

Bartos turned Zaf away from the Break. "Don't look!" he cried. "Look at me instead, all right?" He locked eyes with her. "Look at my hair and tell me how stupid you think it looks. Insult my ridiculous ears. All right? Can you do that for me?"

Zaf nodded miserably, two fat tears rolling down her cheeks. "Your hair," she declared, her voice shaky, "looks like a nest of fuzzy caterpillars who all need a bath."

Bartos smiled. "Excellent."

"Bartos?" Quicksilver fought through the streaming flood of soldiers and the falling showers of black dirt, Ari just behind her. "Which way?"

Bartos waved his hand. "This way!" he shouted over the din. "Follow me!"

Thorn lunged after him, eyes on Zaf, but Noro dashed in front of her.

"Thorn, please, let me carry you!" he cried. "If you fall, I'll never forgive myself!"

Thorn scrambled up onto his back. She set her jaw against the pain that scorched her legs and hugged Noro's slender white neck. With every boom from the Break, the cliffs shook, shards of rock flying—but on Noro's back, despite the pain of riding him, Thorn felt less like the world was trying to buck her off. *Unicorns always land on their feet,* she recited. *Unicorns always land on their feet.* If the mountains knocked them off, they would land safely somewhere below.

She hoped.

Bartos led the way, Zaf safe in his arms. Quicksilver and Ari followed, then Thorn and Noro last of all. Down through the swarm of fleeing soldiers they hurried, darting between bodies, dodging rocks—*down* the cliffs, Thorn noticed nervously. They were moving back toward the Break.

Yes, whispered the shadows roiling inside her, the web in her belly stretching and smiling. *Down you go. Bring the witches to your queen. She depends on you, Thorn.*

"Bartos?" she cried. "Where are we going?"

He glanced back with a tight smile. "Trust me! There's a path!"

Thorn glanced to her right, down, down, down into the Break. She searched its many jagged mouths.

What would the Gulgot look like?

Fresh shadows spilled from the Break, cascading across the dark plains of Estar like an even darker sea. A forest of trees disappeared in the space of a blink, sucked into blackness. Long black ropes like seeking tongues shot out of the Break, snatched squawking flocks of birds from the air.

Thorn's throat tightened. She hoped her parents were far away from the Break's edge, but she knew the horrible truth: they were probably right there at the edge, throwing themselves into danger. *Just like Brier would.*

"There!" Bartos shouted, pointing ahead of them at a narrow cut in the cliff wall, so well hidden that Thorn would have walked right past it.

Bartos stopped, waving Quicksilver and Ari and Noro and Thorn ahead of him. Zaf clung to his neck, shivering, but he kissed her forehead and then put her on Noro. Thorn wrapped her arms around Zaf, hoping she wouldn't squeeze too hard and break her.

"Follow that path, and don't look back!" he shouted. "Climb the steps, take the left fork. Go!"

Quicksilver and Ari, ducking under a cascade of raining pebbles, hurried for the path. Noro followed, but then leaped back with a sharp cry.

The path just behind Ari collapsed, leaving a huge gap between Ari and Quicksilver on one side, and Noro and Bartos on the other.

Noro called over his shoulder, "Hold on, girls!"

Thorn did, ducking low over Noro's neck as he leaped nimbly over the gap to land safely on the other side.

"Jump over!" Quicksilver called back to Bartos, as she and Ari held out their arms. "We'll catch you!"

The cliffs swayed and rumbled. Below, the Break boomed and groaned. Clouds of black dust choked the air. Thorn coughed, searching wildly through the rubble. Zaf's frizzy white hair tickled her nose.

Then she saw Bartos—with ten, maybe twelve feet between him and safety. Thorn's stomach dropped. That gap might as well have been the Break itself.

She watched Zaf blow Bartos a kiss, saw Bartos smile and back up to get a running start.

"Come on!" Quicksilver beckoned to Bartos. "We're ready! We won't let you fall!"

Bartos squared his shoulders, nodded sharply, then tugged straight his tattered uniform. Thorn watched, her heart pounding in her fingers. Bartos seemed suddenly far younger than he'd been when they left the Vale.

"Hurry, Bartos!" Thorn cried.

He backed up a few paces more, eyed the gap, and ran for it.

And then the loudest boom yet shook the Westlin cliffs.

Quicksilver grabbed on to Ari to keep steady. Thorn swayed in her seat, losing her grip on Zaf, who fell into Ari's arms, light as a feather. Even Noro staggered back.

A howl from the distant Gulgot shook the cage of Thorn's ribs.

Bartos's path collapsed under his feet.

With a sharp, choked cry, he fell.

Thorn screamed.

She jumped off Noro, hurried to the gap's edge, looked down the crumbling cliffs—but there was no sign of Bartos, only swirling dust and shadows.

Noro pulled her back to safety. Zaf was sobbing in Ari's arms, her pointy, pale face streaked with dirt.

"We have to go!" Quicksilver called out, beckoning toward the path Bartos had showed them. Her eyes glinted with tears. "Now!"

She waved them on, through the hidden cut of rock and onto a steep set of stairs. Past that stretched a narrow path between sheer stone walls, and then, thin and tall, the mouth of a cave. Ari and Zaf went first, followed by Thorn, Quicksilver, and Noro.

Thorn climbed the stairs on her hands and knees, her body shaking so hard she could hardly keep moving. Bartos's final scream echoed through her body like a bell struck again and again, scraping against her teeth.

Her head spun. She stopped, pressed her cheek against the gritty stone step, felt the rock shudder underneath her. She didn't think it would be so terrible if she stayed there forever.

Noro pressed his nose against her back, pushed her gently on.

Thorn climbed, her vision a soupy fog. The part of her brain that was still working wondered why she wasn't crying. Maybe it was the numb gray feeling rocking through her body, from her toes to her skull. It blocked out the web in her belly and the world beyond too—the quaking cliffs, Zaf's whimpering cries, the distant howls of the Gulgot.

The cave path grew narrow. When they reached the fork, they took the left one, as Bartos had instructed, and Thorn missed him so suddenly, and so terribly, that it felt like her chest was tightening around her lungs, and suddenly the numb feeling inside her popped like a bubble.

The walls shook around them, and the ceiling shook above them, and the floor shook beneath them, and a scream built in Thorn's throat, because she could not remember a time when the world had been still. Her scream rose up, and up, and she feared she wouldn't be able to keep it from erupting.

They emerged into a cavernous room. The ceiling was a tangle of hissing copper and metal pipes, the floor a wet sheet of rock. Stone stairs built against the walls led to high doors, and on the walls themselves were intricate carvings. The same carving, again and again, inlaid with pale jewels, and obviously a work that had taken years to achieve—a tessellation of towers ringed by flying long-tailed birds.

"The Hightower family crest," Noro murmured. "The queen's crest."

"We made it, then," said Ari. Zaf was limp in his arms, her eyes closed. "This must be the basement."

It was at that moment, standing in the bowels of Castle Stratiara, that they heard new sounds, from above—distant, familiar sounds.

First, the snap and crackle of lightning.

Then, faintly, screams.

Zaf lifted her head, looked at Thorn with tired, milky eyes.

"What is that?" Quicksilver muttered, searching the ceiling.

"Stormwitches." Zaf weakly pounded her fist on Ari's shoulder. "That's stormwitches, that lightning sound . . ."

Zaf's voice faded, and her eyes closed once more. She sank against Ari's chest.

His worried gaze found Quicksilver. "She's cold, and so light I fear I'll break her."

And that was when the clever web of shadows living inside Thorn reawakened. It surged past her grief and her shivering fear and snapped its teeth and said, *Hurry. Go help the queen. The others will follow. Lead them to her. Queenie will know what to do. It's the only way you can save everyone.*

Another electric crack from up the stairs. Another stormwitch's scream.

She climbed onto Noro's back and gripped his mane. "Come on, everyone, we've got to hurry! *Go*, Noro!"

The web in her gut kicked its heels. Noro jerked forward.

Quicksilver, Ari, and Zaf followed fast behind them.

That's it, said the web. *Keep going. Almost there. Bring them to her. The queen knows what to do with witches.*

"Keep going," Thorn ordered Noro, her voice low and gravelly. *"Move."*

Noro's long ears were flat against his skull. He took Thorn flying up the stairs, following the frantic screams and the crackling snaps of lightning. They grew louder; Thorn's nostrils burned.

At the top of the stairs, Noro galloped down a narrow stone corridor, torches snapping in silver brackets along the walls, and emerged into a wider hallway with a polished floor. Through the windows lining the hall, Thorn saw a night sky thick with clouds.

"Hey!"

Thorn turned sharply. Four royal soldiers ran at them, unsheathing their swords.

"What are you doing here?" the lead soldier barked. "Where did you come from?"

Thorn recognized the doors beyond the soldiers. She had been there a strange lifetime ago, with a fresh burn painted on her chest and nervous lies on her tongue.

The queen's throne room.

One of the doors stood ajar. Brilliant light flashed from inside. Then, a sharp cry of pain. A child's voice.

Quicksilver and Ari hurried up the stairs, breathing hard.

Zaf wheezed in Ari's arms, but her eyes were wide and bright.

"Go!" Thorn cried, and Noro reared up, blaring out a harsh cry that made the soldiers drop to the floor.

As Noro crashed through the throne room doors, Thorn's eyes found at once what she was looking for—and such love swelled inside her that all the shadows crawling around her bones vanished. The web's voice fell silent.

Brier.

Brier was *here.*

Thorn shouted, her voice cracking but her mind clear as glass, "Wait! *Stop!*"

.35.

THE LIGHTNING GIRL SPEAKS

At the sound of Thorn's voice, the world around Brier spun and slowed.

Zino and the stormwitches, pale and lightless, their power exhausted, were being herded and bound by the queen's singed guards.

The hot stormy scent of lightning lingered in the air, making the hair stand up on Brier's arms.

And Celestyna Hightower, queen of the Vale, was dragging her sword across the floor with one hand—and dragging Brier along by her shirt with the other.

Brier fought the queen's grip, kicking her feet against the

floor, and twisted around to see a sight so beautiful that tears sprang to her eyes.

Noro ran toward her, his hooves striking hard against the tile. Unicorns' hooves were only loud when they wanted them to be, and Brier shivered to hear their sharp, ringing song. The faint dawn light spilling through the throne room's tall windows made his mud-streaked coat glow a bright silver.

And Thorn, wide-eyed and filthy, clung to Noro's back.

"Thorn!" Brier gasped, reaching for her. "No! Run!"

The queen tugged sharply on Brier's collar. "Ah! The second little liar returns."

"Let her go!" Thorn cried.

Only a few frantic minutes ago, Brier had stupidly thought their plan of ambush a good one. Some ambush that had been. Not long after they had entered the castle, thirty feather-capped soldiers surrounded them.

Brier was a fool. She'd brought the stormwitches to their deaths, and she'd betrayed her harvester friends, and for what? For nothing.

"Not another step, Thorn Skystone," hissed the queen, backing them both slowly toward the nearest wall, "or your sister will die."

Then the queen unlatched one of the tall glass doors in the throne room's eastern wall and kicked it open.

From across the room, Zino cried out in alarm. Mazby, trapped inside a royal soldier's coat, squawked and screeched.

A blast of cold wind caught the door. It slammed back against one of the stone pillars supporting the throne room ceiling, and the glass shattered. So many tiny shards went flying that Brier's frantic mind thought: *snowstorm.*

The glass peppered her hands and neck with tiny smarting cuts. The howling wind slapped her cheeks, sucked every scrap of air from her lungs.

Queen Celestyna stalked onto the narrow terrace and shoved Brier's cheek against the railing. The queen was strong—too strong for such a small person. Her burned fingers hissed near Brier's ear.

"It's a long way down, Brier," the queen called out. "Let's hope your sister doesn't do anything foolish."

A blast of wind raced up the side of the castle, making Brier shudder right down to her bones, and her eyes opened against her will.

The drop was so vast that Brier didn't know whether to cry or laugh—the long white wall of Castle Stratiara, the even longer sheer drop of the Westlin cliffs, and beyond that . . .

Brier let out a hoarse cry.

The Break was getting bigger, and darker, like a scrawled line of black ink bleeding across thin paper. Tiny flashes of light zipped through the smoke and shadows. Was that spark of light an eldisk thrown by her parents? Or that one, maybe?

Then Brier heard the sounds of struggle—shouted voices, the thump of fists against flesh, Noro's angry trumpeting cry.

Then, silence.

"Who are you?" the queen asked sharply.

Tears streaming down her face, Brier twisted in the queen's grip and saw people she didn't know.

A pale young woman, a few years older than her and Thorn, with a braid of brilliant red-and-silver hair and a bleeding lip. A young man beside her, maybe a little older, with luminous fair skin and glossy dark hair, his expression mutinous. The soldiers flanking them had wrenched their arms around their backs.

Huddled at the man's feet was a frail girl, who looked to be Brier's own age. White skinned and white haired and milky-eyed, she seemed ready to blow away in the wind.

And Thorn—oh, *Thorn*—struggled to break free of the

guards holding her back, her tear-bright eyes fixed on Brier.

"Thorn," Brier choked out. *"Noro!"*

But several royal soldiers had thrown silver ropes around Noro's neck, and they were tugging and jerking those ropes, even though he gnashed his teeth and shrieked horrible ancient screams that burst open like thunder.

The queen shook Brier. "I told you to shut up!"

"Let the child go," ordered the glaring dark-haired stranger.

"A poor choice of words, all things considered," said Queen Celestyna. Her steaming hand quaked against Brier's shoulders. She pushed Brier over the railing's edge until her head hung unsupported in the chill wind.

Brier stared down the cliffs, her vision spinning. Tears dropped down the end of her nose and vanished into the air below her.

"Wait, please," Thorn pleaded. "We've brought you witches from the Star Lands. Quicksilver and Ari are their names, and they can help us defeat the Gulgot. You don't have to do this!"

For a moment Queen Celestyna was silent.

Then she began to shake with desperate laughter. The sound carved all the warmth out of Brier's body.

"Witches!" the queen cried. "You've brought me mere husks.

You might as well have gone to the Star Lands and come back with a pair of old shepherds."

"It's true we can't perform magic anymore," said an unfamiliar voice—the red-and-silver-haired woman, Brier thought. "But we know how magic works. How curses are engineered." A pause. "Queen Celestyna, what's happened to your hand?"

"My hand is no concern of yours, you miserable, useless piece of Star Land trash."

"Stop it!" Thorn cried. "Listen to me, all of you soldiers! How can you let her do this? How can you let her kill them?"

A silence fell over the throne room, and the queen jerked a little, as if she had been struck. Her grip loosened just enough for Brier to scramble back up over the railing, ready to run for Thorn—but the queen caught her coat and held fast.

Thorn struggled and fought too, and then her eyes locked with Brier's, and time grew slow and sticky. Looking into her twin's frightened brown eyes felt to Brier like slipping into bed at Flower House, their parents downstairs, Mazby asleep on Thorn's pillow, Noro keeping watch in the gardens.

It felt like knowing that, at least for the next few hours, while she slept with her twin beside her, she was going to be safe and cared for.

"Every bolt of lightning we harvest has a witch inside it!" Thorn shouted, looking earnestly around at the royal guards. "And when our soldiers throw the eldisks into the Break—"

The queen grabbed Brier by the collar and heaved her high into the air, too far past the railing for her to reach safety even if she was brave enough to try. It happened so fast she couldn't even scream.

The older boy cried out. The red-and-silver-haired woman struggled to break free of the soldiers holding her back.

Noro shouted Brier's name, his voice collapsing.

The girl huddled on the floor wearily lifted her head. She looked so frighteningly pale, so wan and strange. Was she a stormwitch?

Thorn went utterly, deathly still.

But suddenly Brier wasn't afraid. Or maybe her fear had gone past the place where she could measure it.

Confusion drifted across the faces of the soldiers, and a small hope kicked in Brier's chest.

Thorn had indeed surprised them. They hadn't known the truth.

They hadn't known the truth.

The castle, then, wasn't only full of liars and murderers, as Brier had feared.

Maybe, Brier thought, the queen's soldiers were people just like Brier had once been—doing what they thought was right for their country, getting paid their wages, going home to their Flower Houses and their Mazbys and their safe, cozy beds.

Maybe all they needed was to be told the truth, and then things would start to change.

Maybe what they needed was to see Brier unafraid to speak—even now, with the Break widening fast below her feet.

One of the queen's mistbirds flew down from the rafters, trilling softly. Brier thought she heard, in the rush of wind through its feathers, a faint whisper:

Raise your voice, lightning girl.

A chill raced down Brier's arms. She looked at Noro, saw the familiar sad glint in his eyes, and knew what that meant.

It was the Old Wild, speaking to her, and Noro had heard it too.

So Brier sucked in a breath and lifted her chin.

"Thorn," she said, her voice clear and strong, "tell them the whole truth. Tell them what we have all done."

Then Queen Celestyna released Brier's collar, and let her fall.

.36.

The Tumbling Star

As if stuck inside a lonely dark tunnel where everything was still and cold, Thorn watched Brier fall into the Break.

She heard Quicksilver and Ari's furious shouts, their curses and cries. Noro was shrieking horrible, beastly sounds the likes of which Thorn had never imagined. She turned, slowly, like fighting against a current, to see more guards throwing more ropes around Noro's neck, and she saw the stormwitches fighting their captors, though they were tired and weak and outnumbered.

One of them, a boy with a white bun on the top of his head, was screaming, and clawing against the soldier restraining him, but the man was too big and solid, and the boy was a skinny thing—like Bartos had been when he first started coming to Flower House to help in the gardens, when he hadn't had a soldier's uniform, and when Zaf had still been trapped in a bolt, and when Thorn had known nothing except how to craft art from garbage.

Thorn wanted to scream too. She wanted to scream and run, and smash her knuckles into the queen's face, and then throw herself over the terrace railing after Brier, because she couldn't imagine life without . . . without . . .

Her knees buckled, but two guards kept her upright.

"Brier," Thorn croaked. The word felt fat and strange, like her tongue was already forgetting how to form it.

Queen Celestyna stood alone at the railing. Her shoulders were high and square, and she no longer looked angry. Instead she looked afraid, and bewildered.

Thorn pulled and tugged, she twisted her body, but the guards held her fast. She sucked in a deep, ragged breath and screamed Brier's name. If she yelled it enough, would Brier come back? She would yell it every minute for the rest of her life.

But then, warmth touched her, soft and silken as Noro's mane.

Thorn blinked, not understanding, not hearing, not

breathing. Zaf had limped close, her white hair falling to her hips, her skin gleaming with sweat and so pale it was nearly translucent. Her breath whistled, as if it were escaping from her lungs through the tiniest of holes.

The soldiers holding Thorn shifted uneasily. Thorn heard one of them whisper to the other, "What do we do? These are *children.*"

Then Zaf suddenly, impossibly, began to glow.

"Zaf?" Thorn gasped. "What's happening?"

"Thank you, Thorn," Zaf whispered, "for everything."

Thorn's stomach knotted up. "Wait, what are you doing?"

Zaf's smile was calm. "I have just enough left, I think. The Old Wild told me."

She kissed Thorn's cheek—a slight hot pinch, like the shock of skin to metal on a dry winter's day—and ran away across the glass-strewn terrace. With every step her skin glowed brighter, until she was a girl-shaped bolt lighting up the air. The guards chased after her. The queen's sword flashed.

But Zaf could not be touched.

Thorn, her cheek stinging, watched Zaf throw herself over the railing and fall, spinning fast, like a star knocked out of the sky.

.37.

THE BOUND HURTS

A friend was not a thing Cub had had since the day the Vale split.

And now—lucky Cub—he had two.

Fern and Ford were their names, and it was easier to climb now that they were beside him. They told him he was brave. They sang songs that left all the tired edges of his heart feeling soft, as if he was lying in a meadow on a summer's night, his big furry belly full of sap and clovers.

But the else-hand did not like Cub feeling happiness.

The queen stewing at the other end didn't like it either.

Cub enjoyed two days of quiet stories and slow climbing, and listening to his human friends breathe as they slept curled up in each other's arms.

Ford and Fern. Fern and Ford.

Brier, and Thorn. Their daughters. Cub hoped he would meet them someday.

He was muttering their names to himself, drifting toward sleep, when the else-hand awoke and clenched hard around his neck.

Punch the beast, came the else-hand's voice. *Pound him and kick him and shove him down, down, down.*

Cub lurched upright, clawing at his throat. Through the else-hand's dark magic, he saw a flash of something from the up-above world—Queenie, running through her castle with a sword in her hand.

Ford and Fern reached for him, shouting his name, as if two mere humans could ever keep a beast like Cub from falling.

Then, tugging sharply, tightening like a noose around Cub's neck, the else-hand dragged him down into darkness.

And this time, something was different.

The else-hand felt angrier than it had ever been, and more afraid.

It sank into Cub's neck like a collar of thorns, and pierced him deeper, and deeper, until its nails scraped his tongue.

Cub fell. He slammed into a cliff, and then a cluster of rocks, and then a canyon carved by the rivers made by his own sadness. He lay there shaking and began to cry, huge fat tears that spilled over his paws like oceans, for he had climbed so far and now had to do some of it all over again, and he was *tired* of climbing, and even more tired of falling.

Through his great beastly eyes, Cub looked up. Darkness bled up the walls of the Break, rustling like a forest at night. He saw Fern and Ford leaning out from their cliff, far above him. Fern called out his name and told him not to be afraid. He was brave, Ford said, and they weren't going to leave him. He would never be alone again.

That was when Cub saw the curious thing.

Not the thousand black fingers reaching up the Break for the surface, made of the same wicked meanness as the else-hand. No, Cub was used to seeing those, though he'd never stopped fearing them.

What Cub saw instead was much more interesting.

The else-hand squeezed, its tendrils licking the corners of Cub's mind, and once again he saw the young queen of the up-above world.

Now she was holding a girl in the air—a girl with pale skin and soft brown hair and wide, frightened dark eyes. She looked like Fern, and Ford too.

A word came to Cub's tired mind: *Brier?*

Or Thorn?

The queen dropped the girl.

A spinning star jumped after her.

And the queen . . .

Cub raised his old black nose into the darkness, sniffing. He followed the cord of the else-hand, holding his mind very still around it. Nose quivering, he traced the else-hand higher than he'd dared follow it before. He followed it zipping up the Break, then racing like an arrow up the great black cliffs above, and then, finally, into the white stone castle that belonged to a queen named . . .

Celestyna, whispered the Old Wild, from deep in that soft, secret place buried inside Cub's heart. He had opened it up to tell Ford and Fern his story, and now it whispered inside him, *Her name is Celestyna.*

And Cub saw the queen's ravaged black hand.

She cradled it against her chest and ran, and with every step she took, the pain living in her hand blossomed sharper and hotter.

Cub, far below, struggling to pick himself up, felt it too.

The queen's pain bled down the chain of the else-hand, into the long dark reach of the Break, and pulsed through Cub's trembling body.

He touched one giant paw to the burned, sore flesh of his neck—the band of ruined skin where the else-hand lived.

Slowly, carefully, he wondered:

Was he not the only person the else-hand was hurting?

Was the up-above queen hurting too?

A bright flash interrupted Cub's thoughts. He looked up and saw the two girls, falling. One tiny and dim, the other a softly blooming white light, like the moons coming out from their clouds.

A sharp *smack!* sounded—the slap of bone against bone against rock.

The light abruptly went out.

Cub lumbered over to where the girls had fallen, and when he saw them, he threw up his huge shaggy head and howled.

"Father!" Cub bellowed. "Mother! Hurry!"

But Ford and Fern were so careful, with their ropes and their sharp metal picks, that they weren't going nearly fast enough.

Cub grumbled deep in his throat and found new strength and reached them in two great strides, scooped them into one enormous paw, and deposited them gently onto the ground beside his feet.

"Too important," rumbled Cub, shaking his head mournfully from side to side. "Had to touch. Sorry, Ford and Fern. I'm sorry, I'm sorry."

But Fern and Ford weren't listening. Ford cried out a name: *"Brier!"* And Fern made a horrible sound, so sad Cub wished he could cover his ears forever, but he couldn't, because what if they needed him to cover *their* ears?

They hurried to Brier, who lay very still. The stone beneath her was dark and wet, and beside her was the pale girl, the spinning star. *The witch,* Cub thought, only she didn't look wicked or mean at all. The else of her, the magic, was sweet and good. She trembled, her hair like clouds. Light poured from her hands into Brier, and the girl grew paler and paler, then dimmer and dimmer, until her skin looked as gray as Cub's belly.

Ford touched Brier's arms, her legs, her clenched jaw and closed eyelids. "What's happening?" He looked at Fern, at the pale girl, then up at Cub. "Is she . . . ?"

Cub suddenly felt cold, and wished he were small enough to hide between Fern's legs. "Gone like mothers?" he moaned.

"I wasn't quite fast enough," the pale girl whispered.

"Couldn't slow her down all the way."

She looked up at Cub with eyes smooth and white like stones from the sea.

"But she'll be all right now," the girl said, sighing. Her eyes fluttered closed. She collapsed at Brier's side, soft and silent. A fallen feather.

And then Cub watched, holding his breath, as Brier opened her eyes.

"Papa?" she said. Her voice was rough, like Cub's cracked paws.

Fern and Ford hugged her close, saying her name again and again, crying and touching her hair and kissing her cheeks.

Cub wanted to tell them to be careful. If they were kittens, then little Brier was only a baby bird!

But instead he carefully lay down beside the girl with tired gray skin and brittle white hair. She was not breathing. She was not even as big as his littlest toe. Cub touched her gently with his snout, and when she still did not move, he rested his head on the stone next to her.

Maybe if he held very still.

Maybe if he thought very hard of his mothers, and how much he had loved them.

Maybe then the girl would wake up.

.38.

THE IMPOSSIBLE WHISPER

Thorn lay with her kissed cheek pressed against the cold stone floor.

"Thorn?" whispered Quicksilver, through the tiny crack in the wall between their cells. The witch had discovered it shortly after Queen Celestyna's guards had brought them downstairs to the dungeon. She had planted herself there, speaking to Thorn as loudly as she dared—that it would be all right, somehow, that they'd figure out a way to escape their cells.

That her sister, Brier, had done a brave thing.

That she'd noticed the queen's soldiers looking full of

doubt as they'd locked Quicksilver in her cell.

That Brier's last words had been ones that might very well change the Vale forever: "Thorn, tell them the whole truth."

"But you have to take those words and run with them, Thorn," Quicksilver was whispering. "Honor your sister's memory. Follow her courage with your own. I'll help you. We'll think of something, all right?"

But Thorn didn't want to tell the truth anymore. Since watching first Brier and then Zaf fall to their deaths, she had not been able to say anything at all. She didn't want to. She wanted to lie on the floor and press her palms against the ache in her chest until the Break swallowed the Vale into darkness.

"Thorn, please, say something to me." Quicksilver's soft voice buzzed around Thorn's ears like a fly. "Thorn. *Thorn.*"

But Thorn could not be bothered by the Quicksilver fly.

She dredged up a small scrap of strength, enough to scoot away from the wall. She dragged herself into the middle of the room, curled up beside the stinking metal drain, and said, too quietly for anyone but herself to hear, "I'm sleeping."

Thorn tumbled through exhausted dreams.

She saw Brier falling down the cliffs, and Zaf's light diving after her, and Bartos falling down the cliffs, and Brier falling down the cliffs, and Zaf's light spinning through the air.

She swam through a black sea, sifted through dark waves. She called out their names, and the words echoed across the water:

"Bartos?"

"Zaf?"

"Brier?"

Thorn realized this sea was not a sea. It was the Break, and the waves were churning shadows.

Suddenly she was clawing through air, not water. She fell into darkness, without a scream and without fear.

After all, this was where Bartos and Brier and Zaf had gone.

It made sense to Thorn that she should go there too.

Thorn awoke to the sight of a soft gray sky beyond the one high window of her cell.

It was the violet-touched gray of dawn in the Vale. She had been in her cell for only a few hours, and yet it felt as though she had been lying on the gritty cold floor since the moment of her birth.

"Maybe Zaf managed to save her," came Quicksilver's voice, quiet and hoarse from all the whispering.

But Thorn did not allow herself that hope. She remembered Zaf's hollow cheeks after arriving back in the Vale. The dull white of her skin, stretched tight and thin like old paper across her bones. The pale milk of her eyes.

Thorn's own eyes, swollen and itchy from crying, filled with tears. The web in her belly shifted, grumbling quietly in protest—*You weak simpering cowardly small unimpressive sniffly crybaby,* it sneered—but that mean dark voice seemed far from her now, pushed away by the tight hot ache in her chest, and all the tears she had cried. And anyway, she didn't care what the web had to say just now.

She rolled over onto her other side, turning back toward Quicksilver's voice. The cheek Zaf had kissed met the cold air of her cell, stinging like a pin had pricked her.

"Leave me alone," she pleaded. "I'm sleeping."

Quicksilver did not respond.

But someone else did.

Help us, Thorn.

Thorn's tired eyes snapped open.

The sting of Zaf's kiss blossomed into a knot of warmth on her cheek, and when she touched her fingers to the spot . . . it *moved.*

Thorn sat up slowly, staring in wonder at her hand. A faint white glow dusted her fingers, as though she'd dipped them in a jar of moonslight.

She wiggled her fingers. Would the light disappear? Was she caught in a dream?

The light rolled in droplets down her shifting fingers, collecting in the cradle of her palm. It hovered there, turning slowly in place, like the tiniest of stars pulled down from the sky.

Still alive, Thorn.

Thorn stared at the floating orb of light that spoke with Zaf's voice. Her chest squeezed around her pounding heart. She brought her hand up close to her face, staring at the light until her eyes stung.

A dream?

A trick of her mind?

She exhaled, blew a soft breath across her palm. The light shifted, brightening.

Help us, it whispered, and when Thorn closed her eyes, she could almost imagine Zaf was there beside her—Zaf on one side, Brier on the other, and Bartos watching over them.

Hurry, Thorn.

Hurry.

.39.

THE WAR OF THORNS

Thorn stumbled to the wall, cradling the light in her hands.

"Quicksilver!" she cried, forgetting they were being held prisoner, that there were guards outside in the hallway, that she didn't know where Noro was.

All she knew was that she held Zaf's voice in her palms like a precious jewel.

"They're alive!" Thorn's eyes filled up. She bounced on the balls of her feet. "They're alive, and we have to go get them!"

Quicksilver murmured, "Breathe slowly for a moment, Thorn. And speak soft. Remember?"

"Look at it." She held her palm up to the crack in the wall so Quicksilver could see.

Quicksilver's gray eye blinked. "Great stars. Where did that come from?"

Thorn, realizing the truth, smiled a beaming smile.

"Zaf's kiss," she whispered, her cheeks growing warm. "It came from Zaf's kiss."

The light in her palms shifted, its brightness fading ever so slightly.

Hurry, Thorn.

Please.

Thorn thought of kissing the light, simply to show it how happy it was making her, but she couldn't bear the risk. What if her kiss snuffed it out?

She squinted through the crack. "Did you hear that?"

"I did," answered Quicksilver. "But . . . where can they possibly be? Not in the Break—"

"But it has to be! Zaf must have caught Brier in time, but now they're stuck down there because of course Zaf was already worn out, and I didn't even think she had any magic left at all, but she must have had just enough for that last jump, and now she'll be too hurt to get them all back up, and—"

Fear fell coldly down her back. "What if the Gulgot gets them before I can?"

"How, exactly, do you plan to *get them*?" Quicksilver asked. "They could have fallen for miles."

"Noro. I'll find Noro, and he'll take me there. Unicorns always land on their feet."

"Do they land on their feet even after jumping down into a possibly endless chasm?"

Inside Thorn's belly, between her ribs, in her chest, up and down the tense lines of her arms . . . the dark web grew. Its long sticky legs crept and crawled and latched on and pulled.

Not just a web. Not anymore.

Now, it was a Thorn-shaped, Thorn-size shell that pressed up impatiently against her skin, coating her insides with a hard black veneer, like thick dried paint.

Thorn's eyelids fluttered. Her vision bled black, like ink had dropped into her eyes, and then cleared.

Swaying a little, she thrust the light at the crack and snapped, "I can't just sit here and wait for Zaf's light to go out."

Quicksilver blew out a sharp breath. "All right. Fine. What I'm about to do will sound distressing, but just . . . follow my lead. Don't hold back. We have to convince them. When the door opens, run, and run fast. No matter what you hear."

A thought whispered in the frightened corner of Thorn's mind: *will Quicksilver be all right?*

The Thorn shell, hardening over the frame of her bones, purred happily as it climbed. *Who cares?* cooed the clever dark shell. *All that matters is Brier and Zaf.*

Without further warning, Quicksilver started screaming.

Thorn jumped away from the wall with a yelp.

"Help us!" Quicksilver cried. "Help us, we're *dying*! They're inside! They've gotten inside! Thorn, climb out the window! Jump! Don't let them touch you!"

Thorn's shock was so complete that at first she didn't understand what she was supposed to do—until the frozen pieces of her mind spun into action.

She shouted at the door, "I'm almost there!" She did not have to pretend to sound terrified. Her heart pounded so fast she felt dizzy. "I'm almost to the window! Quicksilver, help! There are *so many* of them!"

Running boot steps thumped outside in the hallway. Chains rattled. Keys jangled.

Ari shouted frantically from his own cell, his voice muffled. "Quicksilver? What's happening? Quicksilver!"

Thorn heard the guards unlocking her door, and Quicksilver's too.

Thorn crouched, licked her dry lips, prepared to run. But what if she couldn't get past the guards? They were storms knew how many strong grown soldiers, and Thorn was just . . . Thorn.

No, whispered the Thorn-shaped black shell shoving her muscles out of the way to make room. *Not just Thorn. Not anymore.*

Zaf's fading light pulsed once in her palm. Still there, still glowing—but for how much longer?

Hurry, Thorn.

The door opened, admitting a frowning soldier with wrinkled ruddy skin. Thorn ran at him fast, closed her fist around the light, then flung it at the man's face. It slammed hard into his jaw. He staggered back, shouting in pain.

Thorn ducked beneath his flailing limbs, dodged another guard's swinging fist. A hand grabbed her sleeve. Thorn spun around, snarling, her vision blazing an angry red.

She kicked the guard who had grabbed her, right in the soft part of his left thigh. He dropped her, howling. Thorn kicked him again—his left knee—and again, in the same spot, and then, when he reached for her, unsteady, his gloved hand coming right at her face, she shoved the heel of her hand hard at his nose.

Something on the guard's face gave way with a sickening *crunch*, like tree bark snapping in two.

Thorn ran. Boots pounded the stone floor, chasing her. She heard Quicksilver shout, "Take that, you brute!" and something heavy drop to the floor.

A fallen guard, Thorn hoped.

Would the guards outnumber and overwhelm her? Would they punish Quicksilver for tricking them?

Doesn't matter, murmured the shell around her bones. *Keep going.*

Brier and Zaf.

Zaf and Brier.

Thorn raced through the winding dungeon hallways, her new strong bones swinging her arms faster, her new muscles pumping her legs harder. In her mind's eye, she was a girl of sleek black enamel, pounding through Castle Stratiara like a storm.

A guard bolted out of a doorway; Thorn dodged his hands. Another guard jumped down a set of stairs and lunged for Thorn. She darted past him, kept running. Slamming footfalls chased her down the narrow stone hallway. Locked cell doors lined the walls.

Where was Noro? She didn't dare call for him. The guards couldn't know what she was doing. Let them think she was trying to escape and run home.

She faked a pathetic-sounding scream.

Let them think she was afraid of them.

Up a narrow set of stone stairs, then out into a wider hallway lined with arched windows. Beyond the windows to her right was a courtyard choked with flowers.

Suddenly Thorn had an idea.

She hurried into the courtyard, toward a clump of wisteria vines. Mistbirds watched curiously from the trees. The sound of boot steps—close, *closer*—drummed against Thorn's mind. She closed her eyes, thought of Noro, held her breath. Then, just as she'd watched Brier do so many times, Thorn dragged her finger along the purple blooms.

Silence, of course, to Thorn's ears.

But her ears weren't the ones that mattered.

A distant crash erupted, followed by shouts, screams, running boots, shattering glass.

Three guards burst into the courtyard, trampling a clump of tiny white snowbells. One raised his sword. The others dove for Thorn.

"Now, girl, just *hold still* for one storming minute," one of them growled.

Thorn spun on her heel and fled back into the hallway, listening hard. Flowers framed every window, spilled out of stone pots perched at every doorway.

She raced down two hallways, then a third, then up a set of blue-carpeted stairs, and then, at last, Thorn rounded a corner and slammed right into Noro, who'd kept his hooves silent as still air.

She stretched up on her toes, wrapped her arms around his neck, and pressed her cheek against his matted mane. Snapped chains and frayed ropes clung to his body. Bright red sores marked his coat, some gleaming with silver-streaked red blood.

Thorn swallowed hard. She'd never seen Noro bleed before. She hadn't known Noro *could* bleed.

"I didn't know where they'd taken you," she whispered.

Noro nudged her shoulder. "Not even royal chains can keep me from you, Thorn of the Vale. Up you go."

Thorn scrambled onto his back, hissing in pain when her legs touched his belly. Running footsteps approached from every shadowed hallway. Bells began chiming from the castle towers, fast and loud. Warning bells. Bells to wake up every soldier in Aeria.

Noro galloped west. "Shall we go into the mountains? We can hide out there, find help—"

"No." Thorn pulled hard on Noro's mane. He skidded to a halt with an indignant snort. "We go east, Noro. We're going into the Break."

After a slight pause, Noro said gently, "Thorn, I understand you're grieving their loss, and I am too, but we can't possibly—"

"Zaf's kiss spoke to me," Thorn said, showing him the faint light lingering on her palm. "She told me to hurry, and you're my only chance of getting down there fast enough. Unicorns always land on their feet." A tiny finger of doubt poked her throat. "Right?"

"Usually. But I've never tried jumping into the Break before."

The gleaming shell of black spreading inside Thorn prickled her every bone.

"Well, you'll try it now," she snapped.

A slammed door. An angry shout.

Thorn looked over her shoulder. Six soldiers were barreling down the hallway, swords out and capes flying.

Noro leaped down a flight of stairs into a grand hall of

indoor courtyards bursting with flowers. Squares of moonlight poured through skylights in the high white ceiling.

"Thorn," said Noro as he ran, "I don't know what light you think you saw, or what that is on your hand, but it can't possibly—"

"You *coward*."

The shell of Thorn's insides pinched her chest and the crooks of her elbows and the crown of her scalp.

She dug her fingernails too hard into Noro's coat. She considered striking him.

"You'd leave Brier lost down there in the dark?" she hissed. "She'd be ashamed, if she could see you now. She'd be embarrassed she ever knew you."

Noro said nothing else.

A line of four soldiers ran at them through the square patches of moonslight. Their swords flashed. One whipped a chain over his head, and it sliced through the air with a sharp crack.

Another soldier, his dark eyes wide, his brown skin slick with sweat, tugged hard on the other's arm and shouted, "No need to *hurt* them, for thunder's sake! What is *wrong* with all of you?"

The chain struck Noro on his back leg. He stumbled, then galloped on.

"Faster!" Thorn growled, even as tears stung her eyes.

She didn't want to yell at Noro.

But she didn't know how to stop. She didn't know how to stop the Gulgot's darkness from growing inside her.

Noro crashed through an east-facing window, horn first. He ran along a narrow stone terrace framing the castle wall, glass crunching under his feet.

Then he called out, "Hold on!" and jumped.

Thorn clung to him with all the strength she possessed, her eyes squeezed shut—until the wind forced them open.

Below them, the Break was a grinning black mouth with jagged stone teeth, smiling wider and wider and widest of all—

Darkness swallowed them whole.

.40.

Two Curls Bright as Blood

Celestyna Hightower the Twelfth, Queen of the Vale, Master of the Realm, Daughter of Westlin, and Mender of the Break, huddled on the floor in her sister's bedroom, her head in her sister's lap, her hands clutching her sister's skirts.

Around them, Castle Stratiara trembled as though it rode a lumbering beast. Which, Celestyna supposed, it mostly did. She hadn't clenched her fist for a few hours, not since ordering that Thorn Skystone and the Star Lands witches be locked in her dungeon. She hadn't pulled at the Gulgot, hadn't made him fall.

She hadn't had the heart for it. She'd only had the heart for stumbling into Orelia's room and falling to her knees at Orelia's bedside.

But none of that mattered. She wasn't any stronger than the Fetterwitch after all. The Break would never stop widening. The world would never stop shaking. Celestyna was beginning to think that, maybe, that was what the Vale deserved.

What *she* deserved.

She pressed her flaming cheek against the cool silk of Orelia's skirt and tried to order her thoughts. On Orelia's bedside table lay a collection of stories written before the breaking of the Vale—stories of witches, and magic, and the great beasts of the Old Wild that had made the mountains and carved out the rivers and coaxed the forests from the ground. She and Orelia had read the stories so many times that their fingers had worn the leather binding soft. They now had to turn the pages slowly, as if cleaning the feathers of a baby bird they didn't want to wake.

Help us, thought Celestyna, reaching for the Old Wild. *Help me.* How many times she'd tried to find it over the years, she could not count. But maybe, with this ripe old witch's curse brewing inside her . . .

She held her breath, searching through the curse for the Old Wild she knew existed at its core. Without the Old Wild, magic could not exist. And the curse was magic, so the Old Wild lay buried deep inside it.

Like trying to recall a memory, Celestyna searched, and stretched her mind, and reached.

But all she found were shadows. A sharp pain pulsing from her tired joints to her pinched belly and back again. A quiet stewing anger that shook like the castle in which she had been born.

If any scrap of the Old Wild did now live inside her, it had nothing to say. All she could hear were the rushing whispers of the curse poisoning her blood.

Strengthening your blood, the curse hissed.

Tears trembled on Celestyna's lashes. They were running out of time.

I'm *running out of time,* she thought.

Master of the Realm indeed.

She was master of nothing, and she was rotting from the inside out.

Orelia stroked Celestyna's hair. "Tell me what happened, Tyna. Say something. Please?"

Celestyna barely managed the words. "I threw a girl down into the Break. I threw her to her death."

Orelia's fingers paused.

Celestyna's gut clenched. Would Orelia run from her now? Would she shove her away in disgust?

But Orelia simply asked, "Why?"

"She was going to tell my soldiers the truth about what I've done."

"Will you tell me, Tyna?" Orelia cautiously resumed stroking Celestyna's hair. "Maybe that will make you feel better."

Celestyna let out a tired puff of laughter. "Doubtful."

Through her every vein, the curse stretched and crawled. Celestyna tried to clamp down on the sensation, but the curse was too slippery, too cunning.

Orelia sounded terribly sad. "You're sick, aren't you? Just like Mama and Papa were."

At Orelia's words, a match struck inside Celestyna's mind. A spark of an idea. As soon as she thought it, a tingling wave of fear flooded her.

The curse hissed in her chest, delighted. *Yes, tell her. Then bring her a knife. You know you want to.*

Celestyna drew in a shaky breath. "I have to tell you a story, Orelia, and you won't like it."

Orelia said nothing for a moment. Then, fearfully, "All right . . ."

"Mama and Papa didn't die of fever," Celestyna began. "They did get very sick, but because of a curse. It's anchored in our family's blood, and has been for generations. There was a witch—the Fetterwitch, was her name—and she carried much of the curse in her own body. She needed our blood to help, to give it power. But she was growing old, and the curse wasn't working as it should have."

"What kind of curse is it?" Orelia asked.

"A curse to fight the Gulgot. To protect the Vale. But the Gulgot wasn't stopping, and more darkness escapes the Break every day. You know this."

"Yes," Orelia whispered.

Celestyna pushed on, before the fear cresting inside her could break. She told Orelia everything the Fetterwitch had told her—and more too.

"Mama and Papa were dying," Celestyna said. "They asked me to help them. They were in so much pain." She closed her eyes, tense rods of grief spanning her chest. "So I did what they asked. I'd known for a few years, since they told me about the curse. I knew I'd have to do it eventually. If they'd died on their own, the curse would have given out with them. The Gulgot would have escaped, and the Vale would have been lost. It had to be me, and I knew it would be."

Celestyna's voice was a hoarse whisper. "I'd just hoped I would be an old woman, when the moment came. Not a girl."

Orelia's voice was so soft it frightened Celestyna. "You killed them."

"They begged me to. They told me . . ." With each breath, Celestyna's throat tightened. "They told me it was all right, that they trusted me to take the throne. That I would be the one to save the Vale."

"Mender of the Break," Orelia said.

Celestyna choked out a laugh. "Some mender I've turned out to be."

"But why does your skin look so sick?" Orelia's fingers traced the dark veiny lines on Celestyna's cheeks—fat and black under her ashen skin. "Mama and Papa never looked like this, not even at the end."

"I thought, if the Fetterwitch was gone, if I controlled the curse all on my own, that I could make this end."

"Tyna." Orelia's voice was mournful. "You killed her too?"

Celestyna could no longer bear the soft touch of her sister's hands. She tried to crawl away, but she didn't have the strength for it.

The curse heaved up against her bones, spitting and boiling. *Who cares what your sister thinks? She's weak. You're strong.*

"Yes, I killed the Fetterwitch," Celestyna whispered harshly. "I'm sorry. I thought it would help. I thought I could save us."

Orelia said nothing for a long time. "What happens now?"

"I don't know." Celestyna shook her head. "I don't know anything anymore."

Orelia gently moved Celestyna's head off her lap. Celestyna watched her go, a lump in her throat that the curse viciously told her to ignore.

Would Orelia leave? Would Orelia banish her? Or maybe Orelia would kill her, now that she knew the truth. Celestyna grew suddenly very still, holding her breath. Maybe this was the end.

But Orelia simply retrieved the rumpled patchwork quilt from her bed. She came back to Celestyna, curled up on the floor beside her, and draped the quilt over both of them.

"I remember when you got these," said Orelia, stroking the

two bright red curls that lay against Celestyna's cheek. "It was the day after Mama and Papa died."

"I've tried to cut them out," Celestyna whispered. "They always come back."

Orelia kissed the smooth red coils. "What did Mama always say?"

"Don't be too nice."

"Don't yell too loudly."

"Don't dress too much like a girlie girl."

"Don't dress too much like a man." Orelia dipped her voice low, like their mother's. "Those boots! Disgusting. You look like a common boy in the streets. Ladies don't wear laces."

Celestyna laughed. "Don't cry. Not ever. Not even in private. You never know who could be watching. You never know when the door could open." She closed her eyes, remembering her mother's voice. "Don't cry. Don't cry."

"I loved Mama," Orelia said thoughtfully, after such a long time that Celestyna thought she had fallen asleep. The windows shook in their panes as the Break widened and the Gulgot climbed and its darkness flooded the world. Bottles of perfume and bowls of glittering beads trembled on the glass top of Orelia's dresser.

"But I don't think she was right about everything," said Orelia, her voice unsteady. "I think it's all right to cry. In fact, I think it's good to cry. Even if you're a queen. Especially when you're a queen."

The curse clawed up Celestyna's arms and neck like a yowling cat.

Wrong.

Queens don't cry.

You weakling.

You embarrassment!

But Celestyna ignored the sharp angry shift of blood and muscles along her cheekbones. Like something gnawing, reshaping her. Like something ready to erupt.

She buried her face in her sister's neck, and for the first time in her life, when she cried, she did not feel ashamed.

.41.

THE SWEEP AND THE CUB

As Noro plunged into the Break, Thorn clenched every muscle in her body, waiting for the crash.

But when his hooves at last touched some kind of ground, it was with a landing only slightly heavier than if he had jumped over a hedge.

In the absolute choking darkness of the Break, Noro sighed happily. "I suppose I can jump safely into a chasm after all. Remind me to gloat to the others, when we're home at last."

If we get home at all, replied Thorn's mind, but she said

nothing aloud. She couldn't have even if she'd wanted to. The darkness of the Break was so thick she inhaled it. Hot and scratchy, it clung to the walls of her throat.

The only light came from the faint glow of Noro's horn. Thorn stared at her fingers, tangled in his mane. She considered apologizing to him for the things she'd said as they fled the queen's castle.

Instead she whispered, "Start walking, Noro," and hoped he wouldn't ask her if she truly thought him a coward.

He didn't.

He obeyed in silence, moving slowly through the whispering dark. Every few seconds, a movement through the darkness, a whisper of touch against her skin, made her look around frantically for monsters.

But she could see nothing.

Noro was taking a strange path—walking in a steady straight line for a few paces, then darting quickly to the left, ducking his head, cutting fast back to the right.

Thorn's skin tingled. She longed to scratch herself, brush off the feeling of tiny legs skittering up her arms. Something was near them. The Thorn-shaped shell living under her skin pulsed outward, as if longing to break free of her flesh.

"What are you running from?" Thorn whispered. "What do you see?"

"I'm not sure you want to know," Noro replied. "I'm not sure *I* know."

Neither of them spoke the words, but Thorn certainly thought them: *the darkness that now lives inside me.*

A tiny glimmer of light winked in the gloom.

Thorn's throat clenched around her breath. *Zaf?*

"Noro," she whispered.

"I see it!" He bounded toward it, leaping over what must have been gorges in the stone under their feet, breaks of ground too dark for Thorn to make sense of.

She watched the glimmer of light grow larger, could almost make out the shape of *something* standing beside it.

But then the light vanished. The air in front of Thorn's face changed. Darker than the darkness. Scorching and stinking.

Noro reared up, turned sharply left to avoid crashing into the *thing* that now stood between them and the tiny glimmering light. Thorn yelped in surprise, and then a roar boomed. Reeking hot air blasted her face.

Thorn's mouth went dry. *The Gulgot.*

A rainfall of tiny rocks peppered Thorn's arms. She ducked,

covering her head with her hands. Noro stumbled with a sharp, bleating cry.

"Noro?" came a shout. *"Thorn?"*

Another voice, so familiar and dear that Thorn lost her breath, said, "Cub, wait! Stop!"

Noro rushed forward, ducking beneath a strange furry canopy, darting between strange hairy trees, each with fat trunks the size of Castle Stratiara's towers.

Thorn slid off Noro's back, choking down tears, and ran toward the glimmering light, because she could now see that it belonged to a man who wore a glowing cloth sack slung around his torso.

"Papa!" Thorn stumbled, feet catching on a ground she couldn't see. "Mama!"

But Brier—Brier, *Brier*, not dead, alive and breathing, limping with arms outstretched, laughing through tears—was the first one to reach her.

Thorn crashed into her twin, flung her arms around her neck, kissed Brier's cheek again and again. Same skin, same cheekbone, same soft brown hair tickling Thorn's neck. Same voice whispering against Thorn's ear, "Thorn, you're home, you're *home*."

Thorn tried to pull away to see Brier's face, but suddenly she couldn't move, and didn't want to. Her father was behind her, and her mother was beside her, and they were both wrapping their arms around first Thorn, then Brier, then both of them at once. Brier found Noro, hugged his slender head. Noro, forgetting himself, nickered and whinnied and whuffed Brier's hair, as any common pony might have done.

"My Thorn," whispered their father, kissing both of Thorn's cheeks. "My brave, brave girl."

But all too soon, Thorn remembered the reason she had jumped into the Break in the first place. With a lump in her throat, she asked, "Where's Zaf?"

Everyone fell silent.

Thorn's mother gently touched her cheek. "Was that her name? Brier didn't know."

Was. Thorn's voice came out strangled. "Was?"

"This way," said Brier, holding out her hand. Noro's horn and their father's bag of eldisks lit a path. Thorn tried not to look at their glow and think about what lived trapped inside them.

Thorn's mother crouched beside a pale, still form on the ground. She turned to Thorn with tears in her eyes.

"Here she is, darling," whispered Thorn's mother. "We tried to keep her with us, but . . ."

Thorn's blood pounded and rushed and roared. "Noro?"

Noro lowered his head, blinked two, then four, then *six* tears onto Zaf's forehead and arms and chest. It was the most tears Thorn had ever seen him use on a single person, and her heart blazed with love for him.

But Zaf remained still as stone. The tears rolled down her skin, useless and wasted.

Thorn knelt. She touched Zaf's hand, her smooth hollow cheek.

"Zaf," Thorn whispered, running her fingers through Zaf's thin white hair. "I'm so sorry."

At Thorn's touch, a wave of light shifted faintly across Zaf's skin. Thorn's heart jumped with hope.

She whirled to face the others. "Did you see that? She's still alive!"

Her mother inspected Zaf's still face. "Thorn, I don't know. We've tried to wake her, but—"

"I don't care what you think," said Thorn, shaking her head fiercely. "I know she's alive. I *know* it."

"Thorn." Her father tried to gently direct her away from Zaf. "Come here, my sweet girl."

The shell inside Thorn shoved hard against her skin, with a sharp spat word. *No.*

Thorn smacked away her father's hand. "Get away from me!"

Her father flinched, his eyes wide.

Brier whispered, "Thorn . . ."

"Don't be angry with her," Noro said quietly. "The Gulgot's darkness has touched her. She's . . . not herself."

Thorn's mother cried out. "Oh, Thorn . . ."

Thorn's father turned away, a hand over his mouth.

Thorn didn't care. Let them be upset. Let them cry for her and pity her and fear her.

She stared at Zaf's still body. "No, I'm not myself," she muttered, her fists clenched. "I'm better than myself. And I'm going to kill her."

Then something shifted behind Thorn—a rough, resounding rumble, like great rocks rolling slowly down a mountain.

A gargantuan voice said, "Who?"

Thorn rose slowly, turned around, and bumped into a mammoth black snout. Two colossal gleaming eyes blinked above it.

The Gulgot.

She took two slow steps away, no more voice in her throat and no more air in her lungs.

The Gulgot's face was a strange one—not quite a hound or a bear, and not quite like one of the sleepy tree skunks that hung from branches and moved slow as tar. Clumps of grass and clover and mud dangled from its ears and chin, like the moss that covered the trees of the Estar swamps when they had still been healthy and green.

Thorn gazed up and up and *up* at the beast's hulking shoulders. "Papa . . . ?"

"It's all right," her father replied. "Thorn, this is Cub. He's a new friend of ours."

Thorn heard the careful note in her father's voice. He believed what he was saying, but he was a little afraid too.

She didn't blame him. The Gulgot's paws were so enormous he could have squashed them all flat with one step. And that was when Thorn realized, a bit dizzy, that the strange hairy forest she and Noro had walked through before had, in fact, been the Gulgot's legs.

The Gulgot—Cub? He had a *name?*—blew a soft breath into Thorn's face. "Who?" rumbled his scratchy, thunderous voice. "Who will you kill?"

Fern interrupted quickly, "No one's killing anyone."

"Well, actually," interrupted Brier, "we've all been killing stormwitches for a long time, haven't we?"

"Brier, I swear to you," said their father, weary, "we didn't know—"

"The queen," Thorn announced, staring hard at the Gulgot. At Cub. She couldn't wrap her mind around the idea of a monster named Cub. She felt very close to bursting out laughing or maybe just lying down and saying, "Forget it," and going to sleep forever.

She pressed her hands against her legs. "I'm going to kill the queen."

Silence. The Gulgot rumbled out a fetid sigh, watching Thorn keenly. "Why?"

"She killed all the stormwitches. She tried to kill Brier. She's why Zaf is . . . why Zaf . . ."

But Thorn could no longer speak.

"Thorn of the Vale." The Gulgot's hot breath smelled worse than the gutters of Aeria, but the shell inside Thorn responded happily to it, rising up inside her like a shiny black wave. "The else-hand has you."

A prickle unfolded along Thorn's spine. "The what?"

"Cub, will you say that again, please?" asked her mother.

The Gulgot touched his neck with one leathery paw. "The queen's hand. It pulls and chokes me. It keeps me from climbing." The Gulgot blinked slowly. "The queen's hand has Estar. The queen's hand has Thorn."

Thorn crept close and saw the sores rubbed raw around the Gulgot's neck. The shell inside her shivered to see the Gulgot's wounds. Thorn's skin bulged around it, reshaping itself.

"See then?" she said. "She deserves to die. She hurt you, and she hurt me."

The Gulgot's nod made a whole breeze. "I understand."

"The queen is only sixteen," said Thorn's mother. "She's a child. Like you, Thorn. Like Brier, like Cub."

"I don't care," Thorn snapped. "She *killed*—"

"She wants help," rumbled the Gulgot. "She asks for help."

"Who does?" asked Brier. She had planted herself beside Zaf's body and was dutifully combing through Zaf's snarled hair. Thorn decided she had never loved her sister more than she did in that moment.

"Queen," answered Cub. His voice tripped over the syllables. "Ce-les . . . tyna. I hear her. She says, 'Help me.'"

Thorn's father frowned. "I don't understand."

With a frustrated groan, the Gulgot swung his head from side to side. "Your words are fast. They run away from me."

Thorn watched the Gulgot's face for a long time. Swallowing hard, she reached for his shaggy cheek.

"The queen wants help." Thorn saw herself in the Gulgot's bright black eye. "With what?"

With a low sigh, the Gulgot leaned into Thorn's palm. His long-lashed eyes drifted shut. Thorn scratched the giant soft underside of his chin.

Then—carefully, her fingers trembling—Thorn placed her hand beside the wet scabbed sores marring the Gulgot's neck.

Heat bled into Thorn's fingers. A voice began to speak to her, and she understood it plainly, though it spoke with no words she had ever heard before. Shivering all the way down to her toes, Thorn knew at once that this was the Old Wild.

Her skin prickled, making her shiver. The Old Wild, gone for so long, was speaking to *her*. It whispered truths to her, just as it had begun to whisper them to Cub. And even though the whisper was faint, even though the Old Wild was still far away, Thorn saw everything it said like a faded storybook unfolding across her eyes.

She saw the queen, wrapped in a blanket with her sister,

lying on a blue carpet embroidered with silver-and-lilac feathers.

She saw the queen's tears, carving shimmering paths down her cheeks.

She heard the queen's voice, telling a terrible story that no one should ever have to tell.

A curse. A sacrifice. A Fetterwitch. A wounded country, frightened of a monster.

A crying daughter, feeding her parents porridge curdled with poison.

But then, Thorn supposed, they all had their own terrible stories—their own sadnesses, their own sharp hurts, their own awful mistakes. It was just that Thorn had never imagined the queen to be someone who could cry on the floor. She had never imagined that a queen's heart could be as heavy and tired and frightened as her own.

And she had never imagined that the monster living in the Break could be named Cub, and that he could miss his parents as terribly as Thorn had missed hers.

Thorn dropped her hand and leaned hard against Cub's leg.

He sniffed her hair. His cold wet snout bumped her head.

Thorn closed her eyes, trying to slow her breathing. The

curse's shadows climbed around her, whispering like secrets and wriggling like worms. The pieces of her mind, now touched by the Old Wild, came together slowly. If she understood correctly, it wasn't the Gulgot that would tear the Vale in two after all.

It was the curse.

Magic crafted by a scared queen and a powerful witch, decades and decades before Thorn was born. Magic made by people who heard an enormous creature trying to climb out of the crack in their ruined land and named it "monster."

This curse was the thing that would devour the Vale at last—and it would do it soon.

And there was only one way to stop this from happening.

"I thought the Old Wild was gone," Thorn whispered against Cub's leg. "How did I hear it?"

"It comes back to help," said Cub slowly. Then, mournfully, "It does not like all the hurt it sees."

"Did you hear what I thought? Did you feel my idea?"

Cub nodded, his great head making a breeze. "I did, Thorn of the Vale. The Old Wild speaks true."

Thorn met Cub's wide black gaze. "If I do this, will you hurt anyone? After? You won't, will you? I know you're angry. I know you've been in pain."

Cub scratched miserably at his neck. "Humans aren't for eating."

The curse living inside Thorn hissed and purred. It had been designed to feed, and it longed for the chance to do more.

Thorn ached to be rid of it.

Thorn never wanted to let it go.

Without it, she would be her old self again—the unremarkable sister, the forgotten sweep.

Cub's voice touched her hair like a kiss. "It is no small thing," he mumbled, "to have a gentle heart."

Thorn's mother gasped in surprise. "I've said that to her, Cub, many times throughout her life. How did you know?"

"Bartos said it too, once," whispered Thorn, her stomach churning, her head pounding, her heart breaking and breaking and breaking again. She hugged Cub's leg, found a tiny yellow flower in his fur.

"May I take this?" she asked.

Cub nodded, slow and heavy. "Bring it to her."

To the queen.

Brier's expression was grave. "What are you going to do?"

"I'm going to break the curse." Thorn plucked the little flower free and squeezed Brier's hand. "Will you watch over Zaf until I'm finished?"

"I promise."

Thorn could not bear to hug Brier again. If she hugged her, she wouldn't find the strength to leave her. She moved past Brier, her eyes stinging.

Stop crying, hissed the curse. *Stop crying!*

"Papa," Thorn said sharply, "you stay with Brier and Cub. Mama, come with me and Noro. Cub's going to throw us out of here, and you're going to tell everyone at the war front to stop launching their eldisks."

Fern Skystone stared at her. "Cub's going to *what?*"

Noro let out a long-suffering sigh, but his expression was gentle. "Unicorns always land on their feet. Didn't you know?"

Thorn climbed onto Noro's back. When her mother settled behind her, she hissed in pain.

"I'm sorry," Noro said quietly. "If I could keep that from happening, I would."

Thorn threaded her fingers through Noro's mane. "Cub? Is this all right?"

Cub held out his paw. As Noro leaped gracefully into his palm, Cub rumbled, "Tell Queenie I'm sorry."

The pang in Thorn's chest was too confusing to decipher. "Throw us as hard as you can."

Cub wrapped his claws around them. Thorn's mother muttered, "Unicorns always land on their feet," over and over, against the back of Thorn's neck.

Thorn looked up, searching for the thin white line that marked the mouth of the Break.

She found it, at last—so narrow and distant it could have been a single white hair drifting in a black sea.

She squeezed her eyes shut. "Go, Cub!"

With a grunt, Cub reared back, flung out his huge hairy arm, and let them fly.

.42.

THE SHIMMERING SPOON

Noro carried Thorn swiftly up the winding switchback trail they'd traveled down only two short weeks before. The path quaked under Noro's hooves, the cliffs of Westlin shedding dust and dirt like falling snow.

Thorn tried her best to ignore the world crumbling around her. At the top of the trail, the Fall Gate stood open. Someone had seen them coming. Crowds of people lined the streets of Aeria. They whispered and pointed. They wondered and stared. A little girl with brown skin clung to her mother, her eyes wide as coins. A pale old man wrung his hat in his hands.

With their whispers buzzing in her ears, Thorn wished she hadn't convinced her mother to stay behind at the war front.

"Noro," Thorn whispered, unable to say more.

But Noro seemed to understand. "You're doing the right thing, Thorn."

"You don't sound like you mean it."

"I do mean it. It's only that . . ." His voice sounded older than it ever had. "I wish someone else could do it for you. Someone else could *tell* her, at least."

"I don't know how the queen will react," Thorn said for the fiftieth time, because saying the words aloud helped steady her. "She could get angry. And if she's going to hurt someone, it might as well—"

"Be you?" Noro shook his head and snorted. "Thorn, say that again, and I will drag you right back down to Estar, no matter how many times you call me a coward."

The curse lining Thorn's entire small, tired body sizzled like meat on a spit, turning ever blacker. It was somehow less frightening to now think of it as a curse, rather than a hand or a web or a shell that she didn't understand.

Not that she understood curses, either. But at least it was a thing with a known name—and at least she wasn't the only one fighting it.

She thought of Cub—his big gentle eyes and his huge rumbling voice—and felt the tiniest bit better.

Noro followed the main road up to Castle Stratiara. Fuzzy-leafed ferns spilled over low stone walls. Thorn inhaled the smell of rain and soft black mud, the fresh green scent of living things and the crisp bite of mountain wind. Vale scents.

Home.

At the moss-capped stone arch that marked the castle's grand entrance, there was a long gray path of rising shallow steps.

One of the queen's gray-haired advisers stood beneath the arch, hands clasped at his waist. His shoulders drooped. His pale face was wrinkled and tired.

Thorn shrank a little. She didn't know this man, and he *did* know the queen. He would not be happy once he heard the news Thorn had to share.

But the curse wrapping up her veins and her bones whispered, *Who cares if he's happy? Plow him down! Are you afraid? You coward! You sniveling lump!*

"I am Thorn Skystone," Thorn declared, her voice shaking. She was tired, and she did not want to do this thing she must do. "I know how to save the Vale."

A flicker of emotion passed across the adviser's face. He

stared at the ground for a long moment before motioning up the stairs. "I am Lord Dellier, Thorn Skystone. Come with me." His gaze flickered to Noro. "Would you wait here, please? I think it might distress the queen to see a unicorn in her castle, given recent events. And . . . I would like to save her what distress I can. She is . . . not well."

Noro stamped one silent, silver hoof. "I will stay with Thorn, thank you very much, and I'd like to see you try and stop me."

"It's all right, Noro," Thorn whispered, sliding off his back. "I don't think anyone will hurt me."

So Thorn said. But her heart still pounded as she left Noro standing rigidly at the castle doors and followed Lord Dellier inside.

There were no soldiers in sight, for which Thorn was glad, for she didn't want to think too hard about Bartos, and how reassuring it would be to have him at her side—his feather cap, his rumpled soldier's coat.

You could hit the adviser, if you want, the curse whispered. *Knock him flat. He'll ruin everything. You can't let him!*

Thorn tried for a brave voice. "Where are we going?"

"You went into the Break and survived," said Lord Dellier. "That's what my soldiers tell me."

"That's the truth."

"You saw the Gulgot?"

His name is Cub. Thorn bit her tongue. "I did."

Lord Dellier stopped. In the clear gray light, the lines creasing his face looked even deeper.

"Do you know how we defeat him?" he asked.

Thorn hesitated, her heart racing. "I think," she said slowly, "that's something I should tell the queen, and the queen alone."

Again, that strange flicker moved across Lord Dellier's face, like the swift passing of a shadow. His eyes were bright, and Thorn wondered if he would cry.

Up in the quiet west wing of the castle—the torches set in brackets of iridescent dark stone, the wide windows framed with soft violet curtains—Lord Dellier knocked on a closed door.

A beat later, it opened a crack.

Princess Orelia's face hardened when she saw Lord Dellier. She clutched a tiny knife in her hand.

Then she saw Thorn. Her eyes narrowed. "Who are you?"

"This is Thorn Skystone," answered Lord Dellier. "The girl your sister sent to Estar, to find more lightning. I think the queen will want to hear what she has to say."

Lord Dellier gave Thorn a small, sad smile, and left her alone at the door.

Orelia glared after him, her knife at the ready. Only after he turned the corner did she relax her arm and turn her piercing gaze onto Thorn.

"You lied to my sister," said Orelia. "She put you in prison. She told me everything."

The curse rose fast and sharp. Thorn felt it in her belly like a whip's snapping cord, and she felt it down in the Break where it wrapped around Cub's neck—and also, for the first time, she felt it tugging on her from inside this room that contained the Vale's queen.

"Did she also tell you that she let my sister fall to her death?" Thorn asked.

Orelia flinched. "She did."

"Then I think I deserve to speak to her, don't you?"

From within, a faint voice called, "Let her in, Orelia."

Orelia, frowning, opened the door to let Thorn pass.

The room was a wide bedroom bordered with walls of windows. Pale periwinkle curtains softened the panes of glass.

On a sofa, facing a cloudy sky rich with sunset, Queen Celestyna sat straight and tall. A thin sheen of sweat covered her face, and thick black veins drifted slowly across her cheeks.

Thorn's throat clenched up. She touched her own knotted, shifting belly. Whatever she was feeling, the queen felt it far worse.

There she is! the curse crooned inside Thorn. *The little Queenie, so sly and cruel. Kill her! This is all her fault! There's her neck, don't you see? Grab it. Squeeze it!*

Thorn swayed where she stood. Her blood wanted her to run at the queen. The curse pushed at her every bone.

"Well?" said the queen, her voice thin but clear. "You have something to tell me?"

"Your Majesty," said Thorn, curtsying. She tried to make her shoulders as square as the queen's. "I know how to save the Vale."

"Mender of the Break," said Queen Celestyna, with a tiny tired laugh. "Tell me, O wise and brave Thorn of the Vale. How do we do it? How do we defeat the Gulgot?"

"Cub is not a danger to the Vale. I mean, the Gulgot," corrected Thorn hastily. "The danger, Your Majesty, is you."

Orelia, standing tensely nearby, whispered, "How *dare* you."

"Let her speak." Queen Celestyna watched Thorn steadily.

Thorn took three deep breaths. She wished Noro had been

allowed to come with her. She wished Brier was standing there, holding her hand.

She wished Zaf . . .

Zaf, growled the curse. *For Zaf. Kill her, kill her!*

Thorn licked her lips, her mouth watering. But she stood her ground.

"The Break grows," she said, "because your family's curse has been tearing it apart for years. The curse you thought would heal the Break and stop evil from rising to hurt us, that's the thing tearing our land in two. It isn't the Gulgot's fault that darkness is destroying us. It's your curse's fault. It's your fault. The Gulgot—Cub—he simply wants to live."

Orelia scoffed, but Celestyna watched Thorn in silence.

"I spoke to him." Thorn pressed on. "I saw the sores on his neck where your curse has hurt him. He gave me this, to give to you."

Thorn reached into her coat pocket and withdrew Cub's yellow flower. She knelt and presented it to the queen. Her mud-caked fingers looked silly next to the queen's pristine silk gown. And the tiny smushed flower wasn't fit for such a room.

"I know it's a small gift," said Thorn, "but he has nothing else. He has been alone for many years, since the Vale split and took the lives of his mothers."

Celestyna considered the flower resting in her palm for a long time.

"If the curse were to somehow disappear," said the queen at last, her voice tight and strange, "what then? Would the Break mend?"

"I'm not sure," said Thorn. "Maybe, over time. But it wouldn't get any bigger, I don't think. It would just be a chasm."

"You don't think," the queen repeated. "And would the Gulgot climb out at last and destroy us all?"

"No. He . . . promised me he wouldn't." Thorn winced, realizing too late how silly that sounded.

Orelia burst out, "He *promised* you? He's a monster!"

"Some might say the same about your sister," snapped Thorn. "Some might say a queen who kills other people to save her own is a monster."

Orelia looked as though someone had slapped her.

But Queen Celestyna only smiled. To Thorn, she looked suddenly very tired. "You're right. Some might say that."

She tucked the flower behind Orelia's ear, kissed her cheek, and looked thoughtfully at Thorn.

"I think I know what you've come here to say, Thorn Skystone," she said gravely, still with perfect posture. "I've been thinking of doing it myself, but . . ."

"But the curse won't let you," Thorn finished.

"It will do anything to protect itself."

"It would freeze your arm, hold you still like a doll."

Queen Celestyna nodded. "Smart girl."

Thorn blushed. "The Old Wild told me."

"It told me too," said the queen, with a sad smile.

"And someone in your family couldn't do it, because then the curse would go to them, and everything would start over."

"And I won't let it touch her," said Celestyna fiercely. "It will die lying dormant in her blood. She will never know its voice."

"What are you talking about?" asked Orelia, glancing nervously between them. "Are you talking about me?"

Thorn could not look at her. She felt more than a little sick to her stomach—from the curse, from exhaustion, from fear, from missing Zaf, and missing Bartos, and missing Mazby, and wanting desperately to go home.

The queen pulled a long cord hanging by her bed. A moment later, Lord Dellier entered the room with a bow.

"Lord Dellier." The queen looked steadily at him, though her voice was hollow and tired. "I wonder if you might prepare for me a bowl of porridge?"

Every inch of Lord Dellier's body seemed to sag, as if soon

his knees would buckle. His gaze was soft on Queen Celestyna's face.

"Let me do this, child," he said. "I would like to help, and Thorn is too young."

"You can't do it," Thorn said quietly.

"He can't do *what*?" said Orelia, frantic.

"The curse wants to stay alive. It won't let you do it, sir, because your family's not bound to it, so it couldn't pass on to you, and it would die. It won't let the queen do it, because without her, without first passing onto another Hightower, it would die." Thorn swallowed, her throat dry. "But it will let me, because it lives in me too. It's gone deep inside me, just like it has in her. And it wants more."

"And what better food can it find than its own power?" Lord Dellier whispered.

"It wants to feed more than anything else," said Celestyna, eyes locked with Thorn's. "It's so hungry it will forget to stop us."

Lord Dellier rubbed his brow. "The curse in Thorn will be drawn to the curse in you."

"Like a starving snake devouring its own tail," added Celestyna.

Orelia paled, her eyes wide. "Devouring?" she said softly.

Devour, devour, yes, devour, whispered the curse in Thorn's ear, its voice rising fast. *Go to her, child, go to your queen. She has power, can't you smell? No! Stay here, stay with me. We don't need her, we two. We are fine as we are. No, devour, devour, do it for Zaf!*

"And once I'm gone, there will be nothing left for it to eat," said the queen. "Without Hightower blood to anchor it, it will leave Thorn, it will fade from the land." Celestyna paused, smiling faintly. "All of it, every scrap of malice, will die with me."

A thick silence filled the room. Lord Dellier stood with his eyes pinched closed, as if he was in great pain.

Thorn rubbed the dip of her left palm until the skin smarted.

The queen reached for her adviser's hand and pressed it against her cheek. "Please, bring me the porridge, Lord Dellier. And thank you for everything you've done for this country. For my family. For me."

Orelia shook her head, put her hands in her hair. "No, no, no . . ."

Thorn swallowed hard. She thought of Noro pushing the dead unicorn into the swamp, Bartos falling with a scream, Zaf so pale and still in the Break.

Hopefully they were right about all of this. Hopefully the

Old Wild had told her true, like Cub had said. Even so, Thorn didn't feel strong enough for it.

And without me, snarled the curse, *you will never be strong again.*

But maybe, Thorn thought, her heart pounding, her palms sweaty, that was wrong. Maybe you could be strong without *feeling* strong. Maybe when you were feeling the smallest and loneliest you'd ever felt, and kept going anyway, that was a strength to be proud of, no matter if you were a soldier or a queen or just a simple, scared sweep.

To that, the curse had no reply.

Lord Dellier bowed. "Celestyna, I'm so sorry . . ."

"Go, Lord Dellier," the queen said, gentle but firm. "For the Vale."

He looked up at Queen Celestyna with such sadness it made Thorn's stomach twist into a knot.

"As you wish, my queen."

An hour later, Thorn sat on Princess Orelia's bed, a steaming bowl of porridge in her hands and a net of nerves stretched tight across her throat. A spoon, glittering with candlelight, rested against the bowl's rim, waiting for her.

She knew the poison would not hurt *her*. Nevertheless, she longed to throw the bowl far away.

But first she had a job to do. The biggest job a sweep of the Vale had ever had.

Queen Celestyna Hightower the Twelfth, Queen of the Vale, Master of the Realm, Daughter of Westlin, and Mender of the Break, lay tucked carefully beneath a silver-beaded quilt at Thorn's feet.

Her head rested in Princess Orelia's lap, and the princess herself was surrounded by pillows. Tears streamed down her face, but she did not protest. That had been done already, during the last hour as Lord Dellier went to the kitchens, and while Thorn watched, wringing her hands from the corner of the room.

Now, the princess was quiet.

"Mender of the Break," whispered Princess Orelia, tracing long soft lines down her sister's cheek. "Mama and Papa said you would do it, and you are."

Thorn's mouth had gone sour. She wished desperately to send for Mazby—the queen had told her he was resting in the aviary—but she couldn't bear for him to see this.

This, she had to do alone.

The queen kissed her sister's hand. Then she faced Thorn,

looking as peaceful as if she were merely settling in for a good night's sleep.

"Go on," she said, "Thorn of the Vale."

Thorn swallowed, which reminded her of what the queen was about to swallow, and made her nearly drop the spoon.

"Go on," said the queen again, gently. "It's all right."

Thorn held her breath and raised the spoon of porridge to the queen's lips. The queen, arms wrapped tightly around Orelia's arms, holding her sister as close as she could, opened her mouth, and swallowed.

"Tyna," whispered Orelia, touching her sister's hair with shaking fingers. Cub's flower sat tucked behind her ear, a bright yellow sun against the golden waves of Orelia's hair. "Tell me that story, about the stars. Do you remember, Tyna?"

Thorn refilled the spoon.

Queen Celestyna accepted it. "Of course I do. From the book. Thorn." The queen glanced at the battered leather-bound book on the bedside table. She winced. Her body twisted, shifting, as if struggling against a great pain. "You should read it, sometime. A collection of stories about the Vale before the Breaking. It's beautifully illustrated." The queen sighed. "Again, Thorn. Another."

Thorn scooped up another mouthful—and then did it again, and again, and again, so many times she thought the bowl would never empty. With each swallow, the queen's body tensed and jolted.

"Once," Princess Orelia choked out at last, "there were two worlds: one of light, brilliant and jubilant, and one of darkness, lonesome and lacking."

Queen Celestyna moaned a little. She turned her face into Orelia's hand.

"Tell me, Tyna." The princess kissed her sister's forehead. "Remember?"

"The world of light pitied its twin," said the queen, smiling faintly as she looked up at Orelia. "It carved out pieces of its own self with a cold silver knife fashioned from a comet's tail . . . again, Thorn."

Thorn raised another spoonful—shaking now, wishing for Noro, wishing for her father, wishing for Quicksilver's strong hand to come and take over for her.

New black veins branched out from the ones already marking the queen's smooth cheeks. Where the spoon touched her lips, the skin began to crack.

"When the world of light shook loose its wounds,"

whispered Orelia, "a thousand thousand embers cascaded down. Like a waterfall catching the sun."

"And the light stuck there, spangling the velvet dark." The queen's eyes fluttered shut, her breathing high and thin. She shivered. Her teeth chattered. Shadows darkened around her eyes and mouth.

Thorn's thoughts were wild. Somewhere inside her, the curse had begun to scream. It had sensed the beginning of its end. Thorn's stomach flopped and twitched like something was desperate to burst out of her.

But the queen's fingers waved at her—*once more, Thorn*—and she found the strength for another spoonful.

"Thus, you shall never be truly alone," said Orelia.

"For I," whispered the queen, pressing her sweating cheek into Orelia's palm, "will always be with you."

"And this was how the stars were made," Orelia finished, tears spilling down her cheeks. "A gift from one sister to another."

Thorn waited, the spoon clutched in her hand. She watched the queen while the clock ticked over the mantel and the mistbirds in the rafters cooed soft and sad, and she waited for movement, for sound, for *anything* warm and real.

But nothing came.

Orelia gave a sharp cry and scrambled out from under her sister's head, as if she couldn't bear to touch her now that she was no longer breathing. She scooted to the edge of the mattress, shaking, and clutched the quilt under which the queen lay unmoving.

But Thorn could not comfort her. Not just yet.

For as she sat there, the empty bowl of porridge in her hands, the Fetterwitch's curse vanished from her body.

Thorn blinked, waiting for more—some kind of violent slap against her ribs, or a wave of sickness that would have her running for the washbasin.

But instead, like a long-awaited sigh, the curse melted tiredly, silently, away.

And in its absence, the first thought that entered Thorn's mind, as she sat there clear-eyed and clear-bodied, was this:

She was, at last, after everything that had happened, the Thorn of the past once more. Already she felt herself shrinking to the weepy, unimpressive girl she had once been.

She wiped her face. She crawled across the bed toward Princess Orelia and held out her shaky arms.

"Did it work?" whispered the princess.

Thorn nodded, tears standing hot in her eyes—because she was glad, and because she wasn't. Because she felt small and weak, and ancient as the mountains.

"It's gone," she replied. "I felt it go."

Then Princess Orelia, with a watery smile, dropped into Thorn's open arms. She knocked her head against Thorn's chin and burst into tears against Thorn's chest.

Thorn's cursed self would not have tolerated such a display. Thorn knew this at once. Her cursed self would have sat there dry-eyed, stewing with disdain, whispering, *Revenge. Pathetic. Weak.*

But the girl of Thorn's true heart—a sweep's heart, a painter's heart, a twin's aching, lonely heart—simply held Orelia, and cried for Orelia, and also cried for the queen lying in the pillows behind them, and for all the witches she had killed.

Somewhere in the fog of Thorn's tears, the door opened. She looked up to see gray-haired Lord Dellier sit heavily beside her and drop his face in his hands.

Thorn gently pulled one of those hands into her own and squeezed it.

Then she closed her eyes and thought words that gave her

a sort of strength she had never felt before—awkward and new, yes, but growing:

It is no small thing, to have a gentle heart.

And at that moment, the shadows rolling fast across the plains of Estar vanished like smoke clearing in the wind.

.43.

THE LIVING WIND

Brier watched the white line of distant sky, waiting for whatever came next.

No eldisks had fallen in hours, and for that she was grateful. For one, it meant that Cub wouldn't be hit by anything, and neither would Brier and her father.

It also meant that Thorn and their mother and Noro had landed safely up above, that their mother had convinced the soldiers of the Vale to lay down their weapons.

But for how long?

Eldisks or no, the Break still trembled, new cracks forming

as the walls shifted and split with shadows. Brier couldn't see the cracks, but she could hear their great sharp tears like the snaps of lightning.

Lightning. Brier closed her eyes, running her fingers through the long white hair of the stormwitch named Zaf. She'd combed it so thoroughly that it now ran like pale silk across her legs. Was Zino friends with Zaf? Did he wonder where she'd gone?

Would Zaf ever breathe again?

Was Zino safe, trapped in the dungeons of Castle Stratiara?

Was he thinking of Brier, as she was thinking of him?

Brier placed one hand over her healed chest. It felt so strange to sit here in this place where she never thought she would be, wondering if the ground would split open beneath her at any moment, with the head of a girl she didn't know resting in her lap. And not just any girl, but a girl who had once burned her.

A girl who had *saved* her.

"What are you thinking about?" asked Brier's father quietly. They sat beside the bag of buzzing eldisks like shivering travelers around a fire.

Brier was thinking too many things for her tired brain

and tired tongue to put them all into words.

But she managed a little.

"I'm thinking," she said, "that Zaf hurt me, but not nearly as much as I hurt her. I'm thinking how terrible and strange it is to know that. To live with that inside me: I have hurt people. I'm thinking it doesn't matter that I didn't know what I was doing." Brier took a deep breath, her fingers gentler in Zaf's hair than they had ever been at home. "What matters is what I did."

Brier's father placed his large, warm hand on her shoulder. Brier leaned into him.

"Do you know what else matters, Brier?" he asked.

She shook her head against his hand.

"What you do next, my love. The before matters, yes. But so does the after, and the tomorrows. They matter a great deal."

As the dust of the Break rained down upon her head and neck and arms, Brier thought about this. She ducked over Zaf's body. It didn't seem right for dust to fall on the witch's still, still face.

Then Brier pulled close the bag of eldisks. Their crackling energy raised the hairs on her legs, made her teeth ache in that familiar way she had so missed from her days in the mountains.

She wasn't big enough to shelter both Zaf's face and the bag, but she thought she could at least keep the eldisks close to her. The warmth of a body, someone looking after them—maybe this would bring comfort to the witches trapped inside those round metal cages.

"I'm also thinking," Brier said slowly, "that I would like to break open all the eldisks we have left, free the witches inside them. Without hurting them," she added quickly. "We could smash them open, of course, but that seems too risky. There must be a way. Thorn brought home witches from the east. Maybe they can help us. They must know many things about magic."

Brier searched the lightning-tinged darkness for her father's thoughtful face. "What do you think, Papa? Could there be a way?"

"If there is a way to do such a thing, my darling daughter," he said, "you will be the one to find it."

Cub huddled close to Ford and Brier and Zaf, but not too close, because that glowing bag beside them smelled like the lightning that had slammed into his snout and his paws and the tough furry hide of his shoulders, again and again and again. It smelled like fire.

It smelled like witches.

Cub eyed the bag as Ford and Brier spoke softly to each other. Cub shifted from his left paws to his right paws. Cub considered his options.

He could move, very quickly, and smash the bag under his paw. That would break open the bag, and also everything inside it. Maybe stomping the bag would burn Cub's foot.

But wouldn't it be worth it? hissed the else-hand. *To hear those witches scream?*

Cub wasn't sure how to answer.

Yes, it would feel good to give the pain that he had gotten.

No, it would not feel good to have a burned paw.

Yes, it would feel good to hear that satisfying *crunch* and *sizzle* as the metal snapped and the bag ripped open. Scattered fingers of light would go flying, and the witches' dying screams wouldn't take long to fade.

No, it would not feel good to look at Brier and Ford after that, and see what they thought of him.

No, it would not feel good to, later, see Thorn. Thorn loved Zaf. That was plain to Cub. His mothers had taught him about love, and his time in the Break hadn't taken that from him. If Thorn loved Zaf, then Thorn might also love all witches. She would not appreciate Cub having stomped them.

In Cub's mind, he saw Thorn, standing tiny and quiet far below his snout, looking up at him with his yellow flower cradled in her palms.

"Why, Cub?" she would ask. "Why did you do it?"

Revenge, suggested the else-hand. *Hurt, and power, and because you can.*

Cub imagined giving Thorn that answer, and even the thought felt wrong in his mind.

"No," he rumbled, in response to the else-hand's hissed words.

Brier and Ford jumped, then turned around to stare.

Ducking his head to meet their eyes, Cub explained patiently, "Witches are not for stomping."

Cub waited for the else-hand to get angry. His body tensed, expecting to be choked and punched, expecting his breath to be stolen from him.

But instead Cub felt the sudden urge to sigh.

So sigh he did, long and slow, like settling down to sleep in the soft meadows of the old Vale, his mothers beside him. The feeling melted him. He laid down, grumbling contentedly to himself. His snout nudged Brier's back. She patted his fur, her hand as light and small as a snowflake's kiss.

By the time Cub had blown all the breath out of his body, the else-hand was gone.

Queen Celestyna Hightower was no longer Queen Celestyna Hightower.

That name was attached to a body, and the body lay in a soft silver bed, in a high white castle, in a city rooted to the ground by brick and old stone.

The thing that left the city of Aeria to drift down the Westlin cliffs and search the Break was not wind, though it moved like a spring breeze.

It was not sad, though it mostly remembered what sadness was, and it was not lonely, though it could sense the loneliness choking the Break like smoke.

This living wind was less than the queen had once been, and it was also more.

The longer it flew and spun and searched, it discovered, happily, that it was not alone in the dark and empty Break.

A strange, familiar voice whispered to it: *welcome.*

And then, *Here you are.*

And finally, *Here you will be, always.*

The wind that was not wind moved swiftly through the Break, listening to the whispers of this strange voice. The not-wind felt a tiny faded warmth living in the darkness like a fallen star, and followed its trail.

First the wind found a beast, and ruffled its matted fur.

Then the wind found a father, and kissed his worried brow.

Next the wind found a sister, and soothed her troubled heart.

Last of all, the wind found a witch, lying still and cool in the arms of a girl she had once hated.

The not-wind sighed gently into the witch's mouth and nose and through her frozen lungs.

Welcome back, it said, trembling.

Here you are again.

And here you will be, for a very long time.

It waited until the witch gasped, until her eyes flew open, until the girl and the father and the beast gathered around her and helped her and held her.

Was that right? asked the drifting joyous thing that was not quite wind and was no longer queen.

That was right, answered the Old Wild that lived in the whole huge world, its whispered voice already not so strange as it had seemed only moments before. *Now, come. Come and see.*

.44.

THE NEW BEGINNING

Thorn Skystone decided she wasn't going to leave her chair.

She was quite comfortable there. The chair's blue pillows were soft and velvety. Mazby purred in her lap as he slept, his bandaged wing quivering with every breath.

She glanced at the chair beside her, in which a snoring Brier slept.

Thorn scratched her left arm until it hurt, and then petted Mazby's tiny feathered head with one finger. Her thoughts were beginning to dip and fret. Worry squeezed hard around her ribs. Unlike Brier, Thorn's worry never slept, and sprouted tears constantly.

Like now.

When Quicksilver and Ari entered the room, they saw Thorn's tears immediately.

"What's wrong?" Quicksilver plopped into the chair on Thorn's other side. "Did someone say something else to you about Celestyna? One word from you, Thorn, and I'll punch them gladly."

"Let's not go punching anyone for, I don't know, a day or two?" Ari perched on the arm of Quicksilver's chair, looking as splendid in his new pressed tunic and velvet-trimmed cloak as Quicksilver looked uncomfortable in hers. He smoothed down the hairs that had come free from Quicksilver's braided knot.

Frowning at him, she wildly scrubbed her hand through her hair until it fluffed out everywhere.

Ari, sighing, pinched the bridge of his nose.

Thorn rubbed her cheeks with her sleeve. "I'm all right, I just . . ."

Beyond the closed gray doors across the room, fiddles and pipes began a solemn song.

Thorn's pounding heartbeat flooded her ears. "I wish I wasn't so nervous."

"Well, stars, I wish that too." Quicksilver blew some hair

out of her eyes. "Strutting around before a giant room full of people is Ari's thing, not mine."

Ari looked rather pleased with himself. "I *am* quite good at it."

Scowling, Quicksilver flicked his leg with two fingers.

"Do you ever . . ." Miserable with embarrassment, Thorn nuzzled her nose against Mazby's soft, warm belly. He cracked open his long-lashed eyes.

"Hello, Thorn," he murmured, a purr rattling his sleepy voice. "Is it time to go in?"

Thorn kissed his head. "Not quite yet." Then she peeked up at Quicksilver. "Do you ever . . . cry?"

"All the time," answered Quicksilver promptly. She jerked her thumb at Ari. "Not as much as this fellow, though."

"When you've got a tragic past," said Ari sagely, "it's expected of you."

"Why do you ask, Thorn? Because you've been crying? That's nothing to be ashamed of."

"Because I cry *all the time*," answered Thorn.

"Your body and mind are exhausted," Ari said. "Tears are a way of relieving stress."

"But even before all this happened, when I was just a sweep, a nobody, I cried at any little thing! When I was happy or sad or scared or angry. I got scared a lot. I never knew what to say. I feel everything. I feel too much."

Thorn rubbed her face. Her eyes were swollen and itchy. She hated the feeling. She wished she would never feel anything again. How was she supposed to go on for the rest of her life, with this ache always in her chest and tears always right *there*, ready to fall?

She even wished, for a dark, stabbing moment, that the Fetterwitch's curse still lived inside her. That pain had made her stronger.

All this pain did was make her doubt and worry.

"I was never brave, like Brier," Thorn continued, watching her sleeping sister. Brier could sleep through *anything*. "People would see her and walk right past me."

"There are many kinds of courage," said Quicksilver. "There's the kind like Brier's, which is loud and bright and obvious. There's the kind like Ari's, which is steady and patient, and a little bit snobby."

Now Ari flicked Quicksilver's shoulder. "When we get home, I'm going to tell Sly Boots what a fart you were."

Gingerly grooming his feathers in Thorn's lap, Mazby let out a tiny chirping laugh. "Ha! Fart."

"*Mazby,*" Thorn said.

"What? It's a funny word!"

Quicksilver grinned. "And there's the kind of courage that you have, Thorn of the Vale. The courage of being kind. The courage of loving others, even those who have wronged you. The courage to see past what a person has done and offer them your hand anyway, and your heart."

Quicksilver touched her cheek. "The courage to journey to a strange land and ask for help, even when you're frightened and overwhelmed and you'd rather stay home in your own cozy house."

"The courage to tell a queen she must die to save her country," Ari added. "The courage to help her do it."

"The courage to keep trying, even when you find out the witches you thought would help you are useless and magicless," said Quicksilver, her eyes sparkling.

Ari sniffed. "Speak for yourself. I'm far from useless."

"We did fight off those guards pretty nicely."

"We have often proved ourselves excellent at fighting off guards."

Mazby puffed up his chest. "I'm *also* excellent at fighting off guards."

Ari bowed his head. "That you are, my little friend."

Thorn's eyes, of course, of *course*, spilled over with fresh tears as she listened to them speak.

"The courage to cry," Brier murmured groggily. "That's a big one. I've never been very good at it."

"It's so easy for you to love, Thorn," Quicksilver said thoughtfully. She wiped a tear from Thorn's cheek. "When I was your age, it was very hard for me to love. I fought it whenever I could. I feared it. To be so unafraid of love, to live so openly and gently . . . what a marvelous thing."

Thorn looked between Quicksilver and Ari, her mouth trembling. "Do you really mean all that?"

"They'd better," Mazby grumbled, fluffing up his feathers.

"I do," Quicksilver said.

"And so do I," added Ari.

Brier sat up and hooked her arm through Thorn's. "And so do I."

Then the gray throne room doors opened, and Thorn's heart skipped and stumbled.

For there was Zaf, whole and shining, her long white hair falling down her back in glossy waves, her cheeks full and her eyes bright blue. Her breathing was strong and her gown was a soft petal purple.

Zaf rushed over to Thorn, grabbed Thorn's hands, and pulled her up into a hug. With a squawk, Mazby fluttered clumsily into Brier's waiting hands.

"They're ready for us," Zaf said breathlessly. "But I wanted to hug you first. Oh, Thorn, I wanted to tell you . . ." Zaf glanced around at everyone, flushing a little. "Well. They're ready for us. We should go."

She pulled away, and Thorn's heart lurched—*no, don't leave*—but then Zaf, beaming at her, leaned in and kissed Thorn's cheek.

Warmth blossomed on Thorn's face and in her chest and down her arms. She touched two fingers to the spot Zaf had kissed. The last time Zaf had kissed her, she had jumped off the queen's terrace to save Brier.

This time, Zaf stayed right where she was.

"Will you hold my hand?" Thorn whispered. Her cheeks were unbearably hot. "I'm nervous."

Zaf's smile was like the parting of clouds. She slipped her hand into Thorn's and held on tight, and together they walked into the throne room.

Queen Celestyna's court had gathered there, dressed in their finest gowns and suits and cloaks and coats. So had citizens of Aeria—hundreds of them.

Thorn looked only once at the watching, waiting, whispering crowd. Even with the strength of Brier's and Zaf's hands around her own, and Mazby on her shoulder, and Quicksilver and Ari at her back, seeing so many people felt a little like that moment when she'd first ridden Noro down the Westlin cliffs to an unknown world.

But then Thorn saw her mother and father, beaming at her from the front row of chairs.

She saw Brier's stormwitch friends in seats of honor beside her parents. The tallest boy among them, his white hair in a messy bun on his head, gazed at Brier with shining eyes.

She saw Noro, waiting for them by the throne, his clean coat gleaming like the far moon. He ducked his head as Thorn approached, and Mazby climbed up his snout to settle in the soft tuft of hair between Noro's ears. His feathers ruffled with pleasure.

Thorn took a breath and faced the new queen.

Queen Orelia was not the youngest queen the Vale had seen, but she was the only one in generations to take the throne with a full head of golden hair. No silver or gray hair mixed in with the rest. No lavender or periwinkle streaks, painted by an old curse.

No bright red curls, colored crimson from a pain no child should know.

Queen Orelia wore a silver gown and a cloak that glittered. Her new slender crown gleamed in her hair.

"Zaf of the stormwitches," said Queen Orelia. "Brier Skystone. Quicksilver and Ari of the Star Lands." The queen, smiling, looked last of all at Thorn. "Thorn Skystone. Over the past weeks, each of you has done extraordinary things in service of the Vale. You have sacrificed. You have listened. You have raised your voices to say things few could believe and even fewer wanted to hear."

Orelia paused. Tears shimmered in her eyes; it had not been long since her sister's death.

"Without your courage," she continued, "we would not be standing here today. The Vale would have fallen. Not to a monster, but to our own ignorance and fear. For many years we looked elsewhere to find the reason for our suffering. But if we had found the courage to look more closely at ourselves, at the things we did without thinking of why we did them, we would have suffered much less." Queen Orelia's gaze moved to Zino and the stormwitches. "And others would have suffered much less because of us."

Thorn squeezed Zaf's hand.

Zaf gently squeezed back.

"Thank the storms, then," said the queen, "that all of you found the courage for us."

Queen Orelia turned to Lord Dellier, who held a violet cushion in his hands. Atop it rested five glittering medallions bound to satin ribbons.

"For you, Zaf," said the queen, "I offer this in thanks: a position in my court, as ambassador to the nation of stormwitches. My hope is that by working together, we can repair the damage my family has done to your people, and bring the rest of them home."

Zaf bowed her head. "I accept this offer, Your Majesty, and pledge to serve both you and my people for as long as I am able."

The queen placed the medallion around Zaf's neck, and then turned next to Brier.

"For you, Brier Skystone," said the queen, "I offer this in thanks: a pardon for the acts you and your fellow harvesters committed under orders of the crown. Your mission, as a member of my royal offices, will be to oversee the exploration of the mountains of the Vale, to search for more stormwitches that may linger lost in the wild. To guide them home. And to work with the witches of the Star Lands, and the royal forgers, to free the stormwitches who now lie trapped inside our stores of eldisks."

The queen smiled, blew out a nervous breath. Suddenly she looked very much the young girl that she was. "That was a lot to say, wasn't it?"

Zaf burst out laughing, as did many in the gathered crowd. The room had been holding its breath, and now the air felt lighter.

"I thank you for your offer and for your words, Your Majesty," said Brier, ducking her head, "and I happily accept this task."

After the queen had placed Brier's medallion around her neck, she turned to Quicksilver and Ari.

"Quicksilver Foxheart and Ari Tarkalia of the Star Lands," said the queen. "I offer this in thanks: a forever friendship. You will always be welcome here in the Vale, and I hope this is only the beginning of our adventures together."

Quicksilver and Ari bowed their heads, accepting their medallions.

"We are honored by your friendship," said Quicksilver, "and have already sent word to the Star Lands about the work yet to come. I will bring my students and friends here, and we will all help you in your efforts to free the trapped stormwitches and heal the Vale."

The queen turned last of all to Thorn and placed the medallion around her neck.

"Thorn Skystone," said Queen Orelia quietly. "I have few words for what you have done for me, and for all of us. What you did for my sister in her last hours."

Thorn would never forget those hours. The pain of them lodged in her chest, a splinter she could not remove.

But as Thorn stood before her new queen, she realized that particular pain was one her heart was strong enough to bear.

And if, some days, she had to sit in her room and remember everything that happened, and cry?

Then maybe that was all right.

Just as Brier had said, that was its own kind of courage.

"In thanks," said the queen, "I offer you a position as adviser to the queen. Together you and I, and Lord Dellier, and anyone else we bring to our council, will decide what comes next. We have much work ahead of us, Thorn. The Vale must be remade. Will you help me remake it?"

Thorn's heart pounded so hard and fast that she couldn't

move. Then Brier tugged gently on her left hand. Zaf's thumb brushed the knuckles of her right. Mazby butted his head softly against her shoulder, and Noro blew out sweet, cool air on the back of her neck.

Thorn bowed her head. "I will, Your Majesty."

She turned to face her friends and family and neighbors, and made herself watch as they rose to their feet and applauded.

"How long do we have to stand here?" Brier muttered out of the corner of her mouth.

With a snort, Zaf's laugh erupted.

It was one of the sweetest sounds Thorn had ever heard.

Cub was too big to fit inside even a building as large as Castle Stratiara.

This was fine with him. He had no desire to squish himself into tiny human hallways and through tiny human doors. What if he got stuck? He would have to lie there while they chipped away the pretty white stone. He would have to hide his face in his paws and not look anyone in the eye ever again.

Cub found that he quite liked looking people in the eye.

So much light, here in the up-above world! So many people and trees and mountains to see!

Ah, mountains. Cub liked them best of all. They were even bigger than he was. When he snuggled down between them and closed his eyes, he could pretend their grassy foothills were his mothers.

That was where he was when Thorn and Zaf found him— lying on his back between two great gray peaks, his soft furry belly exposed. He chewed on stalks of glossy green grass.

Thorn and Zaf weren't the only ones to visit Cub. In fact, Cub was hardly ever alone. The stormwitch children helped cut Cub's hair and claws when they got too long. People from the city brought baskets of flowers and grass and muffins—which Cub had discovered were his favorite human food—and Cub nibbled the stuff from their hands, which tickled so much that even the old men giggled.

But Thorn and Zaf were Cub's favorites.

"Hi, Cub!" Zaf climbed up Cub's arm and sprawled across his belly. "We brought you a present. Thorn made it, but I helped. I told her what colors to use. Well, some colors. But they were important ones!"

Thorn nestled into the grass beside Cub's left eye. She kissed his shaggy eyebrow, then sat beside him with her back against his cheek.

In Thorn's palm, she held a tiny figurine. It was made of wire and tin, painted with so many shades of brown and gray that Cub felt dizzy looking at it. Its eyes were two shiny black buttons. Its claws were shiny black beads. Tiny yellow flowers and tiny green clovers covered its head and back and paws.

Cub tilted his head against the grass. "Cub?"

Thorn beamed at him. "Yes. It's you."

"Isn't she talented, Cub?" said Zaf. "I told her she should open a shop someday. Don't you think she should?"

Cub wasn't entirely sure what opening a shop entailed, but he nevertheless said gravely, "Yes, I do. You should make more, Thorn."

Thorn set the figurine on a nearby rock for display.

The longer Cub stared at his miniature self, the more delighted he became. A tiny Cub! He would take it with him wherever he roamed. He would show it every mountain peak he could find, every river, every downy meadow of the Vale.

"Home," he rumbled happily, gazing at the figurine and the mountains beyond it, and the sky too. Past the gray veil of clouds shimmered an evening of violet and gold. How Cub had missed the ache of colors.

"Home," Thorn agreed. Her voice sounded tired, but in a

good way. A way that Cub liked. It was a high climb to his bed, but she had made the climb nevertheless.

So he gently scooped Thorn close with his paw, and with her head resting against his fur, and Zaf curled up on the mound of his belly, they watched the sky for stars, and for tomorrow.